"Ceej," she says. "You going to answer that? That's the third time."

I run my palm over my eyes and reach for my phone. It's Kerry.

"Yeah."

"C.J." He sounds annoyed.

"What?"

"I've been calling you for an hour."

I lower the phone from my ear to check the time. It's nearly ten-thirty. "I was asleep."

"You obviously haven't heard about Dad, then."

"Yeah, he called last night."

"He did?"

"Yeah. Maybe twelve-thirty. We talked for a bit. Told me he loved me, that was weird."

"Did he?"

"Is he okay?"

It's a good fifteen seconds before he responds with a sigh.

"What?" I ask.

"Mr. Holt found him in the garage this morning. In your old car. With the ignition running."

TWO

I've forgotten just how much I hate O'Hare. Or to be fair, flying generally. Having booked my flights with no notice, I'm forced to connect between two different airlines at opposite ends of the nation's busiest hub. I have eighteen minutes to get from Concourse L to Concourse B. Staggering under the weight of my carry-on, my thigh already bruised from the run through Dulles to catch my first flight, I imagine myself falling, collapsing on the hypnotic white tile, letting the fatigue take its course as travelers step around my prone body. Or roll right over me. By the looks of some of them, they wouldn't bother to swerve.

I realize I'm cursing my dad only after an F-bomb dribbles out loud enough to earn a glare from a woman walking her son on a toddler leash. Is it rational to be pissed off at him for disrupting my daily routine, pathetic though it may be? I had tickets to see a band tonight we catch every time they come through. And the darts tournament tomorrow. True, we play every Monday, but I've been hot lately and was counting on the supplemental income.

Mindy was surprisingly sympathetic. She offered up her credit card without me asking, knowing as well as I did mine was maxed out. Her generosity made me feel guilty for having swiped a check from the box in the top drawer of her desk. For emergency use only. I can still feel her tongue against mine as we parted outside the airport. Like we used to kiss back when she brought some enthusiasm to the endeavor. It's been at least a year since we've kissed like that. Sober, at least

SORRY I WASN'T WHAT YOU NEEDED

JAMES BAILEY

Cover design by www.ebooklaunch.com.

Printed in the United States of America.

ISBN-13: 978-1511840941
ISBN-10: 1511840943

Also By James Bailey

The Greatest Show on Dirt
Nine Bucks a Pound

ONE

From the bay window in the spare room I can see clear into the upstairs bedroom of the apartment across the street. Like ours, it looms over the sidewalk, the center unit of eleven that stretch from corner to corner. The twin buildings were constructed at the same time, in the 1920s when the brick row houses that have since defined the neighborhood sprouted up to accommodate Baltimore's burgeoning populace. Back then it would have been scandalous for a woman to leave her curtains open as the evening darkened the street. Now it's a game. I camp at the window, dangling my cigarette out, she flounces around in just enough to hide the good bits. Occasionally she'll wave, right before lowering the shade for the night. I don't know her name. Mindy calls her Titsy.

This window has become my refuge, the corner I retreat to between rounds. Mindy gets the living room, our bedroom, the kitchen, and the bathroom. It's her name on the mortgage, so maybe that's fair. She might also point out that by a strict dollars-and-cents breakdown what I kick in about covers the bench beneath my bony cheeks. That's selling my contribution slightly short, however. I do all the maintenance. I've saved her thousands on contractors over the past four years. I've replaced two faucets, reglazed a broken window, patched the crumbling plaster in the hall, and will have painted every wall in the place when I finish the four surrounding me.

Tonight's squabble was an amalgam of the usual themes: ingratitude (mine), selfishness (mine), and money (hers). It kicked off on the walk home when I bitched just a little too long about going to happy hour with her office mates, where, as Mindy astutely pointed out, I sucked down six beers I didn't pay for. She claimed she'd be perfectly willing to go out with my co-workers occasionally if only I had some. I had no response for that. I have co-workers, technically, but it's not like we all knock off from the coffee shop at five and go drown out the remains of the day. Weary of playing the losing hand, I bowed out when we got home and headed straight to my corner. As I've been conditioned. If we got along better I wouldn't smoke so much. I suspect that's part of her strategy. She's playing the long game. I could save my lungs by giving in more often, but I'm too stubborn.

Of course, with the toilet behind enemy lines, it's never long before the discomfort of having consumed so freely becomes physically unbearable. If you're ever in the neighborhood, don't pass too close by our building after dusk. I do try to wait until no one's in range, but it's dark and if I were sober enough to aim perfectly I wouldn't be dumping a Gatorade bottle of steaming piss out the window in the first place.

I fire a warning shot in the form of a spent Camel and tilt the bottle out the corner of the window. As it splashes down on the cracked sidewalk below, my cell phone erupts in this horrible laugh I downloaded earlier in the week after a previous binge and brawl. It's been so long I don't immediately recognize the number lighting up the display. I should. It was mine from the time I was first old enough to babble into the phone until I left for college. But it hasn't appeared in my call log for nearly a year now, and it takes three rings before my brain registers the caller.

"Hello," I answer, in the same brusque tone I use on telemarketers.

"C.J.?" My father's voice is fuller than usual, as if he's shouting from across the room. Or drunk. As he was the last time we spoke, which is why it was the last time we spoke. I was at least half gone myself. He said things and I said things and our minds blurred and warped them into a justified moratorium on verbal communication. All subsequent dialogue has come via email or Facebook.

"What's going on, Dad?" It's a legitimate question given it's half past twelve. At least for me. Even three hours behind as he is in Seattle, it's late to be calling. Or so he used to claim when my friends phoned in high school.

"I was just thinking about you. Wondering what you were up to."

"Same old, same old."

I hear his breath and the clearing of his throat, but no words. In the pause I imagine I hear the plup of wine racing back to the bottom of a bottle that's recently been tilted horizontal. "I don't really know what that is anymore," he says at last. I can picture the thin smile flatlining across his mouth and his eyes drawing down at the corners, and I feel guilty for not having reached out at some point before now.

"I'm still at the coffee shop. I had off tonight. Went out with some of Mindy's crew from work. Standard Friday."

"Where are you living?"

I pause before responding. This, nearly word for word, was the seemingly innocent question that ignited the powder keg my sophomore year in college. He can do nothing now, and indeed his tone is merely conversational, not confrontational. "With Mindy." I've posted enough photos of the two of us on Facebook he must know who she is. He even commented on one of them.

"You still writing?"

He's never asked about my writing before. Not even when I was in high school. He always seemed like he thought it was a waste of time I could have spent studying math. So I could be more like him and grow up to be a math teacher. My brother Kerry got the math gene. I got the one that couldn't solve for x. "A little." I had an article in the independent paper this week on one of our local street musicians who has achieved cult status for his harmonica and mandolin performances outside some of the clubs in Charles Village. Aside from that, I mostly tinker with the manuscript of my novel and text my agent with suggestions on where to place it, which he invariably ignores. "Here and there."

"You were always a good writer."

Again, I've never known him to read anything I've written. Ever. So I'm assuming it's the wine, because how would he know?

"Thanks."

"I'm sorry I've not been more encouraging at times." His voice is heavy and slow, as if he's rehearsed this and is having trouble memorizing his line. "I didn't always relate to you like I should have. I'm sorry."

"It's all right, Dad." It's not, actually. But I'm just as guilty as he is, and if we're going to trade apologies for all the ways we've failed as father and son, this is going to be a long call.

"I love you, Christopher."

Before I even realize I'm crying, I can taste the salty mucus washing over my lips. My cheeks are drenched. He hasn't told me he loved me since third grade. In fairness, I haven't said it to him since then, either. And I don't now, which makes the moment more awkward. But it feels like I'd only be saying it because he did, and it might come out insincere. I resolve to work it in where applicable in our next call, or maybe this summer at Kerry's wedding, if I can muster the balls to do it face to face. I mean, obviously at some level I love him. My mom, too, though I talk to her only marginally more frequently than my father.

"I was looking through some old pictures tonight. Lake Entiat. The summer we tried to water ski. Remember?"

He doesn't need to even pin it down that far. At the first mention of Entiat, I know which camping trip he means. As would my brother and sister. We went the next four summers after that, each a little worse than the one before, until even I, the youngest at twelve, unmasked it as a farce. Forced family fun that wasn't. Kerry spent most of that week stoned, and Audra, a year older than me, stuffed her bra to the verge of bursting in an attempt to attract any warm body from a nearby campsite and escape for a few hours.

The last Entiat photos that made their way into an album were from the summer I turned eight. I was still naïve enough to be shocked when Mom left that fall. Her feigned smile is the common thread that ties those pages together. There's just one, of me and her singing by the campfire, in which she looks genuinely happy. In all the rest she's squinting, as if into the sun, forcing the left corner of her mouth up just far enough to fool no one but my eight-year-old self.

"Yeah," I say. "I never did learn to ski."

"Kerry was the only one that ever got up with any consistency. He was a natural."

My brother was a natural at everything, which grew wearisome once I was old enough to realize it wasn't just the three-year age gap setting us apart. He inherited Mom's grace and athleticism. I got Dad's gangly, knock-kneed, lucky-to-make-it-down-to-first-base-without-tripping skill set. Minus the math.

"Okay if I stay with you when I come out for the wedding?" I ask.

He hesitates, almost as if he's mulling it over. "You're not staying with your brother?"

"Didn't get the impression I was welcome there." I didn't have to read too far between the lines, having been left out of the wedding party. Even accounting for the friction that has been a staple of our relationship since he quit tolerating me hanging around with his friends when he was in junior high, you'd think I might rank an usher. Of course, it could still be fallout from having slept with Audra's future sister-in-law the night of her rehearsal dinner. She's never forgiven me for having consummated the union between our two families before she and David did. Maybe Kerry's wise to fear a repeat, given the state of things between me and Mindy, who after showing some initial early interest in making the trip has since claimed she won't be able to take the time off of work.

"Your room will be here for you if you really want it."

"Thanks. Maybe we can fire up the Charger. We'd make quite the entrance driving that thing to the wedding."

My junior year in high school, in a final desperate attempt to connect with my dad, I bought a fixer-upper Charger off a kid in my class for two hundred bucks. We spent a couple of weeks farting around under the hood until it became obvious neither of us knew shit about cars. Nor cared to learn if it meant more time in close quarters with the other. In the end I pounded out a few dents, smoothed her lines out with Bondo, applied a fresh coat of primer gray, and left her to rot in the right bay of the detached garage.

"Yeah, maybe."

"Thanks for calling, Dad. It was good to hear from you."

"You're welcome, Christopher."

"I'll send you my flight information when I have it."

I hear the plup of the wine bottle righting itself before he responds. "Sounds good."

And then he's gone. I thumb my phone dark, then hit it once more to check the time. It's just shy of one. Mindy's almost certainly asleep. The apartment is dark when I crack the door. I'm tempted by the refrigerator, which I stocked this morning with a fresh six-pack. But an empty feeling urges me toward the bedroom. From the doorway I can hear Mindy's steady breathing. I shed my sweater and jeans and crawl in beside her, feeling quite possibly more alone than I've felt since I fled to the East Coast immediately upon finishing college.

It seems like mere minutes have passed, but the room is flooded in daylight when Mindy nudges me awake.

three.

I've fretted all spring over an excuse for coming home stag for Kerry's wedding. Returning alone for my father's funeral seems easier somehow. Almost gallant. There's a certain heroism in grieving. An unassailability I am so seldom afforded. I caught myself wearing unfamiliar expressions several times yesterday, studied them in the mirror, practiced them until I could call them up again on cue. The deep, slow breath, exhaled through the nose. The distant gaze. The subtle, yet firm, nod followed by the Adam's apple-bobbing swallow. I've put so much distance, literal and otherwise, between myself and my father I can't be confident my emotions will respond unprompted.

Kerry and Audra fled before I did. But I went farther. I put six hours between us when I left for college, choosing Washington State University solely because, being nearly in Idaho, it was the greatest distance from home of any of the three schools to accept me. When that didn't prove enough of a buffer, I invested my graduation money in a one-way ticket to JFK. New York spit me out sixteen months later after a series of ill-fitting proofreading jobs. I headed south, not home. I've been back exactly three times in the past decade, brandishing my chronic lack of funds as a rather transparent excuse. That cuts both ways, however. Had either of my parents really wanted me to visit, they could have sprung for a ticket. My father did so for Audra's wedding. That was apparently enough to satisfy their collective appetite. The subject has never since been broached.

The stitch in my left side burning its way up under my rib cage slows me to a trot. I used to be able to run back in high school. I lettered twice in cross country, reaching the pinnacle of my athletic career as a sophomore when I placed fourth in the district finals. Coach quit talking to me when I wouldn't come out my junior year. By then Kerry had moved out, and I didn't have to prove anything to anyone anymore. Or need an excuse to stay away from the house every afternoon.

I'm close enough I can make out the sign for my gate, maybe a football field ahead. When they call out final boarding I pick up the pace again, or try to. The passage is jammed like the mall at Christmas and I'm forced to weave my way through the crowd. I quit apologizing after the fourth time my bag slams someone in the kidneys.

"Hold that door," I shout to the attendant who has just emerged from the gangway. Unlike the rest of the airport, my gate is deserted aside from a handful of squatters waiting for neighboring flights.

She shakes her head and jacks her eyebrows, like a teacher who has warned her pupil too many times already about being tardy to class. I may even look like a student to her. My black jeans are frayed at both knees, and the untucked tails of my shirt stick out beneath the bottom of my sweater. Her eyes settle on the instep of my right foot, where the hole in my sock has conspired with the hole in my Converse high top to expose the chafed skin beneath.

"I need to board." I rake my fingers across my forehead and sweep my limp hair clear from my face.

"Sorry." There's a hint of a sparkle in her eye, as if she relishes this rare opportunity to bust someone's balls in return for all the shit she takes from asshole travelers every day. "They're pulling back."

I want to hit her, or maybe check her into the wall and make a dash for it. Instead I grovel. And bullshit. "Please. I just want to get home before my father dies."

Her smug expression morphs into a sympathetic one. That may even be contrition I read in her eyes. I've scratched her veneer.

"My brother said he won't last until tomorrow morning." The funeral might have done it, but no one with a conscience could deny someone the chance to say good-bye to their dad. "Please, I've got to get there tonight." The tears, affected yesterday, come too naturally. A moment later she's on the radio, alerting the flight crew they'll need to open the door to let one more passenger board.

"Thank you, thank you," I say, as she urges me into the tunnel with a wave.

The flight attendant at the door glares at me as she takes the ticket from my hand, a look I'm well accustomed to by the time she leads me through first class into the coach cabin. Thirty-three rows of fliers take their turn hating me as I pass, my duffel bag nestled to my chest to ensure it doesn't stray across anyone's armrest and give them a legitimate reason to spit on me. My seat, the only open one on the entire flight, is a middle, two rows shy of the bathroom, which I desperately need to use but don't dream of mentioning given the circumstances of my arrival.

The man spilling out of the aisle seat harrumphs when the stewardess leans in and explains the obvious. He'd actually lifted the arm bar between our seats to allow his gut room to roam, and the first thing I do after jamming my bag under the seat ahead of mine is slide it back in place as protection. Seated to my left is a young Arab, in a tunic and linen pants that belatedly set off my "terrorist" alert. He's the only one on the plane that smiles at me. Maybe he's just glad to have someone there to filter out the pastrami and mustard bouquet emanating from our neighbor.

Despite the flab encircling his upper arm like a pool floatie, I clearly feel the bone in his elbow each time it finds my ribs, a recurring event that keeps me from drifting off to sleep as we taxi across the tarmac. And sleep, more than dinner or a good long piss, is what I crave most. I managed less than two hours this morning after lying in bed all night staring at the clock. Every time I closed my eyes, I pictured my dad on the other end of the phone, drinking, pacing—hurting—as we spoke. What if I'd said something different? What if I'd told him I loved him? Would it have made any difference?

Thinking back on it, which I've done a lot over the past thirty-six hours, something didn't feel right. But I could take that final call a hundred times without suspecting my dad would off himself. He was the steady one in the family. By default, perhaps, but steady nonetheless.

I've finally reached that foggy state where dreams flirt with consciousness, just on the threshold of sleep or maybe even across it, when a metal buckle cracks against the knuckles on my right hand. The captain has turned off the seatbelt warning. My fat friend is struggling to extricate his ginormous ass from between the armrests, the one beneath my right elbow rising along with him. I exchange smirks with the fellow to my left, then get up to take advantage of the chance to relieve myself. As it turns out, it is the first of many such trips. For him, not me.

Having given up on sleep, I dig into the bag at my feet for my notebook. I cross out nearly every word I jot down, an inefficient ratio I can't blame on my father. I've been in a rut for months now. I'll go a week at a stretch without advancing my storyline. This never used to happen. In college I was so full of ideas I would stay up all night, writing until my hand cramped. Even afterwards, when I was flunking out of one New York publishing job after the next, I could fill an entire page in the time it took to smoke one cigarette. Now sometimes it feels as though I only cling to this dream to excuse the fact that I'm thirty-two and work in a coffee shop. Everyone at Ruth's is just there to support their art. I work with actors, dancers, cartoonists—none of whom make a dime off their alleged calling.

After the umpteenth elbow to the oblique, I decide to work Tubby into my story as an exercise to kick start my pen. My new character waddles onto the page fully formed, at least physically. It's when I let my mind wander to his motivation that I find myself on the cusp of the zone for the first time since shortly after New Year's. A glance up into his crumb-littered stubble or coffee-stained teeth nudges me forward any time I run adrift. Flipping back through my notebook I realize I've written six pages by the time we begin to descend. Maybe they're all shit and will need to be culled, but they served a purpose of getting me through a couple of hours I could have spent wishing the guy to my left would just detonate his shoe already and spare me the rest of this journey.

There's one new text on my phone when we land. One, to account for the six-plus hours since I last checked it after boarding my original flight in D.C. It's from Kerry, in response to my earlier request for a ride. "All set," it says. I look around for him when I reach the gate, reminding myself when I don't see him that he can't get this far without a ticket. I've forgotten just how long a trek it is to get to the terminal, a train ride away from this satellite concourse. I follow my fellow passengers out of the car and up the escalator, checking my phone for updates from Kerry as the wave spits me out at baggage claim. Our flight made good time. Maybe he's running late. I'm pecking out a quick "where R U?" when I feel a tug on the strap of my bag.

It's not Kerry. It's Keith.

I'd call him my stepfather, but I refuse to give him that much credit. He's just the dickhead who married my mom after she left. I don't blame him for breaking my parents apart. Mom didn't need an excuse so much as an escape plan. In a sense she used Keith as much as he used her. He just got the better side of the bargain. My mother was knockout attractive when she was younger, with lustrous raven hair and exotic, almond-shaped, steel-blue eyes she accentuated with a professional's touch in front of the mirror every morning. Even before men heard her sultry Russian accent, they were drawn to her like a Lamborghini in a parking lot of sedans. I get that she and my father, whose own eyes were magnified by thick lenses secured around his neck by a Velcro strap, made at best an odd couple. The twelve years separating them in age seemed like a generation gap in many ways. Though I was too young to pick up on all this when it was happening, in hindsight I believe my dad always knew that despite his efforts to spoil her it was only a matter of time until she left him.

So, Keith didn't technically steal her. It was more of a right-place, right-time deal. He was convenient. Like my father, he punched well above his weight class. My mother could have done better than a home-appliance salesman, even one who, as Keith will undoubtedly inform you, perennially ranks among the top commission earners in the region.

I saw clean through his façade the minute I met him. I was in third grade and he made a big show of trying to connect, like he needed to win me over to earn my mom's hand. He drove us to a Mariners game in his Vette and flashed a little cash for valet parking, buffing the driver's side door with his shirt tail as we got out. He wore his Oakley sunglasses atop his head, perhaps to mask the thinning hair beneath. I remember my mother rolling her eyes at me as she slipped her arm into the crook of his and let him and his puffed-out chest lead her into the stadium. "What do you fancy, boss?" he asked me at the concession stand, loud enough to make it clear to all around us that he was a big spender. I took him for two slices of pizza, a fried dough, a large Coke, a cotton candy, and a box of Dots. Three hours later I threw it all back up out the window of his Vette as he drove us home across the I-90 bridge. My mom laughed, no sorrier for me than she was his paint job.

He's balder now, individual strands of hair rising from his dome like blades of grass on a newly seeded lawn. His goatee has grayed, but the bullshitter's sparkle in his eye is as fresh as the day he sold his first stainless steel fridge. He cocks his head and spreads his arms.

"Whoa," I say, reluctantly extending my right hand. He bats it away and corrals me in an unreciprocated hug.

"Baggage claim?" he asks, when he finally withdraws.

I shake my head and thumb the strap of my bag. Keith, still grinning like a camel on Novocain, willing to pretend what I am not, nods toward the exit. I follow, giving one word responses and shrugs to his generic questions about my flight. His car, parked illegally at the curb outside, is a lemon-yellow Pontiac Solstice, top down to take advantage of the unseasonably warm early May weather.

"Like it?" he beams.

"It's all right," I nod. I'd give my left nut to drive a car like this, but I won't let him know that. He would let me drive it, and I already hate myself for being this far in his debt.

I can feel the engine racing through my ass as we accelerate onto the highway. Keith winks at me and punches a button on the stereo console. AC/DC rips into me from a dozen different points, most directly through my knee, resting against the speaker in the door. Of their own volition, my fingers begin drumming along on my thighs. Keith does a couple of spasmodic rocker head bobs and shoots his right hand skyward, index finger and pinky extended like devil's horns. Without a trace of irony, as if he expects me to return the salute and cement our secret brotherhood. Instead, I turn and scan the cars we pass, wishing I could trade places with their passengers. He rides the tail of a minivan so close I can see the cartoon playing on the DVD unit hanging from its ceiling, then, just as we pass the exit to the interstate heading north up through the city, noses into the middle lane before there even appears to be a car length of open space.

"Where we going?" I ask, though the answer seems clear as we're now speeding east on the 405 at seventy-five mph.

"Home."

No fucking way am I staying with Mom and Keith. I only ever spent one night there, and that wasn't even technically on their property. I'm suffering enough already, I don't need to open another vein.

"I was going to stay up at Dad's."

"Don't be silly. You can have the couch downstairs. Folds out. You'll have the whole basement to yourself."

"No need to put yourself out. Plus I've got stuff up at Dad's. And I was going to hit up Jimmy Bostic."

Keith lowers his eyelids when he looks at me. Mr. Phony Nice Guy is gone. "Your mom would like to see you."

Sure she would. Until dinner was over and her programs came on. She'd ask about Mindy. I'd make up some shit that sounded better than it was. We'd laugh about one or two of our distant memories, and she'd disappear upstairs. That's how it went at Audra's wedding. Well, it wasn't Mindy then, but they were all the same to my mother, who was unlikely to ever meet any of them.

"I'll see her tomorrow," I offer. "I'll borrow Dad's car and come over for lunch." Do you borrow a dead man's car? He borrowed mine. It's only fair.

Keith's response is to depress the gas pedal. Every time I peek at the speedometer it's pegged further to the right. Eighty, ninety, flirting with triple digits. We blow by cars so fast the faces of the drivers blur. After five minutes of neither of us speaking, he lets off the accelerator just enough the ticket wouldn't automatically cost him his license if we were to pass a cop. I sense him looking at me and glance over.

"So?" he asks, arching his strawberry-gray eyebrows. As if we're now sufficiently off course to break my spirit.

"I was really hoping to go home," I say, emphasizing the final word. "I need to sort a few things out."

He shakes his head and nudges the roadster to the right, banking into the next exit. Unless they've moved, we're still a good ten minutes from where we'd normally get off. I'm not sure where we are. It's nowhere I've ever been. Not that I spent much time down this way even before I bolted town. Keith slows just enough at the red light to ascertain there's no one coming, then punches the gas again. The tires squeal as he veers into a vast and mostly empty parking lot. He pulls to a stop in front of a bank of glass bus shelters.

"It's good to see you're still a selfish prick, C.J." The muscles on either side of his goatee pulse as he turns toward me. I draw back, seeking the door handle with my right hand. He notices and grins. He's hardly a physical specimen, but he's naturally broad shouldered and carries his weight well for a man in his late fifties. And though there's never been a word uttered about it in seventeen years, he remembers as well as I do what happened the last time he took a swing at me. The only shot he intends tonight is to my pride. He reaches into his back pocket and produces his wallet, from which he whips a twenty dollar bill. "This ought to get you to your dad's. I sure as fuck ain't driving you all the way up there."

I want to tell him to shove it up his hairy ass, but I've got less than a hundred bucks in cash to get me through this trip, so I reach for it. He doesn't let go of his end.

"Why don't you use whatever's left to get your hair cut before Wednesday. You look like a jackass." When he releases the twenty I topple against the unlatched door, fighting for a moment to right myself before allowing gravity to carry me down to the blacktop. Laughing, he reaches into the back seat and tosses my bag over the trunk. I cover my head with my arms to protect my face from the storm of pebbles and chipped asphalt as the Pontiac disappears in a cloud of smoldering rubber.

THREE

From my knees, I launch both middle fingers. Keith shoots one of his own back at me as he turns out of the park-and-ride. "Limp dick," I shout, cupping my hands around my mouth as I rise to my feet. He is, too. Has been for years, judging by the Viagra prescription Audra found in his medicine cabinet when she moved in with him and Mom.

It's about now I notice the three boys waiting in the shelter, nearly doubled up in hysterics. They look about fifteen or sixteen, but it's hard to tell with their faces contorted in laughter. I'm just relieved they were too broken up to whip out their cell phones and capture the exchange. Better to be laughed at by three kids in a bus stop than an entire nation on YouTube. I don't even bother pretending to ignore them as I stoop to grab my bag. The worn nylon exterior is mottled black on one side, matching the constellation of oil drippings dotting the pavement. I sling it over my shoulder, greasy side out, and proceed to the timetable posted at the end of the shelter.

There's only one bus that serves this station on Sunday. It runs south around Lake Washington—back to the airport. If I'd spotted Keith before he spotted me I could have saved myself a few miles and some personal turmoil. The palm of my right hand, shredded when it broke my fall out of the car, burns as I dig into my front pocket for my phone to check the time. I gnaw the loose bits of blacktop out of my flesh, probing the deepest scrape with my tongue until the taste of my own blood makes me queasy.

The laughing boys cut ahead of me on the sidewalk when the bus at last appears. Unsure what the proper fare is, I offer up a couple of singles. The driver shoots me an impatient look, motioning with his fingers until I cough up a third. He drops two quarters in my bloody palm and the door grunts closed behind me. The bus is nearly empty. I slump into a window seat near the front and rest my head against the glass. As I watch cars speed past below us, I contemplate whether it would make more sense to get off in Renton or ride all the way back to the airport. The question becomes moot when I fall asleep. I'm still not sure which would have been the better call when the driver rousts me awake at the end of the line.

Groggy and disoriented, I dismount and make my way to the posted schedules. After five minutes of study it finally sinks in there isn't a weekend bus that runs as far north as I need to go. Not even close. I'll have to transfer twice, maybe three times. I'll be lucky to make it all the way home before the buses stop running for the night. Maybe I should have taken the couch at Mom's.

Two buses later, I disembark downtown, feeling as dirty as the panhandler camped on the sidewalk. In black felt tip marker he has scrawled out, "Thank you and God bless" on a scrap of cardboard. I want to make up my own, "Will work for ride home." Not that I feel up to much strenuous labor. My head is throbbing and my eyes want to close. I light a cigarette and suck in scant relief as I tap out a short text to Kerry.

"Thanks for sending Keith, asshole."

He responds almost instantly. "WTF?"

"He ditched me at a park & ride."

"LOL. Mom said she was getting you." A moment later he adds, "Honest."

"Fuck all you."

"Where are you?"

"Sixth Avenue. With the other riffraff."

"You're not home yet?"

"Seriously, fuck you."

By the time my phone vibrates again it's buried back in my pocket, where it remains until I stumble off the bus at the Lake Forest Park shopping center. Despite my exhaustion, I feel a surge of adrenaline being this close to home. It's still a good mile and a half hike, but it's walkable, and there's enough of a moon above to guide me. But as long as I'm here I might as well duck into the Big A and pick up a few groceries. No telling what I'll find when I get to Dad's.

The shopping cart handle feels cool against my skinned palm, a sensation I enjoy until the neurons in my brain start spazzing out about all the germs infiltrating the open flesh. I steer the cart into the store with my good left hand and the knuckles of my right. The girl at the express checkout looks up as I pass, then abruptly turns away. I recognize the pulsing muscles in her clenched jaw. I know that firm, superior chin. It's her. It's got to be. Julianne Wilkes. I'm ninety-eight percent certain of it, though it's nearly fourteen years since I last saw her, at a party the week after graduation. She turned from me in much the same manner that night.

My glances grow more covert each time I swing by, which in all honesty is more than one could plausibly chalk up to a lack of familiarity with the store layout. There's nothing furtive, however, in the way her eyes sweep over my cart, hands, and bag. It feels plainly like suspicion, as though she's determined to catch me stuffing a rib-eye steak down my jeans.

Underestimating the security here is not a mistake I'll repeat. If Julianne is watching me this closely, no doubt the guys monitoring the cameras hidden inside the darkened bowls suspended from the ceiling are as well. I'm counting on them not recognizing me. Simply by entering the store I've violated my lifetime ban. Julianne didn't work here then—though the condoms the night manager dug out of my coat pocket were filched in her honor. I thought I'd thrown them off my scent by bantering casually with the checkout lady as I paid for a king-sized Snickers. Three steps outside the door, I was collared by a Big A goon in a clip-on tie and matching blue vest. After patting me down, he yanked my head up by my hair while his boss, still clutching the purloined Trojans, snapped a Polaroid. I was then physically removed from the premises and thrown clear over the ivy bed onto the sidewalk. I might have had grounds for some kind of excessive-force suit had I chosen to pursue it.

We dated for a week and a half the summer after our junior year in high school. Three dates, the last one concluding in the back seat of my dad's station wagon. She broke my lifetime streak of solo flights with a clumsy hand job. Then it was my turn to explore her goodies. And then we were together, me inside her, so blinded by the sheer brilliance of it all that I had to play it back moment by moment in my head after I drove her home to believe it had actually happened. When the reality sank in, so did the paranoia. I went to bed that night convinced I'd gotten her pregnant. Before the next time, I'd be prepared. And I would have been, if I hadn't gotten caught.

She canceled our next date on some meandering bullshit story that started with her grandma going into the hospital for gallstones and ended with her being grounded for missing curfew. Then she stopped taking my calls. The more she didn't answer, the more I called, until one afternoon I got an automated message saying my number had been blocked. She transferred out of two classes that fall to avoid being in the same room with me, but she couldn't erase herself from my history. My first and forever. At least that's how I romanticized it until it sank in that she hated me.

I wait until the other three clerks have customers and nose my cart into her line. A case of Rainier Beer goes first onto the conveyer belt, followed by a frozen pepperoni pizza, a box of Pop-Tarts, and some store-brand ointment to treat my hand. It's absolutely, one hundred percent, no-doubt-about-it her. Her dirty-blonde hair is cropped shorter, just above the shoulders, diving in toward her face at the temples, and she has toned down the green eye shadow, compensating with a heavier application of mascara that clumps her lashes together like road tar. The badge on her left breast says "Juli." Maybe someone along the way has pointed out to her how pretentiously she used to stress the "anne" portion of her name.

"I.D. please?" She smiles without showing her teeth.

"Seriously?"

"We card everyone." She points to a laminated sign that says exactly that and shrugs unconvincingly.

I tut as I pull my license from my wallet. "Don't act like you don't remember me, Juli*anne*."

She makes a show of scrutinizing my license, eyes darting from my photo to my face and back. "Why?" she smirks. "Do you get that often?"

I do, actually. A girl from Mindy's office plays this game every Friday. At first I thought she was flirting with me, but after three weeks I realized it was her way of conveying I was too lowly for her to bother committing to memory. I make a show of kissing Mindy around her, to demonstrate I have no designs on psychotics like her. But every week it's the same phony fogginess, like she can't quite place me. She's not the only one I get that from, but she's the one I'd most like to slap.

I lay Keith's twenty on the counter along with one of my own. She rubs them between her thumb and forefinger, as if she can somehow intuit counterfeit money with her fingertips, then keys the amount into her register. She silently counts my change from the cash drawer into the palm of her hand, which she holds back out of my reach.

"I'm sorry, but I'm going to have to look in your bag." She nods toward my cart.

"Why for?"

"Standard policy." She reaches one hand toward the switch on the light pole above her register. "Or I can get a manager to do it if you prefer."

"What did I ever do to you to deserve this?" I ask.

Her jaw tightens and she gives me one of those if-you-have-to-ask-I'm-not-telling looks. Then she flicks the switch, causing the bulb above her head to pulse. "Bag check," is all she says when her supervisor arrives. He looks me over quickly while acting like he's not, then grabs at the handle of my bag.

"What the fuck?" I yank it away from him.

"Sir, please watch your language."

"What the hell kind of way is this to treat a customer?" I unzip the bag and force it open, challenging him to probe deeper. He'll lose his hand if he does.

"It's nothing personal, sir," he assures me.

"Yeah, I bet everyone gets this kind of VIP treatment." I zip my luggage shut and grab at the plastic grocery sack on the stand behind Julianne. "You do realize this isn't the only grocery store in town, right?"

"Sir, it's just standard loss prevention."

"So you're going to look through her purse?" I point to the woman behind me in line. Though she's been following this spectacle like she's in the front row at Jerry Springer, she gasps now, aghast at the insinuation she might have stuffed her bag with pantyhose and breath mints.

"Sir, I'm going to have to ask you to leave." He glances up toward the office where my mug shot once hung and steps around the counter toward me.

I hook the strap of my carry-on over my shoulder and ram the cart into his thigh. "Like you're the first fucking guy to ever throw me out of here," I laugh, as I secure my beer under my arm. Looping the handle of my grocery bag around my wrist, I skirt Julianne's boss and the jowly security guy who has answered his summons. When I glance back, Julianne is grinning mischievously, pleased with herself for winding everyone up.

I want to hit her with a railroad tie. Hard enough to knock every last tooth out. But there's some portion of me—and it's not a small one—that wants her. So bad it defies logic. Which car is hers? There are only about twenty in the lot. I'd have a five percent chance of finding it with a random guess. Maybe the aging Celica with the garter belt hanging from the mirror by the cart corral? Cupping my free hand against the driver's window to eliminate the glare from the light above, I lean in for a peek. The security guard starts toward me, swinging something on a lanyard, a whistle or a key, I can't quite make it out. I drop my stuff into a cart and take off across the lot, slow enough he could catch me if he wanted to. Instead he assumes a tough-guy stance and stands there with his arms folded across his chest.

My adrenaline is racing as if I've stolen something. I almost wish I had just to heighten the rush. I'm a couple hundred yards into my escape when it hits me that not only did I not steal anything, I never got my change. That bitch Julianne never gave it to me. They've robbed me, not the other way around. How much is a shopping cart worth? More than nine dollars, surely. They won't be seeing this one again. The front wheels balk as I break into a trot.

The shopping center is laid out in a giant T with an elongated top, the Big A anchoring one wing and the other filled with your average suburban strip-mall tenants. I slow when I clear the leg protruding from the middle, dividing the parking lot into two distinct areas. There are almost no cars over here. I halt a moment to determine whether the echoes I'm hearing behind me in the dark are the footsteps of my security buddy and decide it's only the throbbing of my own tired head. The rattling of the wheels against the cracked and patched asphalt resumes as I push on, not ceasing until I reach the smooth concrete of the sidewalk. Up the hill I turn, the roadway to my right illuminated by a street light mounted on a wooden pole and a steady stream of headlights. The grade steepens when I turn left, facing the long hill I used to dread when biking home as a kid. The shopping cart is now more trouble than it's worth, and if I weren't in such a petty mood I'd leave it here on the sidewalk where it could easily be retrieved. Instead, I cram the grocery sack into my duffel, grab the beer by its flimsy cardboard handle, and kick the cart down a brushy embankment where the creek passes under the road. Fuck you, Big A-hole.

The moon is a sliver no bigger than a watermelon rind, and I lose it frequently in the branches overhanging the road. The vague distance ahead takes on clarity with each cross street and familiar milestone. The yard where the huge German shepherd used to snap and snarl when we passed, praying the invisible fence would really hold him back. The driveway in which I wiped out on my skateboard and needed thirteen stitches in my knee in seventh grade. The bank of mailboxes Jimmy Bostic wrecked his BMX bike into when we were racing down the hill later that same summer. Finally the road plateaus at the intersection of my street.

I shift the case of beer from my left hand to my right for about the fiftieth time and embark on the final stretch. Trees and shrubs dominate most of the yards, several of which appear not to have seen a lawn mower yet this spring. The foliage is so thick, in fact, I can't even see our house until I reach the mouth of the Holts' driveway next door. My stomach churns as I pause to take in the outline of the roof, barely visible against the towering evergreens surrounding it.

There's a light on upstairs in my brother's old room, which Dad converted into an office when Kerry moved out. It strikes me as ironic, given what a utility Nazi my father was. Did he leave it on Friday night when he went out to the garage? How could next month's electric bill really matter at that point? My approach triggers the flood light mounted above the side door, illuminating the driveway from the front corner of the house back to the weedy patch along the garage. The first thing I notice is the rhododendron bush, which appears to be on steroids. It can't have been trimmed since the last time I was home. Heavy with pink blossoms, it rises up nearly to the roof and encroaches upon the concrete stoop.

I set the beer on the top step and fish into the side pocket of my bag for my keys, guesstimating how much time remains before the sixty-second timer on the motion light runs out. Another of Dad's infamous penny-pinching devices. Two keys on my old ring look nearly identical, the one I want and the other one that goes to the back door, too overgrown in ivy to be opened last time I saw it. Just as I raise them to the lamp to compare, it goes dark. I back away from the stoop, waving my arms to activate the motion sensor. My weary brain doesn't register the total darkness until the porch light pops back on. Frozen in place, I count down from sixty, eyes fixed on the second-floor window, doubting myself, wondering if it could have been a reflection I saw earlier. Then the minute expires and I'm back in darkness.

The light in Dad's office is out.

FOUR

The key pings and pops as each individual tooth makes contact with the innards of the doorknob. Hand frozen, I wait for the echo to die in my ears before turning the handle. Why am I trying to keep quiet? If there's anyone here to hear me I've already been spotted. And if it's my imagination it won't matter how much of a racket I raise. I grab an old broomstick from the pantry and clutch it in both hands like a baseball bat. It's one of a pair Jimmy Bostic and I used to play broomball with. The straw bristles are worn to the stitching and the handle was cut down to make it easier to swing. While I wouldn't necessarily want to be hit in the head with it, it pales when stacked up against the arsenal of guns and knives I imagine are wielded by whoever lurks upstairs.

Every couple of steps I pause to listen. The tiniest rustle of clothing would certainly carry throughout, but aside from the thumping of my own heart I hear nothing. The shag carpeting, matted down in the middle of each stair by decades of wear, muffles my steps as I ascend. When I reach the hall I flatten myself against the wall, nodding toward the open doorway of Dad's office as if to signal my crime-fighting partner into position. Everything I know about detective tactics comes from television; none of it is likely applicable to rousting real-life intruders from one's childhood home. Or even imagined ones. With a guttural scream reminiscent of Bruce Willis in *Die Hard*, I leap through the door brandishing the broomstick like a saber. No one shoots or stabs me. I flick the light switch up with my elbow and the globe in the ceiling chases the dark away. Again I signal my imaginary partner to zero in on the closet. After a silent three count I rip the door open. There's nothing there but a metal filing cabinet and three cardboard storage boxes stacked one on top of the other.

I reprise my commando routine across the hall in Audra's old room, which bears little trace of her long ago tenancy. Plastic bins housing my father's prized postcard collection are piled two deep across the bed and on top of the dresser. Who inherits those? Is there a library somewhere willing to take them, or will they feed a landfill? What a horrible thing to say, even inside my own head. Sorry, Dad. But seriously, why couldn't he have collected coins or stamps or Pokémon cards—something with some ready value?

My room is next. I hesitate outside the darkened entrance, wondering more what he's done with it than who might be in there. Forgoing the scream, I spin in and swipe at the light switch. Aside from two cardboard flats of Dad's picture cards, everything looks exactly as I remember it, down to the tennis shoes lined up along the wall next to the closet. Even the marijuana leaf poster I hung above my bed purposely to annoy him the summer after my freshman year at Wazzu is still here. I told him last visit he could take it down. He said he would when he got around to it. Maybe it grew on him. Maybe he was just more forgiving of my disrespect than I was of his.

The bathroom is musty. Dark rings of mildew scar the ceiling, descendants of the ones Dad nagged me to scour in high school. The weathered pump-spray bottle of Tilex on the edge of the tub could date back that far. The shower curtain, once transparent, is so filmy with soap scum I have to kick it before I'm satisfied no one lurks behind it. There's nowhere else to hide here.

I storm Dad's room, feeling a bit silly by now to be playing ninja when I haven't heard so much as a groaning floorboard since embarking on this quest. My TV cop instincts kick in again when I see the drapes flapping against the open window. But upon reflection, it would almost be more suspicious if it had been closed. He liked it cold when he slept. Icebox cold. That window was open almost year-round. Despite the mild evening, I walk over and slide it shut.

Dad's bed is neatly made, the comforter on top drawn as taut as a sail in the wind. Did he go down to the Charger Friday night or Saturday morning? I've assumed all along he never went to bed that night. What if he had? What if he slept the night through, then got up with the sun and ended it? Would it make it any better for me if I knew it wasn't the first thing he did after our call?

Above his dresser hangs the family portrait we had taken shortly before my eighth birthday. I'm all ankles and wrists, growing out of my brown, polyester, J.C. Penney suit, nearly caught up height-wise to Audra, in her sailor dress with the giant blue bow. Kerry looms behind us, piercing the camera with his prematurely angsty, eucalyptus green eyes. Neither he nor Mom is smiling. She claimed later she didn't want her eyes to look wrinkly. She's still beautiful, despite the pursed cherry lips and knitted brows more befitting a sulking teenager than the focal point around which the rest of us were arranged. Dad's beard was still dark and neatly trimmed. It wasn't until Mom left that fall that he let his grooming go. It was our last formal family photo, one of the last times we stood together as a unit. Though it's plain to me now in looking upon it my mother had already mentally terminated her membership. It's a wonder waking to such a memento every morning didn't drive my father to binge on carbon monoxide before now.

I recheck each room as I make my way back to the stairs, then canvass the first floor, examining the living room, dining room, powder room, and kitchen. There is quite clearly no one else here. I'm alone.

All alone.

The solitude suffocates me as I slump against the kitchen counter. I used to relish the nights my father worked late. Every Wednesday, he'd skip out just before dinner to teach an adult education course at the community college, leaving me on my own to microwave something to eat and crank the stereo for three hours. Once, my senior year in high school, he flew to St. Louis for four days for a math teachers' conference. Nerdstock is what I called it when I saw the pictures after he came home, and he didn't dispute it. He called home each night to check I hadn't burned the house down and remind me to empty the dehumidifier or put the trash can out to the curb. I wish so bad he would call now and tell me what to do.

He'd probably start by counseling me to keep my strength up. I set the oven for the pizza and tear into the carton of beer. It's nine hours now since they served us soggy croissant sandwiches on the plane. I've been so preoccupied chasing ghosts I hadn't realized how hungry I was. He would also advise me to wash and treat my hand before it gets infected. So I do, screaming when the water breaks through the thin film that has oozed from the wounds.

There are two texts waiting when I check my phone, both having arrived within minutes of each other nearly three hours earlier.

"Stay there, I'll come get you," turns out to be the response from Kerry I ignored. That might have saved me some aggravation.

The other came from Mindy. "How you holding up?"

"OK so far," I type.

Does she know me well enough anymore to see through that? Do I? I suspect the only thing keeping me from completely breaking down right now is I'm too tired to cry. I don't even have the energy to get drunk.

I awake clutching the broom handle, my feet hitting the floor before my brain has registered the sun filtering through the crack where the drapes in my room don't quite meet tight. Someone is downstairs, in the kitchen as near as I can pinpoint it. In my t-shirt and boxers I creep toward the doorway, straining my ears to make out exactly what is transpiring below. I hear a door creak and then latch. The bathroom off the kitchen, I decide. Awfully ballsy burglar to make themselves so at home.

If I can get down the stairs quickly, maybe I'll have the upper hand. I take a deep breath, nod to my imaginary TV cop partner, and take off down the hallway on the balls of my bare feet. I still know every squeak in these stairs from my days of sneaking in past curfew and make it down to the cold linoleum without giving myself away. Broomstick raised like a club, I position myself outside the closed door and wait, my heart pounding erratically, as if it's sending an S.O.S. in Morse code. I'm almost hyperventilating by the time the toilet flushes. It's only another beat before the door handle turns. I hitch once and unload. Swing first, ask questions later.

Kerry dives out of the broom's path just before it makes contact with the door jamb. A two-count later I'm pinned against the wall, my right arm bent behind my back, a scene played out countless times throughout my adolescence when he routinely practiced his tae kwon do moves on me. Though he no longer towers over me, he's a good forty pounds heavier. I'm just as defenseless now as I was as a gangly fifth-grader.

"What the hell you doing, sport?" he laughs, without loosening his grip.

I hate it when he calls me that. I've always hated it. At least since I was eleven and finally caught on he was using it ironically. He was the sport, not me.

"Defending myself."

He laughs again and spins me around to face him. "From

what?"

"I don't know. I thought there was someone here last night. There was a light on upstairs when I got here, then it was out."

"And?"

"I didn't find anyone."

"Probably your imagination."

Though my fruitless search had led me to that very conclusion, his dismissive smugness pisses me off. Determined not to agree with him, I simply shrug.

"I brought donuts." He lets me go and leads the way into the kitchen.

It's a full minute before I can shake the feeling back into my arm, jangling my hand and elbow as I assume my old spot at the table, the same one we sat around as kids, in the same chairs, which weren't new then. My father inherited them from his grandparents. Credit where it's due, they were built to hold up, and they have, save the occasional crack or cigarette burn in the vinyl protecting the padded seats. The cabinets and appliances are of a similar vintage. If one were to scrape down far enough, they all bear smaller versions of my fingerprints, dating back to the last time Mom cleaned them.

Our coffee has gone cold by the time he broaches the matter we've been avoiding throughout breakfast. "Fucked us over one final time, didn't he?"

It's almost an understatement, but it comes out so completely devoid of compassion I find myself wanting to defend my father. Or maybe it's just habit to take the opposite point of whatever view Kerry espouses. "He must have had his reasons."

"Yeah," Kerry snorts. "He's had them for twenty-five years. He never got over Mom."

"Why all of a sudden?" I ask. "There must have been more to it than that."

Kerry's chin tightens cockily as he shakes his tightly shorn head. "Nah, his note said it all."

I stare hard across the table at him and force the last swig of coffee down my throat. What note? No one mentioned a note. "Said what exactly?"

"I sent it to you."

"No. You didn't."

Kerry grabs his phone, taps a couple of times at the face, and slides it across the table. "They took the actual note, obviously."

It's a photo of a small sheet of paper, about the size of a telephone message notepad. In my dad's handwriting it reads, "Sorry I wasn't what you needed."

It could have been aimed at Mom, sure. But what if he meant it for me? What did I need that he wasn't? And what did he need from me?

"How long you staying, sport?"

"Dunno." Not like I've got a lot to rush back for, though I'm already missing that three thousand mile buffer. "Thursday, maybe."

"Any chance you might be able to stretch that out a bit?"

"Why?"

"Someone's got to go through all his shit." He waves toward the stairs, which I take as a shot at the postcard collection. "I'm so tied up with wedding stuff right now I can barely think."

"What about Audra?"

"She," Kerry sighs. "She doesn't really feel like this is her obligation. She and Dad didn't …" he trails off.

She feels less connected than me? Maybe if we talked more than twice a year I'd have picked up on this before now.

"Well, that's kind of a bullshit way out of helping."

"Why don't you tell her so at dinner tonight?" He grins and pushes his chair back. "Five-thirty at Mom and Keith's. I might be a few minutes late myself. Don't start the fireworks without me."

FIVE

The night Keith hit me I slept in the apple orchard behind Mom's house. It was unseasonably cool for July, and had I been thinking at all I'd have at least grabbed a sweatshirt before running out. I nearly caved when it started raining just before midnight, creeping as far as the backyard, close enough to hear Audra and her friends whooping it up inside. You can't imagine how tempting that was. Half of Audra's former dance team tripping on wine coolers, getting silly, possibly losing their tops or whatever intoxicated seventeen-year-old girls do at slumber parties. Like hooking up with their friend's younger brother if so challenged during Truth or Dare. Damn, I wanted to be in there, acting casual and semi-mysterious in the next room, close enough to be part of it if things broke the right way.

But I caught Keith, and Keith caught me, and there I was outside, freezing my rocks off instead of sneaking into the furnace room with one of Audra's slightly impaired friends. Going in would have meant explaining my crusty and swollen eye, which in all honesty was probably grotesque enough by that point they would have refused any dares to raunch with me anyway. So I stole a wool blanket from the garage and retreated to the orchard to plot my revenge.

I'd wait until morning when the girls had all sobered up and Mom was there, maybe at breakfast, and then I'd tell them all about the tiny camera I discovered tucked into the potpourri dish on the bathroom counter, and how it was aimed right where their good bits would be when they pulled down their panties, which they'd be doing a lot at the rate they were plowing through the two cases of Bacardi Breezers Keith had so generously supplied. And how when I searched the rest of the room I found the second lens mounted in the frame of the shower door. And how when I taped a picture of Oprah Winfrey from Mom's *People* magazine to the wall and aimed the first camera at it Keith came storming down from his lair upstairs and shoved me into the door, called me a fucking smartass, and threatened to hit me if I told anyone. And how he then hit me anyway mere seconds later when I asked how many times he'd already jerked off. His hands were so big the entire left side of my face turned purple.

In the end I pussied out. I'm not sure why I figured he wouldn't be there. Maybe I assumed someone who found such a prominent place in the front hallway to display his Salesman of the Year trophies would spend more time on the showroom floor. I didn't anticipate him taking a vacation day for another wankathon when Audra's friends showered. But there he was at the head of the table when I walked in.

"Geez, kid, what happened to you?" he boomed out, in his back-slapping, everybody's pal voice. "Run into a fence post?"

It's hard to glare when you've only got one functioning eye, but I squinted as best I could at him. He grinned back, betraying not the slightest hint of contrition.

"You oughta know." My cracking voice lacked all the bravado I'd mustered up overnight.

"No. I don't." His eyes narrowed, challenging me to proceed, promising an escalating cycle of ass kicking.

My mother's gaze fell to her plate. Audra shrugged apologetically at her friend Rachel, the only one of the crew to make it as far as the dining room—and she was holding her head in her hands, as if it might somehow stop the room from spinning on her.

"Fuck this," I said, causing Mom's head to snap up. I

don't think she'd ever heard me swear before. I was still the innocent one, at least relatively speaking, and she hadn't seen me in many situations that would have warranted cursing. "I'm going back home."

My mother, who had seemed neither excited nor sorry to learn I was part of the bargain when she "rescued" Audra only eighteen hours earlier, started up after me, her rusty maternal instinct finally cutting through the fog of antidepressants.

"Let him go, Lana," Keith called.

She spun back toward him and summoned the Russian evil eye. "I'll talk to my son if I want to."

That may have been the last time I was proud of her. It was certainly the first time I was afraid for her. She caught up to me in the tiny spare room downstairs, where they'd stuck me for the time being until Keith could clear out his media room on the second floor. She watched me zip my still packed suitcase, then sat down on the futon and patted the mattress beside her. I leaned into her and let her wrap her arm tight around my shaking shoulder.

"*Ya lyublyu tebya*, C.J.," she whispered. *I love you.*

I was crying too hard to say anything, so I just nodded against her neck. She stroked my hair like she used to when I was young. Instead of calming me it only made me sob more.

"I'm sorry," she said, when I finally stopped.

I pushed myself up from the bed and grabbed my sweatshirt off the doorknob. After turning over several choice descriptors, I settled on the simple and undeniable. "He's a prick."

This, Mom conceded with a nod. She followed me back upstairs to the front hall. This time it was her turn to weep. I hugged her awkwardly, clutching my suitcase in one hand and my duffel bag in the other. When she opened the door, I assumed for a moment she would lead me to her car. But she stood aside and let me pass. Within two winding blocks I was lost. I might as well have been in Oklahoma for as well as I knew the East Side. Issaquah, where they lived, was a ritzy suburb off a ritzier suburb across Lake Washington from Seattle. For a kid two weeks short of his sixteenth birthday, with tears drying on his puffy, aching face, it felt like a thousand miles from home. I spun around twice trying to determine whether I was going the right way, then continued in the direction I'd started. Sooner or later, I figured, I'd come to a bus stop. Before I made it that far, I heard the friendly honking of a horn as a car pulled alongside me. Rachel smiled at me sadly and popped the trunk on her dad's Saab.

I told her everything. She got so furious about the cameras she nearly drove up on the curb. She swore she'd get her father, an attorney, to press charges against Keith. I asked her to just make sure Audra knew what she was getting herself into by moving there. She wouldn't take it seriously from me, I knew, but she might listen to her friend.

Not that there would be any chance of changing her mind. She hated living with Dad. The burden of replacing my mother fell most heavily on her. From the time she was nine she was expected to make dinner for the rest of us. On the random occasion she felt adventurous enough to try one of Mom's old recipes, she'd wind up in tears after Dad made the inevitable tone-deaf comment about how it was close but just a little off somewhere. That quickly curbed her enthusiasm for cooking, reducing our menu to a rotation of chicken fingers, fish fillets, and frozen pizza. Even still, if Audra couldn't find an excuse not to be home, it was her job to move dinner from box to oven to table. When she got her driver's license the day she turned sixteen, it came with the stipulation she'd fetch the groceries as well. Dad briefly added her to his Visa account when he realized she was pocketing a cut of the grocery money. A four hundred dollar charge from Nordstrom ended that experiment, but not the constant fighting over money and responsibility that never seemed to entangle me or Kerry.

Like Mom, she plotted her escape for weeks before finally executing it. I went along on the spur of the moment because I didn't want to be the only one left. The one who had to try to make conversation on the nights Dad didn't want to exist outside his own head. The one who caught the sharp comments when he got in a wine mood. He was a wiseass drunk. Once or twice a month he'd dull his inhibitions enough to loosen his tongue and let you know what he really thought. It was never cruel. More the kind of stuff that might have been funny if it came from your buddy, but not so much from your old man. Like, "The guy from Foo Fighters called. He wants his hair back." Or, "Next time you use my computer can you slip a Trojan in the disc drive? All that porn, something's going to catch eventually."

I was also kind of hoping for a fresh start in school. Maybe being the new kid wouldn't be as bad as being the scrawny longhair on the cross-country team who hangs out with the scientifics to look cool by comparison. Which wasn't why I actually hung out with them. We'd all been friends since grade school. It's kind of dickish to suddenly break away and trade up to a new clique of supposedly hipper kids. Whereas if you start over at a new school, voilà. Right?

Fortunately, I wasn't gone long enough to have to explain this to any of them. If Dad hadn't actually seen me leave, he wouldn't have known, either. He probably would have just figured I was over at Bostics', because half the time I went to Jimmy's I forgot to call home and let him know. Or more like I didn't figure he'd even notice I was missing.

But he was home. When he saw me hauling my suitcase down the stairs he looked so hurt I almost turned around on the spot. He could expect it from Audra, or even Kerry, who had finally left in the spring after threatening to move out every few weeks since his sophomore year of high school. But not from me, the semi-reliable one, who until recently had even shown the occasional interest in his postcards. "Et tu, Brute?" was all he said.

He looked up from the kitchen table when I entered, then dropped his eyes and resumed reading his newspaper as I shuffled past with my bags. By the time I showered and changed he was gone. He barely spoke at dinner that night. Maybe if you couldn't literally see Keith's handprint on my face I could have claimed I simply changed my mind. But you could. Clearly. I'd run back because I'd had no choice.

Our relationship was never the same again.

SIX

Someone has hung the keys to the Charger on the hook by the kitchen door. Maybe Kerry, maybe the sheriff's deputy who responded to Mrs. Holt's call Saturday morning, maybe Mr. Holt, who wrapped his fist in his jacket and punched out a small pane of glass so he could reach through and unlock the side door into the garage. He found Dad slumped against the driver's side window, completely unresponsive. He killed the engine and dragged my father outside, no easy task considering he's at least five years older and thirty pounds lighter than Dad is.

Was.

I'm still having a hard time putting things in the proper tense. When you haven't seen someone for five years it takes a little longer for it to sink in that they're not around anymore. Particularly when their house is frozen in time. Nothing has changed in this kitchen since my last visit. The linoleum Dad claimed he was going to replace is still worn in the same traffic pattern, smoothed by decades of feet shuffling from refrigerator to table to sink. The faded flyers crammed in the top slot of the bamboo mail rack on the wall could be the same ones that were there when I left for college. The Charger keys dangle just below, bound to the same plastic Knott's Berry Farm souvenir pendant I inherited from Jerry Dugan when I bought the car. The metal feels cool against my palm when I wrap my fingers tight around them.

The broken glass has been swept up and the window crudely repaired with plywood, but the smell of exhaust still hangs in the dank garage air. Not wishing for a copycat sendoff, I press the control mounted on the wall and the four-panel, double door ascends upon its track. My father's cypress green Outback wagon is parked closest to me. To its right on the pitted concrete floor sits my old junk heap, soft tires rotting out from under it. The renewal sticker adhered to the rear plate denotes it was last street legal in 2002. I'm amazed it even started up for my dad. It was always a fumy beast. It's half a wonder I didn't wind up like him back in high school.

When I bought it off Jerry, I thought it was cool my car rolled off the assembly line the same year as I did. But things can be old without being classic. No one looks back now and marvels over the '80s as a great decade for automobiles. Had it been a souped-up Shelby model at least it would have had some muscle. Mine was one of the anemic 1.7-liter models Dodge dumped on the market in 1983. New, it would have had a clean body going for it. By the time it sputtered into my driveway, the rust was flaking off the undercarriage and there was a long gouge in the passenger-side door where Jerry's older brother once sideswiped a concrete planter. I exorcised a lot of frustration pounding out that dent and several smaller ones. Stereo cranked to antisocial volumes, I filled and sanded the dings, reapplying new layers of putty when the lines came out uneven. Again. And again.

That was after Dad and I gave up under the hood. We tried following along with the Haynes repair manual, but struggled even changing the belts, which should have ranked on the easy end of the scale. That quickly scuttled my grandiose plans to rebuild the engine and cured me of any delusions I was some kind of automotive savant. When I grew bored of the cosmetic work I abandoned the project, reverting to a mooch lifestyle of bumming rides off Jimmy Bostic and begging my dad for the keys to his wagon.

My hand lingers on the driver's door, fingers poised but

unwilling to lift up on the handle. I'm not sure why I've come out here, why I'm clutching the keys in my fingers. The car is clearly not road worthy. The stressed tires wouldn't last the length of our gravel driveway. Dad exploited its only use Friday night. Or Saturday morning. We may never know exactly when he came out here and fired her up. Mr. Holt told Kerry all was normal when he put the trash out around ten on Friday night. Sometime between then and six o'clock Saturday morning, Dad walked his final steps to where I stand right now.

The door groans and lunges at me when I pull it open. The air inside is damp and heavy and smells faintly of Old Spice. I fan the opening with my hand to encourage the death-infused particles to disperse into the surrounding air. Many of them cling still to the faux sheepskin covers like dew, infiltrating my pants and sweatshirt almost immediately upon contact as I sink into the bucket seat. A shudder runs up my spine when my foot touches the gas pedal. It's almost enough to make me clamor out, but I slowly exhale and the creeped-out sensation subsides. I finally grasp why I'm here. Basic curiosity. I want to understand.

I pull the door tight and slide the key into the ignition, turning it just far enough to bring the dashboard to life. The speakers emit soft but modern music that sounds vaguely familiar, something I would only ever have listened to long enough to reject and change the station. A woman's passionate, almost operatic, voice, backed by a sweeping orchestra. I punch the eject button and the stereo spits out the *Titanic* soundtrack. Holy hell, he choreographed the whole thing, down to the music he'd drift away to.

How long did it take? Was there a fleeting moment in there when he reconsidered? Was it too late by then? My eyes roam the cab, seeking what he saw as he drew his last breaths. I start when I catch the outline of his head in the side window, his hair and beard smudged into the otherwise even film of CO-laced condensation coating the inside of the glass. I don't realize I'm hyperventilating until I've fled the car. I pace the driveway until my breathing returns to normal, then return to fetch the key from the ignition. As I lean in, a sparkle draws my gaze to a crease in the matted seat cover.

It's a woman's earring in the shape of a teardrop. I'm hardly an expert on expensive jewelry, but I'm fairly sure it's a real diamond. A big one.

My mother used to have a pair just like it.

SEVEN

I recognize the two pig-tailed girls chalking the walkway from photos Audra has posted on Facebook. I sent a card and a little unicorn onesie Mindy picked out when Chloe was born four years ago. My sister's response, as filtered through the family grapevine, was pure snark about how she'd be sure to frame the outfit to memorialize my generous gift. She was apparently hurt I didn't drop everything to fly out for the big event. When Naomi was born the following year I sent nothing. I can be petty, too.

I can't tell which one's which. They're both coated in pastel-colored dust from their cheeks to their shoes. They stare at me as I approach from the driveway, then retreat to the covered porch and the safety of Grandpa Keith. By his grin, he's just scored a point on Uncle C.J. There's something grossly ironic in the way their ingrained fear of strangers sends them to him, in whose company they've apparently been entrusted. By all rights his voyeurism hobby should have landed him on the sex-offender registry. Then again, Audra was willing to overlook such faults in her own youth, so why get all protective now?

I crouch a little to draw myself nearer to their height and hold out my palm as one might when encountering a strange dog for the first time. They scrunch closer to their grandfather, who wraps an arm around each.

"Hi, Chloe," I say to the one nearest the front door, in the patronizing tone I detested myself as a child. "I'm C.J." I leave out the formal "uncle" title to convey that I'm really just a big kid, like her.

Her forehead creases as she shakes her head at me. "I'm Naomi, stupid." She doesn't actually say the "stupid" part, at least not out loud, but it's definitely implied in the eye roll.

Keith chuckles and pats her shoulder. Game, set, match. Start the bus.

"Wow, you sure have grown, Naomi," I say, emphasizing her name as I rise back to full height. "I'm going to go see your mommy now."

"She's the one in the black sweats," Keith calls out as I open the storm door.

If I held the weight advantage over him that he enjoys on me I'd hurl him over the railing into the juniper bed. Then I'd leap down upon him like Hulk Hogan and pound his head into the bird bath until one or both of them cracked. I'm not sure it's possible to hate anyone more than I hate him right now. It's all I can do to pretend I didn't hear him.

Audra's husband, David, is camped on the couch Indian style, his tassled loafers lined up on the floor next to the ottoman, upon which sits his open laptop. Bluetooth jammed in his left ear, he grunts out one-word answers and taps at the keyboard. Heir to the Swain family printing empire, comprising two East Side locations as well as the flagship his grandfather launched downtown in the early 1970s, he took half a dozen business calls in the limo the night of his bachelor party. His own father finally confiscated his phone. We made it our mission to get him out of his skull on tequila, which took longer than I figured it would. Turned out he'd been in some Alpha Beta Drinka fraternity at the UW. Judging by his best man, it was one of the nerdier houses on campus, though it had the same ready access to alcohol as the cool-kid frats.

He puked in the parking lot of the strip club three times, which made me feel a little guilty, though he did pay me back by spattering my shoes with his insides as I steadied him. Between heavings, he lauded Audra's virtues, delving much deeper into the physical attributes than one might typically go with their fiancée's brother. I forgave him—actually pitied him—when he let spill how he was counting down to the wedding night, when he'd finally graduate from the hand jobs he'd settled for since proposing. Had he any inkling of my sister's history, he would not have suffered those blue balls so patiently.

Midway through her junior year in college, after a late-night run to the pharmacy in search of a home-testing kit, Audra reclaimed her virginity. She even showed me the "Worth the Wait" card she kept in her purse, as if humiliating herself to her family was one of the twelve steps required to recover her chastity. I never figured she'd even last that summer, but it took. She lost her virginity the first time way back in junior high. Then lost it, and lost it, and lost it. She was a very busy girl. Through two high schools, community college, and a semester and a half at the university, she earned a reputation as a safe bet. As sure as the sun rises in the east, as sure as birds will shit on your freshly washed car, Audra Neubauer would put out for the price of dinner and a movie. Sometimes just a movie. She saw more films than Siskel and Ebert.

Dad made a crack one night about two weeks after she moved out about how she ought to install a turnstile down there. I told Kerry, who blabbed it to Audra, who didn't speak to Dad again until well after Christmas. I think she was most pissed off she hadn't fooled him. He was never as oblivious as he led us to believe. Maybe that's why we resented it so much when the wine loosened his tongue.

You'd never guess any of this by looking at her now. She's the picture of the upscale, suburban housewife, leaning into the granite-topped island, attacking a cucumber with a ten-inch Ginsu knife. Her shimmery, black track suit hugs the curves of her body so tightly the zipper strains against her breasts, at least half again as big as I remember them. Her nails and ponytail holder match the fuchsia piping along the seams of her jacket and pants. She's tanned and toned and wearing so much lipstick she reflexively wipes the spot next to my mouth with her thumb after greeting me with the kind of perfunctory kiss you get from a friend's wife or a cousin's girlfriend, with no bodily contact and no intimation of affection.

"Christ, you look like shit," she says.

And so it begins.

"Thank you for noticing."

"No, seriously," she insists. "Mom, be honest."

My mother, clad in a low-cut blouse and tight jeans that would unfailingly fetch an "older sister" line were she to walk into a bar with Audra, places her hands in the crooks of my elbows and gives me an arm's-length onceover. "He does look a bit tired," she shrugs. And if anyone should know tired, it's her. Try as she might, no amount of makeup can conceal the fleshy, gray bags under her eyes.

"Maybe because I am," I say.

Mom pulls me to her and slips her arms beneath mine and up my back until her fingers rest on the tops of my shoulders. "I thought Keith said he gave you some money for a haircut."

"Here's what Keith gave me." I hold up my shredded palm. "Sorry I didn't put a lot of effort into my appearance. Not sure if you heard, but my father just died."

"Oh, please," Audra sniggers, her lips clamped tight together. "Like that's kept you up all night."

I eye her in disbelief as I swipe a beer from the door of the refrigerator. She betrays not the slightest hint she's bothered Dad is gone. I'd expect more emotion if one of the Kardashians OD'd.

"Well, clearly we don't all feel the same, but I've found it a bit unsettling." I watch her watch me take a long pull on my beer. "You could at least show him some respect."

"Respect?" Audra slams the knife into a tomato, cleaving

it in two with a resounding clack as the blade meets the cutting board beneath. "Like he always showed me?"

"Dad had his faults, but he sure as shit wouldn't be laughing if it was you who died."

"He didn't die," she says, pointing the knife at me, ignoring the juice and seeds trailing it across the counter and down to the floor. "He killed himself."

Her eyes are the same almond shape as Mom's, though a shade grayer, making them almost green as they catch the light from the twin pendant chandeliers above. I got Dad's eyes, standard-issue walnut brown. It's not the color that makes mine weak. It's the resolve behind my stare. I blink before she does. When I bow my head, my much maligned hair falls midway down my chest. The ends are a bit split and would benefit from a trimming, though I'll be damned if I'm cutting it this trip. I toss it back and try to reengage Audra's gaze, but she's suddenly engrossed in her salad again.

"You say that like it's not worth mourning," I say. "To me that actually makes it sadder."

"Yeah," Audra says. "Sad as in pathetic. Manipulative to the end. He gave up and blamed Mom on his way out the door. How do you think that's made her feel?"

"Why are you guys so confident it was Mom he meant? Like I said to Kerry, why now, after all this time? It could have been anyone. Maybe something happened we don't know about."

"And why are you always defending him?"

"What?" I laugh. "When have I ever defended him? I ran just as far from him as I did from the rest of you."

"Because you're selfish, just like he was."

This is turning into a typical Audra argument, every statement a right turn from the one before it. Eventually she'll wind up right back where she started.

"So I'm selfish for wanting to get as far away as possible from the most dysfunctional family this side of the Rocky

Mountains? Excuse me for wanting a fresh start."

"You exaggerate so much to justify and rationalize your immature decisions. Look at yourself. You're thirty-two and barely employed. You dress like you're still in high school. You're the dysfunctional one, C.J. You and Dad."

"I'm the dysfunctional one? Do you even remember our childhood or have you had it hypnotherapied out of your head? I won't even go into how Mom abandoned us and wound up with the pedophile who's out front watching your girls, because that's so far off the fucked-up scale—sorry, Mom, but it is." My mother's head sags, and I feel like a dick because this wasn't supposed to be about her, but our family didn't really begin unravelling until she left, so it's kind of hard to leave that part out. "Kerry had an affair with his Spanish teacher just to keep his grades high enough to stay eligible for football, then got kicked off the team anyway for failing a drug test. It's a miracle he ever passed one. He was stoned from junior high straight through college. And you, you slept with half the able-bodied males in King County. That is not normal. Dr. Phil, or whoever the hell you watch every afternoon, would probably blame that on an absence of love at home."

I've scored the most direct hit I've ever landed. On anyone. I've said a few things that have turned Mindy into a tsunami of curse words. She once threw a phone at me when I told her she was turning into her mother. Audra is armed with more than a telephone, however. The knife, now protruding from the wooden carving board into which it's been buried, is certainly more than I can fend off with a beer bottle. Fortunately, she begins her assault with the bag of carrots next to it. I turn and duck, covering my head with my empty hand, and they crash harmlessly to the floor at the feet of David, gaping in the doorway. From the way his twisted mouth hangs open, I can guess with some degree of precision how long he's been standing behind me.

"Fuck you, C.J.," Audra shrieks. "God, I fucking hate you."

She looks past me, at her husband, then claps her hand to her mouth and runs out the opposite exit and upstairs. David glares at me and starts after her. His former position is immediately assumed by Kerry, grinning like he's auditioning for a toothpaste commercial.

"Damn, sport," he chuckles. "I thought I told you not to let it all kick off without me."

EIGHT

Audra's old bedroom sits directly above the kitchen. Had she taken acoustics into account, she'd have continued down the hall to Keith's sound-insulated media room. He claims the wall panels absorb ninety-six percent of the television output at normal viewing levels. I never bought his purported concerns about disturbing my mother when she was trying to sleep across the hall. I suspect his true motivation was preventing the bassy soundtracks of his porn DVDs from carrying throughout rest of the house. Of course, given what Keith has invested in equipment, even at wholesale prices, it's probably best Audra and David are squaring off in a room in which the most expensive hurlable electronic is a clock radio.

It's David's voice we hear first, or rather his fist, beating on the very recently slammed door. Three times he asks to be let in. Three times she tells him to go away. By the pitch of her voice when the door finally opens, I guess he forced the handle until it popped. It's the last thing we'll have to guess at for a while. Audra is a screamer, and the seemingly mild-mannered David has the lung capacity to match her.

"What did that all mean?" he demands.

"Your wife's a whore," Kerry cracks, his head tilted back, eyes trained on the ceiling. As are mine. And Mom's. We follow the verbal volleys like a tennis match, shifting our gaze from one side of the elevated court to the other.

"It's not important, David."

"Is it true? What C.J. said?"

"My brother doesn't know when to keep his mouth shut."

"Right though she may be," Kerry says in a tone not unlike a color commentator on a football telecast, "that is a diversion, not a denial."

"How could you lie to me all this time?" David bellows.

"How could you possibly not know, you ignorant, self-important douche?" Kerry lampoons.

"I am not a liar."

"What do you call it, then, when someone doesn't tell the truth?"

"I never lied. I did not lie to you."

"You told me you saved yourself for me. Turns out you didn't. How is that not a lie?"

I glance at Audra's handbag on the counter next to the wine rack. Is her "Worth the Wait" card buried in there somewhere? Maybe the fine print on the back could help her wriggle out of this on some technicality.

"Not everything that happened before we met is relevant to our life together. I didn't really feel like it served much purpose to go into detail about things I did in high school."

"And college," Kerry says. "Folks, she was still very active well into her college years. Let the record show, she was quite popular on campus."

Hand to her brow, Mom shakes her head. But when she peeks up it's a smile she's suppressing. She is finding humor in the resurrection of her own daughter's sordid past. This moment in time sums up our family dysfunction better than I ever could. Shame Audra's not down here to see it. Even she couldn't refute this.

"The relevant part is the part where you told me I was your first. That our wedding night was the first time for both of us."

"Oh, dude," Kerry chuckles. "You just lost all credibility right there. Ouch."

It's probably just as well our entertainment is interrupted by Chloe—or is it Naomi?—bounding into the kitchen, one hand clutching a sparkling tiara to her head. "Mommy, look what Auntie Lauren brought us." She slams on the brakes, halting in the middle of the tile floor, turning confusedly from my mother to Kerry to me. Her sister scampers in a moment later sporting a twin crown, tugging at the hand of a perky, tight-bodied redhead who doesn't look old enough to buy herself a daiquiri.

Auntie Lauren, I presume by the rock on her left hand the size of a Peanut M&M. And why should this surprise me? When my brother wasn't copulating with the high school faculty to maintain a passing GPA, he cultivated a harem of nubile freshmen to satisfy his urges and ego. He claimed they came free of the baggage that burdened most of the girls in the senior and even junior classes, which I took to mean they lacked the wherewithal and self-assuredness to say no when he started pawing under their blouses.

I run some calculations in my head. The first mention of Lauren reached me the Thanksgiving before last, when he brought her here for dinner. Mom described her in an email as a "delightful young lady," an apt, if understated, description. So they've been dating at least a year and a half, maybe two, which would put her barely out of high school when they met. No wonder he's reluctant to get too ensnarled resolving Dad's estate. He needs to keep an eye on this one to make sure she doesn't wise up and skitter away before she's matrimonially obligated to a man nearly twice her age.

She belongs to that class of girl I write off instantly when I'm out. Not that I'd approach one, even if I stood half a chance of avoiding public humiliation. Mindy knows enough people, she'd hear about it. Maybe if I'd had enough to drink that I wasn't thinking through the consequences of A) getting shot down, or B) my girlfriend finding out, I'd give it a go. I'd bolster my confidence by ticking off her flaws as I worked up the stones to introduce myself. For starters, she's several inches shy of the minimum height for a model, there's a hump in her nose about the size of an intense mosquito bite, and … that's all I can come up with. If they made a petites edition of *Sports Illustrated's* swimsuit issue, she'd be a candidate. Either she's cloaking some serious self-esteem issues or my brother must make a lot more money than I ever guessed. Triple, maybe. He sells insurance for an independent outlet I'd never heard of until he started there and was encouraged to reach out to friends and family. When he tried to recruit me to join the force last time I came home, I pegged the operation as a pyramid scheme. That he's pulling down the coin to entice Lauren doesn't necessarily prove I was wrong.

She heads straight for my mother, bouncing up on her toes to kiss her on the cheek. Mom whispers something in her ear and drops her head on the girl's shoulder. I wish I were ever hugged like that. On either side, really. I know I haven't brought such comfort to my mother since long before I was Lauren's age—however old she is. Kerry winks at me and nods toward his fiancée, then gives me a what-do-you-think shrug. She may be young enough to be his daughter, but she has surpassed him already in maturity.

"Where's Mommy?" Chloe/Naomi asks no one in particular.

"She's upstairs, sweetheart," my mother says. "She'll be down in a minute."

Audra's muffled voice reaches us once again, her words indistinguishable but clearly barbed. As is David's response.

"Is she fighting with Daddy again?" The girl's tone is so matter-of-fact it's obvious this isn't an isolated incident. I don't recall my parents fighting. Maybe they hid it better. Or maybe Mom just bottled it up inside until she left.

"No, sweetie," Mom says. "They just went up to—"

CRASH. The chandeliers sway like pendulums as the thump of what sounded like a fish bowl hitting the floor above echoes in my ears.

"Dammit, David." Audra's voice is once more clearly audible. "I've had that fucking thing since I was eight."

"Me?" David yells back. "How's it my fault? You pushed me into it."

"And down goes the crystal unicorn," Kerry intones.

This time Mom's not laughing along. She brought the unicorn back from Sevastopol on her last visit home before my grandmother died of pancreatic cancer. We never met her. Or any of Mom's family. I still have two uncles and some cousins over there. I wonder how fucked up they are. Is it biological or environmental?

"Would somebody go separate them, please?" my mother sighs. Her eyes tremble beneath their drawn lids. I can see her chest filling and falling as she pulls deep breaths in through her nose.

Kerry waves a hand at me, index finger extended toward the hall.

"Not me." I shake my head. "I'll be in pieces smaller than that unicorn if I go up there."

"Well, she's still pissed at me from yesterday," Kerry says. "It's got to be you."

"What happened yesterday?" I ask.

"I'll go up," Lauren chips in. One can almost see the halo encircling her head as she starts across the room. What the hell is she doing getting involved in our family? I should spin her around and tell her to run out the front door before it's too late. But I let her pass and she disappears into the hall. A moment later we hear the rap of her knuckles against the door above.

David is the first one down, several minutes later. Clearly chagrined, he pauses in the doorway, one hand nervously massaging the back of his neck as his eyes dart around the floor. "Sorry you all had to hear that," he says.

Kerry and I shrug in unison. What is there to say in response? The awkwardness is so thick you could cut it with the knife still protruding from the board on the counter. I sense David would rather plant it in my chest as he passes by on his way back out to the living room. Tellingly, neither of his daughters move toward him, clinging instead to my mother's legs.

When Audra and Lauren appear, their arms are wound around each other's waists, shoulders touching, heads angled inward. Like siblings who actually like each other. I step timidly forward, unsure of what to say, but knowing I should say something. It turns out to be, "Sorry, Audra. I didn't know he ..."

I leave the sentence hanging there. It could end two very different ways. I didn't know he was so clueless as to not have caught on by now that you were such a slut in your younger days. Or, I didn't know he was there. Neither really seems like much of a remedy here.

Audra glares at me, mulling over her potential replies. She settles at last on the familiar. "Fuck you, C.J."

Damn, it's good to be home.

NINE

Audra has arranged a kid's table in the kitchen for the sole purpose of avoiding the rest of us, leaving three empty chairs in the dining room where she, Chloe, and Naomi were to have sat. Instead they encircle a green, plastic table borrowed from the basement playroom. She has strategically located it on the other side of the island, out of the line of sight from the dining room.

I park myself at the opposite end of the table from Keith, who spends the first five minutes of the meal congratulating himself on the swordfish he grilled out in the garage while the rest of us were witnessing (and/or contributing to) the crumbling of the mortar holding together Audra and David's foundation. I grudgingly nod in acknowledgement—the first time. It's marinated in an olive oil, vinegar, and lemon juice concoction and is actually quite good, but he carries on so long even Lauren wearies of complimenting him.

To my right, my mother pounds ice wine like lemonade. Every time I glance at her she's either picking up her glass or setting it back down, her eyes growing glassier by the sip, the alcohol's effect amplified by the cocktail of prescription meds that enable her to tolerate Keith. And the rest of us. Across the table from me, David taps and swipes at the smart phone lying just to the right of his dinner plate. He's not even pretending to care if he looks rude, which he does even by my standards. Lauren and Keith are the only ones making conversation. Try as they might, they fail to lure anyone else into the dialogue with the exception of Kerry, who interjects the occasional off-color joke, because that's what Kerry does.

With my sister camped in the swing path of the refrigerator door, I ration the final sips of my beer like a man crossing the desert. Inevitably, it runs dry before I finish my dinner. Kerry, who uncapped a fresh bottle when we sat down, drains the last third in one long chug and burps into the sleeve of his leather blazer. As he pushes back from the table, I motion with my empty. He returns a moment later, a single bottle in tow.

"Thanks," I mutter.

"What?" His grin implies he knows exactly why I don't want to make the run myself.

"That's all right. I wouldn't want you to strain yourself."

"What do you need, C.J.?" asks Lauren, an empty chair down from me, on the opposite side of the table from the kitchen.

"No, it's nothing," I say. "I just figured as long as he was up."

"Babe," she says to Kerry, seated directly across from her. "You should have gotten your brother a beer."

"He can walk," Kerry says. "He's a big boy."

Lauren tsks at him and rises from her seat. "I'll get you one, C.J. What kind do you want?"

"No, you don't …" I start up from my chair, but she's halfway around the table by the time I get to my feet. "Uh, whatever. First one you grab is fine. Thanks."

She's way too nice for Kerry. There has to be some catch, some heinous flaw I just can't see. Physically, she's a solid nine. She's kind to children, seems to be the only one capable of putting a smile on my mom's face, and can even make conversation with a Cro-Magnon like Keith. The only blemish I can spot is her taste in men. From the kitchen her voice rises as she greets the girls and asks if she can get Audra anything. Audra, who could literally open the fridge from her seat. She returns clutching two open longneck bottles, with a third pinned to her ribs. Circling the table, she delivers one a surprised David, one to me, and the third to Keith.

"Anyone need anything else while I'm up?" she ask "Mom, are you okay with your wine?"

Mom? She called my mother, "Mom." She honestly show more affection for her than Kerry, Audra, and I put together. Then again, Mom didn't skip out on her when she was in grade school.

Elbow planted on the corner of the table, my mother extends her fingers toward Lauren. "*Solnyshko*," she smiles. There's a word I haven't heard in decades. It was something she used to call us when we were little. When Lauren takes her hand, Mom whispers something else in Russian that I can't quite make out. By Lauren's expression she can't either, though the affectionate tone makes the precise words incidental. As Lauren helps steady her to her feet, my mother, nearly four inches taller, leans forward and kisses her on the forehead. Arm in arm, they disappear into the living room, Kerry eyeing them proudly. His fiancée has just indirectly scored him some points. She is good, and by extension he is the good son.

Mindy might have done the same. It would all have depended upon how she and I were getting along. If she was in a mood to please me, she would ply my mother with drink and lend a shoulder to lead her to her television. If she was pissy, she'd be in the other room with Audra, cataloguing my shortcomings.

Kerry swirls the remains of his beer like a snob at a wine tasting and sucks it in until his cheeks fill. When he at last swallows, he lifts the bottle to his lips and blows across the top, emitting a moan like the wind through a broken attic window.

"What's the plan for Wednesday?" I ask, when he finally lets the somber note drop.

"Eleven o'clock, Sanford's," he says. "Pretty standard

stuff."

I don't know standard. I've only ever been to two funerals, one in college and one last fall when Mindy's great uncle had a massive coronary. I wouldn't toss that one in the standard category. There were so many mourners we were relegated to an auxiliary room across the hall, where we watched the memorial service on closed-circuit television. We had to park down the street.

"It's just the funeral, then? No calling hours?"

"Ceej," Kerry shakes his head. "Who the fuck would come?"

It's a legitimate question. Dad's brother and sister, who both moved to Southern California before we were born, are gone. Neither of their surviving spouses was all that close to my father. I can't picture them making the trip. Dad must have had some friends at the college, though. He taught there for forty-three years.

"Someone might."

"Who?"

"I don't know," I confess. "I don't really feel like I know who Dad was anymore, so it's hard to guess. But obviously he knew people."

"Well, that's what happens when you move three thousand miles away from your family," Audra calls from the kitchen. She's talking to me again. Well, taunting anyway.

"I'm not sure I really knew him when I was here," I say. "And I doubt you guys did, either."

"Where the fuck is this coming from?" Kerry says. "I'm picking up some strange 'poor misunderstood Dad' vibe off you today, and I don't know where you get off throwing that around. I can guarandamntee you I made more of an effort than anyone to see him on holidays and Father's Day and shit. You ever even send him a fucking card? So don't come around here and accuse me of not being there. I was there. Dad just didn't talk much. If I didn't understand him it wasn't for a lack of trying. He didn't reciprocate. You know how many times he came over since I bought my house? Once. One fucking time in four years."

"That's one more time than he came to our house," Audra yells from the kitchen.

"And probably one more than you've been to visit him since you moved out," I say.

"What's that?" she hollers.

"Come in here if you want to be part of the conversation," I yell back.

She appears in the doorway, arms folded across her chest, eyes fixed on me. "What was I supposed to go back for, C.J.? To make him dinner and wash his dishes? He treated me like hired help when I lived there. The minute Mom moved out, everything got dumped on me. You don't make a fucking nine-year-old cook your dinner. Unless you're a chauvinist asshole."

Behind her, one of my nieces exclaims, "Mommy said another bad word."

Audra turns toward them. "Outside, you two. Go play out back on the swings. Daddy will go with you."

"Awww," they groan in unison. And who could blame them for not wanting to miss a fight that for once doesn't pit Mommy against Daddy? If only they'd have kept silent they might have been able to stay.

David looks up from his phone as if he's just heard his name called in his sleep. Eyes still glued to the screen, he rises and vacates his seat at the table. After supervising his withdrawal, Audra takes his place.

"If you're so keen to host calling hours, C.J., you can do it yourself," she says. "I don't even want to go to his damn funeral."

"Oh, come on," I say. "He wasn't that bad. You make it sound like he abused you."

"Yeah, sometimes it felt like it. You laugh, but you and

Kerry never had to do shit. I had to do everything. That's abuse."

"Okay, but you're making it out like he hauled you into the closet and made you—"

"Fuck off, C.J. I never said anything like that. Don't put fucking words into my mouth."

WHEEEET. Kerry whistles long and loud at us, two fingers wedged between his lips. "Solid points raised on both sides, but you guys are getting a bit off topic."

I offer an exaggerated shrug in response, as if none of this is my fault, when in fact it mostly is.

"Sorry," I say.

Audra responds with a glare, then turns toward Kerry. We've ceded him control.

"Let's just try to get through the next couple of days without more of this," he says. "I asked C.J. if he could try to make sense of Dad's stuff this week. Maybe go through some of his papers and at least figure out if he had a will, who his lawyer is, stuff like that."

"What if he didn't?" I ask.

"Just split it all three ways and be done with it," Kerry says.

"Or," Keith pipes in. I've spent so much energy ignoring him I actually forgot he was still there at the head of the table. "Five ways."

"How do you figure?" I ask.

"One share for each of you, one share for each of his grandchildren."

"You can't assume that's what he would have wanted to do," Kerry says.

"And if there's nothing saying otherwise, you can't say he wouldn't have," Keith argues, as if he's been watching too many court-room dramas on television.

Until now, I've honestly not given a moment's thought to what I might get out of my father's death. Aside from all the aggravation of dealing with it. He wasn't wealthy, and half of what he had he spent on those stupid postcards. But seeing Audra turning sums in her head across the table, suddenly I'm damned if she's going to walk away with sixty percent of whatever the pot turns out to be.

"Keith, you know this has nothing to do with you, right?" I say. "It's actually none of your business."

"Don't talk to me like that in my house, you punkass prick." He juts his jaw out and challenges me with his dark, boring eyes.

"Why, you going to hit me again?"

As Keith starts up out of his chair, fight or flight plays out in my head. My only hope would be cracking him across the noggin with my beer bottle. Of course, if I miss he'll carve me up with it. Still, I don't want to run, even though I could easily outpace him. The internal debate is stifled when Kerry slams the butt of his own bottle against the table.

"Grow up, man," my brother scolds Keith. "And C.J.'s right. This don't concern you."

The vein winding into the thinning garden of follicles atop Keith's dome twitches as he faces Kerry. "I'd like to knock the both of your heads together. If it weren't for your mom I'd never let either one of you ingrates through the front door."

"Yeah, it's a real fucking treat being here, Keith," Kerry smirks. "Appreciate the hospitality. But while you might be able to kick C.J.'s ass up and down the block, I would drop you like Tyson on Spinks, okay? So whenever you want go, let me know."

Keith's glare travels from Kerry to me before he finally breaks eye contact and heads for the kitchen. He pulls a bottle from the liquor cupboard above the stove and continues on out the other exit. A moment later we hear the glass door to the patio slide open. We've chased him from his own house. Well, Kerry has. I can't take any credit for it.

"So much for Christmas dinner," Kerry says. "Take one last good look around, sport. I don't guess we'll be back anytime soon."

"In that case," I say, rising unsteadily, the racing in my chest only halfway ramped down to normal, "we better drink all his beer tonight. Want another?"

Kerry nods. Audra's left hand shoots up as I pass her. I instinctively jump back, assuming she's taking a swing at me. But she's laughing, and for the first time all night it's not in a bitchy way.

"Make it three, C.J. And keep 'em coming."

TEN

I probably shouldn't be driving home. I've got that kind of buzz on where I'm fine as long as I focus, which I have to remind myself to do every thirty seconds. I feel it most in my bladder, ready to burst even before I merge onto the interstate. Dad's Outback has some balls to it, certainly more of a kick than any of the wagons he owned when I lived at home, and the needle nudges up beyond seventy-five. I lighten my foot and change lanes, preferring the anonymity of the middle column, where I blend into the stream of SUVs and sedans traveling at a more prudent speed. I have no idea what I'd blow on a breathalyzer, and I don't want to find out. That's the beauty of not owning a car in Baltimore. I'm never the designated driver unless Mindy outdrinks me. It happens, but not often. With a dozen bars within a mile walk of our place we rarely take the car, anyway.

It feels late, but the clock on the dashboard reads just 9:27. Mom was asleep in the living room when we finally broke from our powwow. Audra, adamant she doesn't want any of Dad's stuff, seconded Kerry's motion that I dispose of things as I see fit. Money aside, obviously. She's all in on that, with a keen eye on the retirement account she and Kerry figure sits at half a mill, minimum. I don't have a 401K. If I'm honest, I don't have the vaguest notion how they work. To imagine a regular guy like my dad would build up such a nest egg kind of blows my mind. Accurate or not, the speculation temporarily put Audra in a good enough mood that the last time I apologized for initiating the shitstorm with David she just sighed and shook her head, as if there was a whole lot more to the story. That's no guarantee I'll be close to forgiven when she sobers up tomorrow morning, but it beats the f-bombs she was lobbing earlier.

The analyst in me says somewhere not far beneath the surface superiority Audra regularly wields over me, there's a hint of jealousy. That she's nostalgic for the days when she could close down the bars with her girlfriends, and the resentment she dishes me is really meant for herself, for choosing a path that eliminated such options. Then again, I barely passed Psych 101, so it's possible I'm completely full of shit.

By the time I pull into Dad's driveway I have to piss so bad my back hurts. I won't last until the house. I duck just far enough into the shadows that I can't be seen from the Holts' side window. My stream hits the garage wall like a pressure washer, flaking off old paint, creating a dark spot in a sea of dusky gray. As it tapers to a trickle, my phone buzzes in my pocket. It's a text from Jimmy Bostic.

"Just heard about your dad. Sorry. You coming home?"

"I am home," I write back. "Since last night."

"Fucking A." He actually spells it out like that, and I wonder if his response was delayed at all while he deliberated proper syntax. "You've got to come join us."

"I'm beat."

"Come on. We're just down the hill at Izzy's. First round's on me."

First five rounds were on Keith, actually. But the cool evening air has a bracing effect. I slap my cheeks a couple of times and talk myself into it. Jimmy was the brother I wished I had growing up. We were inseparable. And he never once kicked my ass. Never even tried. He was a docile—dare I say, sweet—kid who lacked the competitive gene that turned most other adolescent boys into assholes, a sin for which he received no end of crap from the pathetic excuses for alpha males in our class.

"On my way," I text back.

Izzy's sits across the street from the parking lot I fled last night, a journey that seems a week ago already. I squint and can almost make out the Big A security guard still looking for me. Jimmy's at the bar with Patrick Seegar, who was a year behind us in high school. He had a younger sister I may have fancied briefly as a senior. At least until she rebuffed my invitation to the Homecoming dance. I figured it was in the bag. What freshman would turn down an upperclassman? Kerry's playbook never worked for me.

"Neubs." Jimmy rises and spreads his arms wide. His somber expression is meant to be respectful, which actually makes it more comical than if he'd been playing for a laugh. He taps me on the back twice with his fist as we embrace, then in one continuous chain nods, shakes his head, and lifts his hands in a shrug I can only interpret as "eh, what do any of us mere mortals know about death, anyway?" I reach beyond him and shake hands with Patrick, then settle onto the stool to Jimmy's left.

Patrick leans forward far enough to see past Jimmy and says a little louder than is necessary, "Your old man, huh?" The bar is so sparsely populated I can make out the conversation of the couple fifteen feet away. They, and everyone else in the building, can no doubt hear Patrick.

"Yeah," I say, quieter than usual, hoping to recalibrate his decibel level.

"Was it sudden?" he asks.

That all depends on whose side of things you're seeing it from. By definition, anything you don't anticipate happens suddenly. For all I know, Dad could have been planning this for a year. Or since the day Mom left, to hear Kerry and Audra tell it. "I don't know."

"Was he ill?" Jimmy asks.

"I don't think so."

"What did he die of?" Jimmy asks, adding a hasty, "if you

don't mind me asking."

"Carbon monoxide poisoning."

He cocks his head quizzically. For a kid who tallied a 1420 on his SAT, he was never actually all that quick when it came to everyday life. Ask him for the square root of the distance to the sun in kilometers and he'll give it to you to the third decimal place. Ask him something that can't be measured on a multiple-choice test and he was dumber than most of the potheads I hung out with in the smoking section outside the gymnasium.

"He killed himself. In my old Charger. Remember that piece of shit?"

Jimmy nods. He helped me replace the calipers on the front brakes one weekend shortly after my dad bailed on playing automotive rehab. I was still hot to show my father I could do it myself, without his help. That fervor, like most of my passions, didn't last long.

The bartender finally takes my order, having nonverbally made his point that those of us who don't profile as big tippers aren't worth being pulled away from the Mariners game until the commercial break. Not that I would have tipped him much, but he couldn't have known that for sure. I don't have any history here. Never been thrown out. Only been inside once, a few months before I turned twenty-one, and that was only because the bouncer at the place we really wanted to go rejected my doctored ID. It's a family restaurant with a bar that caters to soccer moms and their chino-wearing dates, the kind of people that actually enjoy the John Mayer spewing from the speaker above my head.

"You guys come here very often?" I spin around on my stool to survey the clientele.

"It's close by," Jimmy says. "Why?"

"No reason."

To our right, a fortyish woman in mousy glasses and winged, wavy, eighties hair sips a glass of white wine and listens as the guy seated across the small, round table from her prattles on about his job as a 911 dispatcher. He's talking so fast his face is going pink, and she's nodding every so often. I'm bored just overhearing him. She deserves an Oscar for looking as interested as she does. Two tables past them, a much quieter couple picks at a tray of wings, gazes fixed on opposite televisions. He's watching the game, she's eyeing some *American Idol* ripoff. I wager myself a thousand bucks they're married. Beyond them, on the other side of the oak railing separating the bar from the restaurant, three women chitter and titter over a bucket of margaritas. They appear to be about our age, at least based on the faces of the two I can see. I catch one of them looking at me. She turns away quickly, bowing her head conspiratorially, as if she's calling plays in a huddle. It breaks a moment later in an eruption of catty laughter, all three girls glancing in my direction. I dribble beer down my chin when I realize the third one is Julianne.

"Oh, fuck me," I mutter, turning back to face Jimmy.

"What?"

"Julianne Wilkes. As if I ever needed to see her again."

"Oh, yeah. She's here a lot. We see them probably every other time we come in." Aside to Patrick he adds, "C.J. had a little thing for her, back in the day. 'Til she dumped him."

"Yeah?" Patrick perks up.

"Something like that." I pat the front pocket of my jeans and pull out a crushed, nearly empty, pack of cigarettes. "I need a smoke. Patrick?"

He shakes his head as if I've just offered him herpes. I didn't peg him for a smoker, but figured it would be impolite not to at least ask. I down what remains of my beer and head for the door, purposely and obviously training my eyes away from Julianne's table, which sits about ten feet to the right of the step down from the elevated bar to the main floor. My shoulders and back tense when a new wave of laughter reaches my ears.

Outside, I lean against one of the support posts that hold up the awning over the entryway and thumb through the icons on my phone. There's a text from Mindy. "What are you doing? Thought you might have called by now." It came in forty minutes ago. No point in responding. She'll be asleep. I consider writing Jimmy and telling him I had to take off. But why should I slink away? What I really ought to do is march up to Julianne's table and demand the nine dollars and change she stole from me last night.

I settle instead for a casual strut back to the bar, firing a quick glare at the girls as I pass. None of them are looking—until I catch the toe of my shoe on the step and momentarily lose my balance. Jimmy and Patrick exchange a sly glance as I plop back down on my stool, my ears still burning hot enough to melt butter.

"What'd I miss?"

"Nothing." Jimmy's eyes get large and his jaw crimps tight. He was always shit at playing pranks in high school. He couldn't keep a straight face. I investigate the full beer on the counter in front of me. There's nothing floating in it. When I lift it to my nose it smells like beer.

"What'd you guys do?" I study Patrick now and can read nothing in his shrug.

"Suspicious much?" he asks.

"Just around Jimmy," I say.

"C.J.?" A woman's voice comes from behind me. I turn to find a waitress in a white shirt and black vest holding a frosty margarita.

"Yeah?"

"Sorry, hon. She's not having it."

"What?"

"She offered me a twenty to dump it over your head," she says, handing me the drink. "But that would probably cost me my job, so I'll let you boys fight for it."

The laughter comes at me in stereo, from Jimmy and Patrick to my left and the girls' table down below to my right. I doubt either group knows precisely why the other is laughing, but I think I can piece this one together. The only part that confounds me is why someone would hate me so much they'd decline a free drink on the grounds I might have been the one to send it over.

ELEVEN

Jimmy's five minutes into his apology before the fact I answered the door in my boxers registers. "Oh, man. I didn't wake you up, did I?"

"Nah."

"You sure?"

"I was meaning to get up about now, anyway." Per the clock on the stove against which I'm leaning, now turns out to be ten before noon, not an unreasonable hour for him to have expected to find me awake.

"Son of a bee, I should have texted first or something. Sorry. I'm not really thinking too good this morning. I almost puked on the way to work. I haven't been hungover in so long I forgot how crappy it feels. I told my boss I thought I might have the flu. She took one look at me and sent me home."

The right side of his mouth curls up into a sheepish grin. I'm guessing this may be the first time he's drank himself into a sick day. I can't recall having ever banked enough goodwill at any job to have been sent home with well wishes. It seems to be generally assumed when I call in sick there was a devil in a bottle to blame. If I'm not hungover at the moment, it's only because I'm still drunk. The line can get a little fuzzy sometimes.

"Coffee?" I draw a nearly full bag of dark roast from the pantry.

He shakes his head. "No, didn't go down good this morning. Man, I shouldn't have drank that margarita. We never would have even ordered it if I knew what happened Sunday. I still can't believe she did that."

"How would you have known?"

"Still, I feel like such a dick."

"Forget it," I say. "And quit apologizing. It's actually kind of funny in a way."

In the way things are funny that happen to other people. Unfortunately, this is my circus. These are my monkeys, and the excrement they're flinging is aimed at me.

"You make it home okay?" Jimmy asks.

I glance down at my body in search of any evidence to the contrary. Outside in the driveway, Dad's Outback lacks any major dents or mailboxes protruding from the grill.

"It's a pretty straight shot up the hill. And I wasn't all that bad off when I left." Rubbing my face with my palm, I aim an elbow at the five empty cans congregating in the sink. "I was fine until I ran into them."

"Fucking A, Neubs."

"I know. I should have just gone straight to bed. But I was kind of worked up."

"On account of Julianne?"

"On account of everything. My dad … it's been a shit week." I stoop to dump the old filter into the can under the sink and feel a breeze through the fly of my shorts. There's more visible down there than most old friends would want to take in. "Let me go throw some clothes on. I'll be right back."

I return in the same outfit I wore last night. My shirt is damp and smells of beer. Jimmy's on his hands and knees poking the old sawed-off broomstick under the table, batting at a wadded paper towel trapped beneath the legs of a chair.

"What are you doing?" I laugh.

"Practicing."

Broomball, like most of our favorite adolescent pastimes, was born of boredom one summer afternoon when we were in junior high. My father taught a full load even during summer, making our house the choice hangout for my friends. Jimmy spent so much time here, he would let himself in if I was still sleeping. When it was nice out we rode bikes and threw stones at cans and sat up in my tree fort pounding Hostess Ho Hos and flipping through Kerry's old *Playboys*. When it was lousy we hung out up in my room chucking bottle caps into a jar or playing full contact, no rules, Nerf basketball. One afternoon when my brother and sister were off doping or whoring or whatever they did when they left, we marked off a soccer field in the living room, rolled up a tube sock for a ball, wrapped it in duct tape, and took turns kicking it as hard as we could, equally pleased to nail each other in sensitive body parts as to sneak one into our opponent's goal. Within an hour we had our first casualty, a ceramic vase Audra had made in art class. As I swept up the shards of pottery, Jimmy peppered me with the sock. I fended off his shots with the broom and the light bulb went on. Broomball.

When other friends came over we'd hold tournaments, round-robin format, Jimmy keeping track of wins and losses, goals scored and allowed, and whatever other statistics his computer brain could compile. Kerry played occasionally. He brought a lacrosse mindset, hacking us mercilessly until our forearms and shins were bruised and welted. He lacked skill, however, so despite his tremendous size and strength advantage, Jimmy and I fared well in our matches against him.

We clear the center of the room, pushing all furniture to the wall by the front window. Out of habit, I remove the framed M.C. Escher print from its hook. Impossible staircases were Dad's idea of fine art. I thought he was going to cry the day we broke the glass my freshman year in high school. He docked the cost of replacing it from my allowance. While I tape up a sock, Jimmy lines a pair of kitchen chairs up on opposite walls. A valid goal must pass through the two front legs. I roll the ball to him to initiate the action. His eyes are keen and clear now, his hangover evaporated, as he taps the ball back and forth in front of him. He feints left and starts up the right side of the field. I step forward to meet him. He jukes one way and moves the other. I mirror his movements, shuffling my bare feet across the hardwood floor. Having worked his way to midfield, Jimmy winds up, drawing his broom behind him for a shot. I spread myself wide to maximize my reach, just as he's anticipated I will. With a flick of the broom, he pops the ball between my legs, cuts around me, and sweeps it into the goal.

"One zip." The self-satisfied smile on his face is the same one I've seen right here in this room a thousand times before, after each clever maneuver that either led to or prevented a goal.

My gameplan has always been a bit more helter-skelter, reliant mainly on passing to myself off walls or other handy objects, confident I can anticipate the angle of the ricochet better than my opponent and advance downfield with an unimpeded path to the goal. I fake to my right, where we've lined the back of the couch up as one sideline, then slap the ball off the wall to my left. Warding Jimmy off with my right elbow, I collect the rebound and dribble it near enough to tap it easily home and knot the score.

The contest grows more physical as we proceed. Even compared to me, Jimmy is slight. While I have filled out somewhat in the shoulders, chest, and gut since our broomball heyday, his ribs are still prominent through his sweat-drenched tee when he sheds his dress shirt. I feel guilty about lowering my shoulder into his to clear some space, but he's quicker than I am and I'm forced to adopt Kerry's strategy to keep it close.

"Sorry," I say, after driving in my ninth goal to draw within one. "That was kind of a cheap shot."

"It's fine." He grimaces, rubbing his chest where it absorbed the impact. "It counts."

"You sure?"

He eyes me like I've just offered to cut the crusts off his peanut-butter sandwich. Batting the ball out of the goal, he dribbles to midfield and waits for me to get set. By now I've seen all his moves and he's seen and felt mine. He opens his attack with a spin move I counter by stepping back. The last two times I tried to spin with him, he pirouetted into a clean shot. He appears surprised by my conservative approach, so I cross him up once more by lunging forward. It works. I pop the ball just far enough away from him that we both have an equal shot at it. I swing hard, hoping to bounce it to myself off the couch, but it sails high. Our mouths fall in concert as the ball slams into the blown-glass lamp on the end table. Racing gravity, I charge after it. The lamp wavers and topples. I'm half a step too slow, grasping vainly as it crashes to the floor.

"Oops," Jimmy laughs.

"Sorry about that, Dad," I chuckle. It was a hideous lamp, shaped like a phallic mushroom, its glass shade rounded like the tip of a fully engorged, erect penis, etched in gold with a representation of our solar system. The base was likewise done up with a moon and sun. It was one of a pair my parents bought in an antique shop in Bulgaria the week they met. Kerry broke the first one with a football twenty years ago.

Jimmy runs to the kitchen to fetch a waste basket, and I kneel to pick up the big pieces. The moon side, which hit the floor, has shattered, but the sun side is still one unbroken piece. I pinch it with my fingertips and drop it in the trash. Beneath it, amid the shards of smoky glass, lies a long, narrow, manila envelope. I pick it up by a corner and blow the tiny fragments of lamp away from the flap, tucked inside the opening.

"Fucking A," Jimmy mutters, when I spread the envelope wide to reveal a thick stack of bills.

There are twenties, fifties, and hundreds, some so stiff

they cling together, others soft and worn. I line them up by denomination on the floor. When we add them all up there is $9,740. I'm tempted to bust open the rest of the furnishings, but we settle instead for shaking and feeling our way through the remaining downstairs décor, finding nothing of interest. The base of the broken lamp was held in place by screws, making it an ideal place to hide money. The question is, from whom?

"What are you going to do with it?" Jimmy asks, after we've cleaned everything up and have counted the loot a third time.

"I don't know." I know what I won't be doing, and that's telling anyone else about it. I wonder for a moment if Jimmy can be trusted not to say anything tomorrow. "Find another hiding spot, I guess."

TWELVE

I can still button the pants from my high school band tux. It requires some slight adjusting of my internal organs and a significant sucking in of breath, but they fasten, which moves them to the top of the list of possibilities for tomorrow's formalities. The jacket's sleeves are short but close enough they won't draw attention. It pinches a little in my armpits as I pace back and forth across my room, pantomiming a witty interaction with one of the many guests Kerry has insisted won't materialize. If the funeral doesn't run long I might survive. For now I've had enough. My liver, pancreas, kidneys, and bladder scramble back into place when the pants are unbuttoned.

I don't own a suit. The last one I had was the one immortalized in that final family portrait. I had a navy blazer in college that was supposed to have come in handy for all the highbrow extracurricular events I was meant to attend. I sold it at a consignment shop my sophomore year for twelve dollars.

My father's suits are no better. The pant length is close enough, but I can't keep them up any better than I could a hula hoop. He was thirty-five pounds heavier than me last time I came home. The gap may have grown since. I cinch the trousers with one of his leather belts and the cloth around my ass flares out like I'm smuggling balloons back there. The jacket hangs loose around me, the wool rustling as I raise and lower my arms. In the bathroom mirror I look like a child playing dressup. Buttoning the jacket causes the lapels to billow away from my chest. When I plunge my hands into the side pockets to flatten the front, I find two ticket stubs from the Paramount Theatre for *The Lion King*, dated March 20th of this year. He never went to the theatre when I lived at home. I thought he hated it. Not that he ever had anyone to take. Who did he go with in March?

I shrug the jacket off my shoulders and shuffle back to Dad's room on my tiptoes to keep from tripping over the cuffs. Just as I let the pants fall to the floor, I hear the muffled booming of a car stereo and the popping of tires on the gravel driveway. Slacks in hand, I rush down the hall in my boxers. Parked below the office window is a black Acura sedan. The music ceases as the door opens, so simultaneously it's as if the one controlled the other. An oversized handbag swings out through the opening, followed by Lauren, who heads straight for the side door. After waiting a moment to see if Kerry emerges from the passenger side, I yank Dad's pants back on and scurry down the stairs.

"C.J.," she laughs, as we enter the kitchen from opposite sides. "What are you doing?"

"I was just …" I pause to notch the belt and guide the end through the first loop on the pants. I then smooth my t-shirt, tucking it in tight, imagining myself as she's seeing me, as one who has been caught in a guilty moment. "I wasn't jerking off or nothing, I swear."

"Oh my god," she squeals. "I didn't figure you were. Not that I've never caught your brother going at it. I only meant what are you wearing? Are those Warren's?"

"I was trying to find something for tomorrow. I don't really have anything."

"Nothing? Not even a nice pair of slacks?"

As I shake my head, it's Audra's taunting voice I hear. Only I had nicer clothes when I was in high school than I have now, so technically she was wrong.

"Well, you can't wear those. Have you got a nice shirt at

least?"

"Kind of. I guess. I mean the shirt from my band tux—"

"You can't wear a tux shirt to a funeral. Good night, you're worse than Kerry. Look, help me find some pictures of your dad and we'll go shopping, okay."

"I'm kinda …" How do I explain broke to a girl who apparently is not? Oh, but wait, I'm not, either. If only I can distract her long enough to raid the envelope buried in the bottom drawer of my dresser. "All right. Cool. Pictures, huh? What kind of pictures?"

"Anything nice, especially with you guys in them. Framed, or we could mount them on poster board. It'd be a nice tribute. Kerry wasn't planning anything. I said you have to do something. That was three days ago. So here I am, because he found yet another excuse."

"He doesn't seem to think anyone's going to come."

"Augh." Lauren taps her hand to her forehead. "I've had it up to here with him on this. A, he's wrong. And, B, so what? It's his dad. Your dad. How's he not worth just a little bit of effort? Even if nobody shows up—which they will—it's still not a big ask."

She waves her hands when she talks, raising them in animated shrugs and bringing them down in short chops like an orchestra conductor. Her cheeks flush the more worked up she gets. With her cream-colored pants and blouse, pink face, and red hair, she looks like a matchstick. No one in our family is this passionate about anything. When she marries Kerry she'll instantly become both our conscience and heart by default.

I lead her upstairs to Dad's room. A small wooden bookcase under the window is lined with blue and gold photo albums. He filled two a year when we were young with prints from an old Canon single-lens reflex he used to take every time we left the house. The year after Mom left the pace was cut in half. We stopped posing and he stopped taking pictures. The entire four years I was in high school are captured in one binder. There have been just two added to the shelf since. At some point, he took to tossing loose prints into a shoe box on the top shelf. I start with these, pulling out a fat handful and sitting down on the bed. Lauren sits next to me. She smells of minty Listerine breath strips and lavender perfume. I hand her each photo as I work through the stack. Most are of other people. Me and Mindy at a party last Christmas. My late Uncle Dax sporting a triumphant smile on his weather-beaten face as he dangles a marlin from a thick fishing line. My grandpa scowling from behind his walker. There are a bunch of people I don't know, half a dozen shots alone from a picnic at a park I vaguely recognize. In the last of this group, my father stands next to another man in a Northpoint College t-shirt, each resting a baseball bat on his shoulder. He looks genuinely happy, like he just scored the winning run in the department softball game.

"Use this one," I say. She sets it aside.

We pull two others from the box. The first is my father in his office at the college, wearing some kind of metal contraption on his head, like a tiny jungle gym illuminated by Christmas lights. The other is one Lauren took of him and Kerry at a restaurant.

"What about this one?" she asks, as I kneel to pull the most recent album from the shelf. She's pointing to the family portrait above his chest of drawers.

"With my mom in it?"

"She's so beautiful."

"Yeah, she was really pretty."

"She still is." Lauren lifts the frame gently off its hook. "I'd kill for her hair even now."

"You really think we should use that one, though?"

"She was part of your dad's life. Tomorrow's about him. No one seems to get that. This is actually perfect. Are there more like this?"

I pull out the Entiat-era albums and she opens one on her lap after resuming her place on the bed. Every so often she plucks a photo from its plastic sleeve and adds it to her stack. As she completes each binder she hands it to me and I swap it for a new one.

"That's probably enough," she says, glancing at the silver watch on her left wrist. "We've still got to get you some pants."

She drives like she does everything else, confidently and efficiently, shifting between fourth and fifth gear as she picks her way north on the interstate. She tells me about her job managing a Tenzler's menswear shop, about the associate's degree she earned at the community college, about her five-year plan to open her own boutique, and her ten-year plan to open two more. She has more ambition in her big toe than has cumulatively circulated through my entire body over the course of my lifetime.

Tenzler's is one of those pretentious upscale men's clothiers I've always avoided because I would probably feel the urge to start punching the people I saw inside. Half their clientele is made up of guys who hook their mirrored sunglasses in the collar of their buttoned shirts, always handy for a quick hair check before they approach the ladies who work here. Is that how it went down with Kerry? I can see my brother pimping his bangs by the reflection of his shades as he works out what smarmy line might woo a girl like Lauren. Fortunately, there's no one for me to hate on. Aside from a girl arranging a display of golf shirts, the store is deserted.

"Don't even look at the prices." Lauren drapes a pair of black dress pants over my shoulder. "I get everything at cost." She piles three more pairs on and leads me to the fitting room. It's got one of those Old West slatted doors that only comes down to my shins. I can see her feet outside as I unzip my shredded jeans. She steps away, says something to the other girl that I can't make out over the techno music, and returns.

"So?" she says.

"They're all right." I'm still, against her advice, trying to calculate what cost is on eighty-nine dollars.

"Let's see."

I turn the metal knob and she pushes the door open. "No," she shakes her head. "They don't fit you right in the hips. They're too … try these ones." She lifts a second pair off the chair and slips back out the door. These go for ninety-four bucks. Is cost half? I only took $200 from my secret stash. Even adding what was already in my wallet, it's going to be a stretch if I get a shirt and shoes. Never mind a jacket or tie, which I could frankly do without. If she'll let me.

I haven't even buttoned them before she's rattling the handle again. The door, which apparently didn't latch tight, swings open. "How do they feel?" she asks. "They look better. Not all bunched. Do you have enough room down there?" She waves at my groin.

I widen my stance and squat halfway to the floor. "They're a little tight, actually."

"Okay, try this one." She hands me the next pair. Instead of stepping outside, she nudges the door shut behind her.

I hesitate before unbuttoning, trying to conjure up any thought that might ward off the erection budding in my boxers. Funeral, funeral, funeral. It's not helping.

"It's okay, C.J., we're family now," she says, as she collects the first reject from the floor. With a deft turn of her hands, they're neatly lined up again seam to seam and folded in even thirds.

I let out a breath and drop my pants. She reaches for them before I've even stepped clear. If she notices anything growing, she doesn't let on. I turn away as I pull up pair three, not rotating back until they're buttoned and zipped. "These are good," I announce, before even trying to move in them.

"No, look at that. They're all floaty in the front." She

grabs at the flaring crotch and draws her hand back as if she's just touched the burner on the stove. "Ah," she winces. "Maybe I'll go find you some shirts. Gray, I think, unless you prefer a light blue?"

"Whatever you think goes best."

The lock clicks crisply into place this time when she closes the door. I watch her feet until she's out of range, then slump into the chair, wishing I could disappear. But what's to be embarrassed about? It's an involuntary, autonomic reaction. That's just the way the human body works. Mine's no different than anyone else's. So she knows—ugh, stop thinking about it. It's not going away. Think about pants and shirts and socks and food. Especially food. I realize I'm starving. It's after six and I haven't eaten since Jimmy left. In the absence of sustenance, the walls of my stomach are starting to size each other up.

She's gone so long I have time to try the last pair of pants, which seem to fit best everywhere but in the wallet. The tag reads $119. I haven't paid that much combined for all of the clothes I've bought in the past year. Granted that may be why my wardrobe is disintegrating.

"All clear?" Lauren calls from outside. When I open the door she's holding two gray shirts and a sport jacket the exact shade of charcoal as the pants I have on. In the end the damages on the pants, shirt, jacket, and a silk tie come to $165, which I suspect she somehow manipulated below even her cost, though she claims the jacket was marked down because it had been returned. I can sense pity. Usually I don't object when it nets me a free pint or two, but it stings slightly coming from Lauren. I don't want her to view me as a pity case. She wouldn't pity someone she respected.

I insist she at least let me buy her dinner. She refuses, until I start laying twenties down on the counter to pay for my new duds. We grab a couple slices of pizza and some breadsticks in the food court and claim a table near the fountain. I study her face as she watches a small boy tossing pennies into the water. There isn't a wrinkle on it anywhere, not even around her eyes.

"Okay, I have to ask."

She grins at me as if she already knows the question.

"How old are you?"

"Guess."

"Twenty-one."

Her emerald eyes shimmer when she shakes her head. Without the slightest hint of self-consciousness, she rakes her forefinger down the front of her teeth and pops out a transparent mouthpiece.

"Twenty?" I ask, pretending I don't notice the string of saliva trailing from her plastic mouth guard.

Another shake. She liberates a lower tray with her thumbnail and sets it on the napkin next to the first.

"Oh, shit, please tell me you're not nineteen. That would be impossible, right? You were at least out of high school when you met my brother, right?"

She slaps me on the shoulder. "You are nothing at all like I thought you'd be."

"Is that good or bad? Good, right?"

"I didn't say good or bad." She bites into her folded pizza slice and leaves me hanging while she chews and swallows and washes it down with her ice water. "Just different."

"Yeah, well, Kerry didn't even ask me to be in the wedding, so I can only imagine the kind things he's had to say. Then get Audra in your ear. You won't hear anything nice from her."

Lauren's laugh confirms I'm right on both accounts. "You want me to talk to him? I couldn't believe he left you out. He said something about—"

"David's sister, right?"

She nods.

"I can't help it she liked me. Did we go too far? It was nobody else's business. Until she apparently talked about it. I didn't say anything. But let me tell you, she's the one in their family that got all the personality. He sure doesn't have any."

"He's kind of stiff." She bites down on her lower lip and giggles. "Well, not like you."

"You won't say anything about that, will you?"

"Of course not. It was my fault, anyway. I shouldn't have been in there."

"I didn't mind."

"That much was obvious." Her eyes twinkle with mischief when she flirts, which is undoubtedly what she's doing now. Maybe she likes the attention, maybe she's just being playful. My heart is beating too off rhythm to care either way. I haven't had this much fun talking to a girl since college.

"Can I ask you something?"

"You already did. And I'm twenty-two. You didn't really think I was younger than that, did you?"

I shrug. I did, but I'm ready to move on to new ground, so I'll leave that one alone.

"What are you doing with my brother?"

"You mean why aren't I with you?" she laughs. She leans back in her seat and stretches her arms down to her sides, heaving her breasts up in such a manner the pink lace of her bra is visible between the buttons of her blouse. I can't help but peek, and she can't help but notice.

"Get a good look?"

"Yeah," I say. "I'm good. That's not really what I meant, though. About me. Girls like you don't usually talk to guys like me. I get that. But why him? He's kind of a … lunkhead. And a misogynist. You could do so much better. I mean, look at you."

"Some people might point out that's a rather misogynistic thing to say. That a girl's appearance should factor into who she marries. That an attractive girl should … you meant I was attractive, right?"

I nod.

"That an attractive girl should have more choices based on her appearance doesn't really place proper value on her intelligence or work ethic, et cetera. Guys don't judge other guys by the same criteria. So some would say you're a misogynist, too. Or that all guys are to some degree. I'll take it as a compliment, though, which is how I think you meant it."

I've taken it on faith thus far that what I've said won't travel back to Kerry. I'm not picking up any vibes off her that she'd like to see him kick my ass. So I push just a little further.

"I just meant you're too good for him."

"Thank you. But I'm not. Your brother's a good guy with a great sense of humor. Sophomoric at times, yes, but he's got one at least He works hard. He treats me well. He paid for those." She points at the mouth guards sitting next to her plate. "After my parents split, we couldn't afford braces. My sister got them, I didn't. He's very generous. I have no complaints."

"You admit he's a lunkhead, though?"

"Sometimes," she shrugs. "But a lovable one. My turn to ask you something."

"Shoot."

"Why can't you guys get along better? All of you."

"I don't know. We never really have."

"That's a copout. If you wanted to you would. And I wish you would. It'd be more fun to be around everyone if it wasn't always like, well, last night."

"I'll try."

"Promise?"

"Not Keith. But everyone else."

The breadsticks have gone cold, congealing to their paper plate in a puddle of yellow grease. I fold the dish in half, wipe the crumbs off the table with a napkin, and toss it all in the trash barrel. Lauren leads me to a discount shoe outlet where she negotiates a further fifteen percent cut off the price on a pair of black Oxfords with her mall employee credential.

She talks mostly about the wedding on the ride home, going into every infinitesimal detail on choosing florists and DJs and bakers and bridesmaids. Things I may never actually need to know about but have no trouble showing interest in. She could go into chapter and verse on cross-stitch patterns or tofu recipes and I'd pay close enough attention to keep her talking, which is what I do for fifteen minutes after we pull into the driveway. When the conversation finally flags, I collect my bags from the back seat and say good night. I'm already lonely as I wave from the stoop.

THIRTEEN

Kerry stole a girl from me once. Elizabeth Dunning. She was in half my classes first semester of my freshman year and we'd occasionally swap homework answers on the bus to school. I was working up the cojones to ask her to the Homecoming dance when my brother swooped in. Two weeks after deflowering her, he cut her loose. Suddenly none of her friends would talk to me. I was sullied by association, relegated to the fringe of desirable society. In a sense, he skewed my entire high school experience by hijacking Elizabeth. Then again, she might very well have shot me down anyway, in which case her friends would all have mocked me behind my back for having presumed I was somehow worthy of taking her to the dance.

It's Elizabeth I cite as I defend myself to myself while smoking the very last cigarette in my possession out in the driveway. So I'm in love with his fiancée, he stole Elizabeth Dunning. Maybe it's time to even the score. Karma's even bitchier on ice.

And I'm an idiot. Worthy or not—and it's a stretch to chalk my name in the plus column here—Lauren's not available. I might as well try my luck courting the Duchess of Cambridge. I need to disregard the ache in my chest that began when she appeared out of nowhere this afternoon. That wasn't chemistry sparking when she laughed at my jokes. She was just being polite. She laughed at Keith's jokes for fuck's sake. This puppy lust is stupid and reckless and must be snuffed out like my cigarette butt before it sparks a conflagration that will undoubtedly scorch me.

But part of me craves the rush of holding the match as it burns toward my thumb. The selfish part. The part that lives down to the universally low expectations harbored by virtually everyone I've ever had the opportunity to let down. When was the last time I did anything for anyone without expecting something in return? Or worse, without already being in their debt. Like all the work I've done on Mindy's condo to pay her back for not casting me out on the street.

Dammit, I meant to call her this afternoon.

It's nearly eleven-thirty back in Baltimore. Will she be more pissed off if I wake her up or if I don't call? It's been three days. I have to at least leave a message. Maybe something about how sorry I am I haven't called, about how it's been so crazy out here seeing everyone, about how I've been so busy dealing with things at my dad's that I lost track of time, about how I'll absolutely, one hundred percent, no doubt about it call her tomorrow no matter what.

But it's not her voice mail I get. She answers on the second ring.

"Oh, so you are still alive." Her voice is about a six on the frosty scale. I've triggered ten so many times six hardly phases me.

"Sorry I didn't call last night. Never felt my phone buzz. By the time I saw your text I figured you were probably in bed."

"I'm in bed now. Reading, waiting for the phone to ring. Just in case you didn't forget me."

"I didn't forget you. I've just been busy seeing everyone and getting ready for the funeral. Had to go buy some decent clothes tonight. None of my old stuff still fit."

"Who paid for that?"

Shit. She, of all people, knows I barely have two nickels to rub together. Kerry might believe I have enough on hand to afford a shopping spree; Mindy knows better.

"My dad. Kerry figures we'll all see a chunk of his retirement account. I took a little advance. Don't worry, I'll pay you back for the ticket. And everything else."

"I'm not worried, C.J. I quit worrying about money with you a long time ago. I know I'll never see it again."

How am I supposed to respond to that? As much as it stings, I can't pretend to be offended. I owe her so much it would be futile to even track it anymore. Needing to say something to pierce the ballooning pause in the conversation, I ask, "How's work?"

"Fine. When are you coming home?"

"I don't know yet."

"Funeral's tomorrow, right?"

"Uh-huh. Eleven o'clock. That is going to be weird. I can't wait until it's all over."

"So are you coming home Thursday, Friday?"

"I really don't know. Probably not until the weekend at least. I have to go through all my dad's stuff."

"Why can't your brother and sister deal with that? You don't even live there."

"Kerry says he's got too much going on with his wedding. And Audra, I don't know, she's got some serious issues. She doesn't even want to set foot over here."

"So they're dumping it on you? How's that fair?"

I sigh. It's not fair, but the only truly equitable solution would involve the three of us looking through everything together and that would probably result in at least one additional funeral. I know Kerry's excuse is bullshit, because Lauren is clearly doing all the heavy lifting on their wedding. So we'll chalk his reticence up to laziness. Audra's is rooted in bitterness. "Someone's got to do it."

"And someone's got to finish painting the front room."

"I'll do it when I get back. Don't worry, it'll get done."

It's always gotten done, since the morning she asked if I knew anything about repairing a garbage disposal. The morning I woke up in her bedroom, unsure exactly where I was, fuzzy on most of the details from the night before, like her name, for starters, or why she had wandered into the coffee shop on her way home from work. Or how I'd managed to latch onto her and her group of friends by the time they left for the bar down the street. I bluffed my way through the audition, plunging my hand through the rubber gasket and groping around until I detected a mangled bottle cap wedged between the blades. Based upon that fraudulent act of handyman heroism, I never went home. Not overnight, anyhow. Long before my lease expired the following month, everything of use had been moved from my apartment, one armload at a time. Nothing was ever discussed. She never formally invited me to move in, and I never asked if I could. It just happened.

"Well, you left everything all—"

"Don't make it sound like I'm on vacation out here. I didn't tell my dad to kill himself so I could get out of painting the spare room."

"I didn't mean it that way and you know it." I've nudged her to an eight on the frosty-meter. Eight is where she tries to sound dispassionate to mask the pissiness frothing up inside. She rarely stays at eight long. From here it's a short journey to ten and airborne objects. "Of course you'd have been done a week ago if you didn't waste so much time spying on Titsy."

This last bit is meant to be a joke, judging by the sudden change in her tone. Which makes the Titsy reference ironic given some of the comments she's made about my voyeurism habit, as she calls it. She sure wasn't kidding last month when she burst into the spare room and "caught me in the act," rekindling the seemingly fizzled out argument that had sent me to my window bench in the first place. I stare out the window because there's nothing to look at inside. If my eyes happen to wander to our exhibitionist neighbor, well, Mindy's free to relinquish the TV room next time we fight.

"How's she doing?" I ask, playing along. "Does she miss me?"

"I do."

"I'd be working until close tonight anyway, so just pretend I'm at Ruth's."

"I was being serious."

"Sorry. I miss you, too." It comes out flat and unconvincing.

"Sure you do," she sighs. "Let me know when you're coming home, okay. I'll come get you."

"Thanks." Not having dug myself in deep enough, I tack on a hollow "I love you."

I love you. Those are three little words we don't practice saying much. Neither of us. When they do come out, they're usually panted as we collapse on the mattress after makeup sex. In the early days of our relationship, I used to say it in Russian, *Ya lyublyu tebya,* the way my mother whispered it to me when I was small. It was the last thing she said to me the day she left. Of course, I didn't realize then that she meant it as good-bye. "I love you" was more foreign than the foreign translation. Maybe that's why it sounds so awkward when I say it. Or maybe it's the absolute lack of conviction in my voice, the way it comes out almost as an apology. Or that an hour ago I said good night to someone else who stirred more inside me in one afternoon than Mindy has in four years.

FOURTEEN

The top drawer of the file cabinet in my father's office closet is jammed so tight I can barely read the labels, inscribed in his blockish handwriting. He kept everything. There are folders for AAA, American Airlines, Amica Insurance, and on and on. Some bulge so fat the manila tabs no longer reach high enough to be seen. Others contain only a single sheet of paper, like the receipt filed under Carpets from when he had the stairs cleaned. "Poor job," he wrote on it as a reminder presumably to his future self. "Don't re-hire." He's got a thick folder labeled Ford Taurus, with service records detailing every oil change and inspection for a car he sold when I was in college.

Every time I think I've found something of interest it turns out to be a false start. The collection of monthly statements from Cascade Federal Credit Union runs through June 2001, when he closed the account. I find a receipt for a deposit to an IRA in a folder labeled Ameritrade. He opened it with $400 in 2005 and evidently never touched it again. I toss the folder toward the middle of floor. I'll have to follow up and see if it's still there.

If it's left to me, most of this can be shredded. Or burned. Maybe a bonfire in the backyard, a symbolic funeral pyre fed by the receipts of everything Dad ever bought. There's nothing remarkable here. No secret stashes of hundreds and fifties. No leads. No answers to any of the questions I came here with.

Until I hit drawer three. Here we are, lined up alphabetically. Impersonally. As if we were simply three of his thousands of students. "Neubauer, Audra." "Neubauer, Christopher." "Neubauer, Kerry."

I pull mine first.

The top sheet is a printout of a story I wrote for the weekly paper in Baltimore last Christmas on a local photographer who was raising money for his son's leukemia treatments by selling calendars featuring his own black-and-white images of the city. It wasn't anything I'd have included in my own portfolio if I kept one. Just a quick fifty bucks for two phone calls and a couple hours of work. Somehow it made my permanent file here. As did half a dozen other articles I'd written over the previous two years, a couple of which I'd actually forgotten about. Below them I find the flight itinerary from my last trip home, a shipping receipt for a package he sent for my twenty-fifth birthday, and the brochure I mailed him of my first apartment in Baltimore. It was meant to show him I was doing just fine, moving to a fancy new complex after having enough of New York. Shame I was evicted seven months later for overdue rent.

That's ten items to represent the last ten years of my life, none of them personal. I know I sent him a couple of Christmas cards in there somewhere. Definitely the first year Mindy and I were together. Maybe there's a specific folder for those. I never wrote him any actual letters, though. Not since college, at least. October of my sophomore year, to be precise. And no surprise, here it is, mixed in with the receipts for tuition and meal plans. The single most regrettable collection of sentences I've ever committed to paper. The letter that made me feel like John Hancock flipping King George the bird when I signed it in large, looping handwriting—and a sniveling little shit when I came to my senses an hour after dropping it in the campus mail.

Dad,

This may come as a shock to you, but I'm an adult now and I would prefer to be treated like one. I'm old enough to vote and fight for my country. I'm certainly old enough to make my own living arrangements. So thanks for listing your top ten reasons why Deanna and I shouldn't room together. Maybe you should send it in to David Letterman, because everyone here found it pretty hilarious.

If you really are going to withhold my room and board next semester because of this, I won't come home over the summer. I'll have to stay here and work to make enough for us to get by together. And don't count on seeing me at Christmas. I'll probably just go to Deanna's mom's. She treats us with respect. She's totally cool with it. I don't get your hangup.

I think it's hypocritical for you to make a big deal of this. Kerry had girls (yes, plural) living at his place almost all the way through college. And you send Audra checks without ever asking any questions about where she's sleeping and who with, probably because you know as well as I do the answer is the entire school. So it seems I'm being punished for being in a monogamous relationship.

I love Deanna and she loves me, and as long as we're going to be together all the time anyway, we might as well share a place. If you're bitter about being the only one in the family not getting any action, don't take it out on me.

I'm ashamed all over again to be reminded what a punkass bitch I was. If I were him I would have coldcocked me the next time we met. But he never even mentioned it. I wondered for a long time whether it had gotten lost in the mail. I returned home that spring with a chip on my shoulder, prepared to defend my poor choices and complete absence of gratitude. It never came up. By then he'd had seven months of wine nights to vent. It was out of his system long before I let it out of mine.

Of course, I never sent him a letter when she broke up with me over Thanksgiving weekend. I never shared with him how awkward it was to co-habit with my ex until the semester ended. Or how I got stuck in a duplex full of foreign exchange students after the holidays because no one else had an opening. Or how he was essentially right about everything he said. Had I been half as worldly as I claimed to be, I wouldn't have hesitated to share the painful reality with him when it all fell apart. I wasn't, and he knew it.

Maybe we'd have been closer if he had called me out once in a while. We could have fought and I would eventually have apologized and we could have moved past it. I kept my conscience busy with some of the awful things I said to him in high school and college. I was sarcastic and mean, and he was my most convenient target once Kerry and Audra moved out. Frustratingly, he turned the other cheek almost every time. How could I say sorry when he didn't even have the decency to show me how much it had hurt?

I've depressed myself so much I'm not sure I'm up to looking through Audra's folder. It's much thinner than mine, which makes sense, as to hear her tell it they've barely spoken since the day she moved out. I'm surprised he even came to her wedding, though maybe she only invited him to make him watch Keith walk her down the aisle.

The first item is a program from Naomi's baptism. Was Dad there? There are newspaper clippings of the birth announcements for both girls. And a card in my sister's handwriting, thanking him for his "generous gift," whatever it was. It's not specified. Maybe a lamp full of cash?

None of that is enough to prepare me for the next document in her dossier. "Loan Agreement," it reads in all caps across the top. There's a brief legal-sounding paragraph, identifying the parties involved. My father is listed as the lender. Opposite him are listed Audra Swain and David Swain, the borrowers. It's dated June 4, 2011, almost a year after their wedding. It's the amount of the loan that triggers a series of cranial explosions as an entire layer of my cerebrum detonates. *Thirty-two thousand dollars.*

And I'm the ingrate?

How does one go from borrowing thirty-two grand to dancing on their own father's grave? Unless—did Audra welsh out? Did he send the mob around to threaten David's kneecaps, or the tender fingers of his granddaughters?

If my memory can be trusted, that was the summer she and David built their house, about a mile from Mom's. She turned her Facebook stream into a time-lapse documentary on the birth of a modern suburban home, posting photos from the day they dug the hole in the ground through the night of the housewarming party. I don't recall seeing my father in any of them. Considering his contribution, they should have painted a mural of his face on the living room wall.

Beneath the loan contract I find Audra's wedding invitation, a receipt from Nordstrom for a two hundred dollar crystal salad bowl, and then a gap of six years until her college graduation announcement. She apparently never wrote him any sassy letters when she was at school.

I flip open Kerry's file. There's no suspense here. The first page on top is a loan deal, laid out much like Audra's. It's dated just last fall and the principle is ten grand, a pittance compared to my sister's. Wedding expenses, maybe. Perhaps my dad put that diamond on Lauren's finger. On the back of the sheet he has recorded six payments, each for $300 made the first of every month. It's the first of three such documents in the folder, with two other loans having been made for $6,500 and $8,000. Both were repaid in full according to my father's handwritten notes. Without interest. It certainly casts a new light on Kerry's sense of obligation and the regular visits he endured.

Curious, I reexamine Audra's loan. There are five sporadic payments logged on the reverse side in amounts varying from $350 to $500. If this is the complete record, she hasn't made a payment in more than three years. She owes him nearly thirty thousand bucks. Sort of makes the dough we found downstairs look like loose change. I guess I won't feel so guilty about keeping that windfall to myself.

FIFTEEN

The look on Audra's face when I walk into the funeral home pays for my new suit all on its own. Even had it been my money, it would have been well spent just to see her eyes spring open as if George Clooney had strolled in. It's not her approval that tickles me. It's knowing she's giving it grudgingly. She would have loved it if I'd slunk in wearing my old band tux, or with Dad's pants drooping down below my waist. That would have given her something to talk about until the next family member was laid to rest.

"Look at you." She reaches up and tugs at the knot of my tie.

"It's not a clip-on."

"It's crooked." Nudging my chin up with the back of her hand, she pulls at my collar until the thin end of the tie clears the knot. Unable to find fault with my clothes, she settles for lecturing me on how to properly tie a double Windsor.

I'm partial to the schoolboy. Not because the Windsor is too challenging to tie. The simple, off-center knot, preferably with at least two finger widths of breathing room, conveys a more casual attitude toward formal wear that sets me apart from, say, David, standing on the other side of the room, tapping away at his phone while his daughters chase each other around the podium, atop which sits a pewter urn I can only assume holds my father's mortal remains.

Lauren enters in a black dress, a crocheted shawl draped around her shoulders. I can hear my brother's voice from out in the vestibule, where a thin, white-haired man in a black pinstripe suit nods at everything Kerry says.

"Don't you clean up nice." Lauren takes my left hand and tugs on the cuff of my shirt until it pokes just beyond the sleeve of my jacket. She repeats the exercise on my right wrist. "Looks good all together. Very handsome."

An innocent compliment at a funeral shouldn't quicken my pulse like this one does. It was Lauren I thought of when I trimmed the ragged ends of my hair this morning before banding it neatly into a ponytail. I don't often wear it back, but it looked more sophisticated with the jacket and tie, like a junior-level Mafioso.

"Thank you. You look very nice as well."

She extends her arms and rises up on her toes. I count off the duration of our embrace in breaths, relieved when each one ends that she hasn't yet broken away. I finally let go when I realize I'm stiffening up below the belt. From her smirk, she noticed as well.

"Hey, easy there, sport." Kerry enters toting a poster-board tribute to my father under one arm and a wooden easel in the other. "She's with me. She's got a cousin you might like, though. Bit of a Bohemian type, but awfully nice to look at."

Lauren offers me a cheeky eye roll and relieves Kerry of his load. As she sets up the easel, Kerry props himself on a chair, ass on the back rest, feet on the seat.

"What's the over-under on attendance?" he quips. "Five?"

I shrug. I have no reason to expect anyone will show, but just to prove him wrong, I'm rooting for a big turnout. Not that it would shut him up. "I'll go high."

"All right. You're on. That's five aside from us, I mean. Non-relatives. You can buy me lunch. We're going to Bernard's after."

Nothing in his demeanor would lead anyone to conclude we're about to bury our father. He's chatting like we're waiting for a graduation ceremony to begin. I'm embarrassed for him, and for our family, when I catch the funeral director looking at us. I want to step away, physically disassociate myself from him. What would my father think if he could see us?

"Get down off there," I say.

"What?"

"He's looking at us funny."

"So? My shoes are clean."

"That's not the point."

"Who am I meant to be impressing, sport? There's no one here."

"Who's that?" I nod toward the entrance. An older gentleman in a corduroy sport jacket is hunched over the visitor's registry. It's ten minutes to eleven and he's the first actual guest. I'm guessing he worked with my father at Northpoint. "Should we be greeting people?"

"That's calling hours, which we didn't do. We're just going to sit up front. Vic is going to say a few words, and that's pretty much it. If someone wants to talk to us afterwards, that's fine, but it's not going to be anything formal."

"You're not going to say anything?"

Kerry shakes his head dismissively. "I gave Vic a few bullet points. That's good enough."

If my dad had been more popular, Kerry would have written a monologue worthy of a Friars Club Roast. He wouldn't cede the floor to the funeral director. He'd work the crowd and slip business cards into every palm on the way out.

Two more guests, a guy and girl who both look younger than Lauren, bring the crowd to three. They sit in the last row and whisper to each other as their eyes roam the room. I'm sure they're talking about us. I recognize the next man to enter as the one with my father in the softball picture. He signs the guest book and takes a seat up front, beside the first fellow who came in.

"That's four," I say. "One more and you owe me lunch."

"No, one more's a wash. It's over-under, not equal-under."

We both check the time on our phones. Ten fifty-eight.

"Let's get this over with." Kerry nods toward the front of the room. I follow him, still unsure what to do or what will happen. Audra herds her girls toward the first row of chairs on the right side of the aisle. They climb up onto their seats and survey the twenty mostly empty rows behind theirs.

"Grandma!" Chloe screeches. As they scramble down from their perches, Kerry and I rotate toward the entrance. My mother, face shrouded by a black veil, advances slowly, her long, white fingers clutching her handbag to her side as if it holds the balance of her life.

"Did you know she was coming?" I ask.

Kerry shakes his head.

Mom stoops to receive the girls, lifting her mask just long enough to kiss each of them. They skip back to their seats singing, "Grandma's here, Grandma's here." Lauren, predictably, is the first adult to greet my mother. They whisper in each other's ears briefly as they embrace. Audra hugs her next, then Kerry, and finally me. I peek in through the side of her veil. Despite her grieving widow getup, her eyes are dry. Perhaps that's what she's intent on hiding.

As we separate, I turn smack into Jimmy. He looks even thinner in his three-piece suit, his vest suppressing what little flesh there is around his midsection like a girdle. "Neubs," he says, extending his hand, "sorry for your loss."

"Thanks, man." Aside to Kerry, I add, "There's five."

"Jimmy doesn't count," my brother says. "He's family." He claps Jimmy on the shoulder nearly hard enough to topple him.

"I don't count for what?" Jimmy asks.

"He bet me lunch there'd be more than five people we don't know," Kerry says.

"No, five non-relatives," I correct him. "Doesn't matter if

we know them."

Vic approaches and motions toward the podium. Kerry nods and takes a seat in the second row, directly behind my mother. I leave an opening for Lauren and sit half turned toward the door, too stubborn to give up on our wager. A solitary girl enters, head covered in a black and gold scarf. When she unknots it and shakes her hair loose, Kerry and I lock eyes. His expression is as befuddled as I imagine my own. She looks exactly like my mother in the photos from when we were kids. From the row ahead, Audra slaps at my arm and mouths, "Who the fuck is that?"

We're still studying her when Vic opens the ceremony, fourteen minutes late by my phone. His voice echoes off the back wall as he welcomes everyone to the memorial service, greeting us as I imagine he would a packed house. As if they were waiting for things to officially kick off, a stream of college-aged kids enter. They fill the back row first, then the next to last, until eight rows are nearly full. There must be at least seventy of them, maybe more.

"If everyone can get settled," Vic calls, his deep voice reaching the back of the room without the aid of the microphone, "we can get started here."

"Sorry," one of the kids blurts. "It said eleven-thirty in our school paper."

Brows knitted, Vic turns to Kerry. "Shall we wait?"

Kerry sighs as if his lunch reservation is at stake. "Yeah, whatever."

Vic nods and reaches under the podium. The sound system begins playing soft saxophone music. In the ensuing ten minutes another two dozen kids enter, as well as several older folks who reek of academia.

"Aren't you glad we made the memory board now?" Lauren asks.

Kerry just shrugs and nods. He doesn't snap at her as he would at any of the rest of us for rubbing his nose in his wrongness. Staring down at the sharp creases of my pants, I'm grateful all over again Lauren prevented me from dressing like a clown.

Vic resumes his position at precisely half past. He too looks anxious to be done. Maybe he's double-booked the room.

"Welcome, everyone. Thank you for joining us today as we remember Warren James Neubauer, beloved father and friend. Warren was born in Snohomish and spent his entire life here in the Pacific Northwest. He raised three children here, and taught mathematics at Northpoint College for forty-three years. He was a good friend and strong family man."

Audra and I simultaneously turn to Kerry, who stares straight ahead pretending he doesn't notice. Then again, what else was he supposed to tell Vic to say?

"At sixty-nine, Warren leaves us too soon. But he leaves behind a legacy of friendship and love. And at this time we invite those who have special memories of Warren to step forward and share them with all of us."

I reach across Lauren's lap and poke my brother in the leg. His glare answers my question. There's no point in asking Audra, too absorbed in smoothing Naomi's curls and fixing Chloe's collar to even meet my eye. If one of us is going to say anything, it's up to me. But I have nothing to say. The pause extends to fifteen, twenty, thirty seconds. Have all these people come for this? I'm assuming they're at the right memorial, as they haven't gotten up and left. I start up from my chair, my brain racing for any anecdote that would portray my father in a positive light. I'm spared the spotlight when Dad's softball companion rises and makes his way toward the podium.

He looks to be about ten years younger than my father. Thin on top, his wiry, gray hair runs wild over his ears. His forehead is wrinkled like a beach after the tide recedes. He dabs at the corners of his mouth with a handkerchief and adjusts the microphone.

"Twenty-five years ago, I moved into the office next to Warren's. I had just driven three days from Waco, Texas, and was staying at a little motel right off campus while we waited to close on our house. It poured down cats and dogs that morning, and I showed up sopping wet, having hiked in all the way from the north lot, halfway across campus. Warren took one look at me and burst out laughing. Then he fixed me up with some dry clothes and called someone to have mine laundered in time for my ten o'clock class. So much has changed in the department since then, but I could always count on Warren for a quick wit and a strong cup of coffee. Every Tuesday morning during office hours we'd dig out his beat-up, old backgammon set and play for nickels. He was a keen competitor and a dear friend, and I'm going to miss him sorely."

There's a smattering of applause from the student section as he steps away from the stand and returns to his seat. It gets louder a moment later when an Asian kid whose white shirt is bisected by a narrow black tie makes his way to the front. He runs a hand through his spikey hair and flattens a sheet of notebook paper on the podium.

"Two weeks before I started my freshman year, my father lost his job. All we had was my mother's salary from the recycling center. I arrived at Northpoint convinced I would have to drop out at the semester break. When Mr. Neubauer found out, he took me to the guidance office and helped me apply for every scholarship in the book." He holds his thumb and forefinger about four inches apart and grins. "He coached me through the submission process and kept my hopes up as I waited and waited for positive news. He saw something in me, in my love for math, and wouldn't let me quit. He was more stoked than me the day I finally got my first grant. Thanks to him, I received enough aid to pay for my tuition and room. He sponsored a team of four of us to participate in the mathematics Olympiad last spring, and we finished second place out of forty-four teams from fourteen different schools. He has been my advisor for four years, and I cannot believe he won't be there next month to see me graduate. Thank you, Mr. Neubauer."

Next up is a girl with purple hair who tells how my dad sat after class with her for two months until she finally picked up the basic concepts of geometry. She went from a D on her first quarter progress report to an A and made the Dean's list. She's followed by a kid whose first words are, "Mr. Neubauer was the bomb." And he failed my dad's trigonometry class. Even after having to retake it, he still stopped by my father's office a couple of times a week just to chat about his job at a movie theater and his girlfriend's kid and whatever was in the headlines that morning. He concludes by pounding his chest twice with his fist and saluting with two fingers. "Peace, Mr. Neubauer."

Kerry stares at the back of my mom's chair, as he has since this parade began. Audra's shoulders quake like a sputtering Volvo as she leans into her tin-man husband. One of us should say something. We can't leave his story to complete strangers. But who are the strangers here? I rise to my feet and stumble past Jimmy, hypersensitive that more than a hundred people are watching me mount the dais. My mouth is dry and my eyes are moist as I survey the crowd. I wipe my forehead with the back of my sleeve and tug at the knot in my tie.

"I didn't know any of this." My eyes roam the audience seeking a comfortable face on which to focus. It was a trick suggested by a speech teacher in college. Find someone sympathetic and block out everyone else. The problem now is everyone looks sympathetic, aside from my brother, who looks like he wants to set the building on fire. There are too many to choose from. Instead of picking one I drop my gaze to the pewter vase before me, inscribed with my father's initials in sweeping cursive letters, WJN. "My dad never talked much about work. Or maybe I just never listened. We weren't all that close. I wish I would have kept in better touch with him. I wish I would have called him more. Maybe I'd have seen what you all saw."

When I glance up, the guests before me have melted into a watercolor of indistinct faces atop shoulders clad in a somber rainbow of navy, gray, and black. Digging at my eyes with the knuckle of my thumb only makes my vision go hazier.

"Even though we didn't always get along, he was a good guy and I miss him." I focus on the urn and blow a breath so long and heavy into the mic it echoes back at me through the sound system before I'm done exhaling. "I miss you, Dad. I love you."

The last three words come out like a mother orca calling for her lost calf. I may be the only one in the room who knows what I said. But I said it. Finally. I collapse face down, the front edge of the podium digging into my chest with each sob that ripples through my body. I'm aware of nothing but my own grief until I feel a hand on my back.

"Nice job, Neubs." Jimmy lifts me to my full height and slides his pipe-cleaner arm beneath mine and around my back. "Come on. And let's leave that up here, okay?"

He grasps the neck of my father's urn and gently twists it out of my quivering hands.

SIXTEEN

As I've pointed out to Mindy any number of times, I can't read minds. But it doesn't take Carnac the Magnificent to divine what everybody else around the table is thinking as our waitress takes our drink orders. Kerry's disgusted I broke down. He's always thought I was a pussy, but this tops everything, even the day I cried when I was sent to the vice principal's office for cutting class. Lauren is appalled by his lack of empathy, which should really have been apparent long before now. She's turning the word "lunkhead" over in her mind every time she looks at him. Audra is embarrassed we got outgrieved by a bunch of college kids and wishes none of them had shown up. My mother is toughest to gauge, still cloaked as she is behind her veil. The vibe I'm picking up is a perplexed one. She can't reconcile the outpouring of affection by the students. If Dad was so beloved at school, why did he want to end it all, and how did she get dragged into it nearly twenty-five years after divorcing him?

Her cranberry vodka travels straight from our server's hand to her shrouded lips without detouring for an instant to the table. She's got one in the books before I even lift my beer off its tiny napkin. At a nod, she sends the waitress off in pursuit of a second.

"You okay, Mom?" Lauren asks.

My mother simultaneously shrugs and shakes her head.

"What the hell does that mean?" Kerry demands. "Would you take that damn thing off so we could at least see your face?"

I'm torn between watching Lauren slap my brother's shoulder and my mother struggle with her veil. I need a split screen. Mom wins in the end, if only because everyone else is watching her. I don't want to be the only one to miss the unmasking. She extracts a bobby pin from each temple and slides the curtain back until it clears her face. Her pupils are as big as dimes, the whites of her eyes a maze of pink squiggles.

"Happy?" she asks.

"No, Mom," Audra squeals. "You're a mess."

"Jesus, put it back on," Kerry says, earning another strike from his fiancée.

My mother makes a show of stuffing it into her purse instead, snapping the clasp loudly and dropping the bag to the floor between her feet. She bows her head and massages the inside corners of her eyes with her thumb and forefinger.

"Did you sleep much last night?" Lauren asks.

Without removing her hand, Mom shakes her head and utters a soft, "No."

"Would you like me to stay with you tonight?" Lauren asks. "I can read to you until you fall asleep."

A faint smile flickers across my mother's mouth. She has found someone to play her game. I have to roll my eyes at someone, and Audra, seated to my right, seems the safest target. Her default scowl softens to a smirk and she nods in assent. For a fleeting moment, at least, we are in agreement on something.

"I know I'm the last to know just about everything because no one ever tells me jack shit," I say, "but are you basing this on more than Dad's note? Because I still think that could have been intended for any of us. Could have been me, for all I know."

"Is there something you're not telling us?" Kerry asks. "Or why would there all of a sudden be an issue? You said you hadn't even talked to him in a year. Is there something you left out?"

"No. And you could make the same point about him and Mom. Only more so. He at least had a right to be hurt I never called. But he couldn't have expected Mom to reach out, could he? After all this time? It doesn't make sense."

"Clearly he wasn't in his right mind or we wouldn't be here right now." Kerry switches to his lecturing voice, the one I imagine he uses to convince reluctant insurance purchasers that only a true idiot wouldn't prioritize the financial security of their dependents in the unlikely event they were to become too disabled to provide. "Dad had a hard time letting go. He never moved on."

"What do you base that on?" I ask.

"We've been over this, C.J.," Audra interjects, without looking up from her phone. Her thumbs hopscotch across the pullout keyboard so quickly I can't string enough letters together to crack her text. "Leave it now. You're just upsetting Mom."

"How is telling her it's not her fault upsetting?"

"Is this a bad time?" Our waitress sets Mom's drink down on the table. "Should I come back?"

My brother, sister, and I shake our heads. Mom switches her smile on and orders the pepper steak salad with vinaigrette dressing. By the time the girl has taken the rest of our orders my mother has drained her drink and is holding her empty up to be refilled.

"It was lovely what you said about your father," Mom says, when fortified with her third cocktail. "I hope someone can find such kind words when it's my turn."

"Oh, Jesus, Mom, of course we will." Kerry preemptively draws his shoulder away from Lauren who has given up on slapping sense into him. His tone leaves some doubt, however. One can easily picture him raising a toast to being done with the drama.

"I don't expect such a big sendoff as Warren had," Mom

says. "Though maybe the girls could sing for me. I like the one from *Mulan.* That would be pretty."

This time it's Audra's turn to roll eyes at me. "You're seriously planning your funeral, Mom?" she says. "How old do you envision the girls being when they serenade you? You're only fifty-seven."

"Only," Mom scoffs. "Imagine how you'll like it. Too old to be what you once were, too late to start over."

"Start over?" Audra glances up from her phone, which has been buzzing with incoming texts every couple of minutes since we first sat down. "What do you mean start over? Without Keith?"

Mom closes her eyes and shakes her head and suddenly I can see exactly what she was talking about. She used to be so beautiful. Now she just looks tired. And not the kind of tired a good night of sleep will cure. She has aged even since I saw her Monday. She strikes me as an old fifty-seven. I never thought of my mother as old for her age before. When she came to my college graduation, my roommate dubbed her a MILF. Not to sound all Oedipus, but she was. Even Monday, one could have made a weak case. She's not even a GILF today. She's closer to old maid.

"It would have been nice to have a career," Mom says. "I thought about real estate once. Or cutting hair. I'm too old to go to school, though."

"No you're not, Mom," Lauren says.

"Yes, I am." And as she nods it's impossible to envision her keeping up in a class full of kids. My mother has always been more clever than book smart. "Yulia Janokov offered me a job in her boutique. I might take it, but that's not a career. It's just an excuse to get out of the house for a few hours."

She has just summed up my job at the coffee shop. Succinctly. "You should take it," I say, trying to sound encouraging. "It might be fun. Make a few bucks, meet some new people."

"I might. I'd like to save up a little so I can go home."

"Keith won't pay for it?" Audra asks.

"No."

"You mean for a visit?" I ask. "Or …"

Mom's shrug can only be interpreted as confirmation she's at least entertained the thought of a one-way trip to Sevastopol.

"You can't just leave," I say.

"Why not?" Kerry says. "You did."

"That's hardly the same. I'd just graduated. I wanted to see the world a little and get out on my own. I can come back any time I want."

"And yet we haven't seen you for five years." Audra brandishes a smug smile and sets her phone, which has finally gone quiet, on the table next to her mojito.

"My point was I could have, assuming I had something to come back for. It's a lot easier to get here from the East Coast than from Ukraine. And don't pretend anyone gave a shit when I left. Ten years, no one's ever come out to visit. Planes fly both directions."

"I did." My mother's voice is barely louder than a whisper. "I cried when you left."

"And I cried when you left us," I say. "Every night for a month until I accepted you weren't coming back. The difference was I was eight when you abandoned us."

"You're still crying about it," Kerry says. "It was twenty-five years ago, let it go already. Jesus H. Christ on a fucking crutch."

At the head of the table my mother is openly weeping, moaning softly with each pained intake like a rusty bellows. I wish she'd put her veil back on so the people at the next table might stop staring. Throwing a disgusted look at my brother—and an only slightly less harsh one at me—Lauren gets up from her seat and kneels by Mom's chair. She wraps her arms awkwardly around my mother's shoulders and whispers something I can't make out. She then helps her to her feet and leads her away toward the restroom.

"Nice going, sport."

"Fuck off, Kerry." I shove my chair back from the table. "You cried, too. Don't act like you never did."

There are just enough ones in my wallet to feed the cigarette machine in the entryway. It's drizzling outside, the sky a fitting dull gray that extends to the horizon in all directions. I nod at a fortyish woman in low-rider jeans and too much eye makeup. She returns the gesture awkwardly, lips flat and pursed. Clearly she has witnessed too much of our family kerfuffle to bother making chitchat about the weather. She takes one final long drag and snuffs her butt in the industrial-sized ashtray, lipstick end protruding from the sand like a pink turd in a litter box.

As she opens the tinted-glass door, Lauren and my mother are passing through the foyer on their way back from the lavatory. Then the door closes tight and I'm left alone, to watch the mist sneak under the awning and settle on the arm of my jacket. This transient peacefulness is half the reason I smoke. If it were socially acceptable to light up indoors, I'd probably quit. The ban has provided a valid excuse to walk away from any situation. What would happen if I kept on walking, just got in the car and left? Pack my bag and let Kerry deal with Dad's shit. Go back to Baltimore where I can argue one-on-one.

The door opens behind me and Lauren steps out, clutching her tiny purse.

"Hook me up with one of them," she says.

I hike an eyebrow at her as she beckons with her right hand.

"Yes, I know, it's not good for me. It stunts my growth, yada, yada. Heard all the jokes before. Just give me one."

I fish the pack out of my pocket and hand it to her. She

shakes it a couple of times until one pokes above the rest, and draws it slowly out. "You promised you'd behave," she says, as she hands the pack back.

"I didn't start that. Talk to your fiancé."

"Oh, I will. And he knows it. Light?"

I hold my lit cigarette to the end of hers. Lauren stares into my eyes as she sucks the flame in through the tip.

"He's always been an instigator," I say. "And you're an enabler."

"What?"

"You're playing right into my mom's hands. That's why she loves you more than us."

"Stop." Lauren playfully slaps my arm. "I feel sorry for her. She's been through a lot."

"She's put herself through a lot. Us, too. She didn't always used to be so manipulative, though. Not when we were young."

"She's not manipulative. How?"

"Are you serious? Everything she says is loaded. I shouldn't have bit on that B.S. about her going back home. It's a damn war zone now. She ain't going there. And fuck her if she does. I'm not going to visit."

Lauren tsks me. She's got a beautiful tsk. Her eyes pop just a smidgen and her mouth hangs open almost, but not quite, in a smile. I've forgotten how fun it can be to banter with someone who doesn't take everything I say as the opening line of an argument. "You don't visit her now."

"Touché."

She drops her cigarette into the sand pit and digs into her purse for a Listerine strip. "We better get back in there. They must have brought our food by now."

I flick my butt toward the parking lot. It emits an orange spark when it bounces on the sidewalk.

"Remind me again why this ashtray's here," she says.

"Have you any idea how unsanitary those things are?"

"Go pick it up." Her expression is playful, but her tone isn't. I grin and step toward the door, but she stands her ground, hands on her hips. "Seriously, go pick that up. The world's not your garbage can."

I feel like I'm back in grade school, being scolded for accidentally on purpose knocking all the whiteboard markers to the floor. Only by a much prettier teacher. Shaking my head in mock disbelief, I trudge down the walkway and retrieve my cigarette.

"That's better," Lauren says, when I drop it in the sand trap. "Now behave yourself in there. You promised."

Our lunch is waiting on the table. Kerry is halfway through his steak, and Audra has made a noticeable dent in her pasta. Mom's salad looks nearly untouched. She's leaning forward on her elbows, staring into a new cranberry vodka.

"How are you doing, Mom?" Lauren asks.

"She's drunk," Kerry grumbles. "That's her fourth one."

"Fifth," Audra says.

"Oh, no," Lauren says. "Are you feeling okay, Mom? You want me to take you home?"

Her eyes as impenetrable as frosted glass, my mother nods. Leave it to her to upstage my father at his memorial luncheon. I still don't understand why she even came, other than her unquenchable thirst for drama. A week from now we'll all have returned to our daily lives. Dad will be forgotten, and so will she.

SEVENTEEN

We emerge from the restaurant into a steady rain shortly after two. I can barely see the lights on the storefronts across the street through the fog. By the time I reach Dad's car I'm wet to the skin without having felt the individual drops hitting me. In Baltimore the rain comes down in sheets, like someone on a nearby roof is aiming a fire hose at your head. Here it's more like walking through a cloud. I'm slowed on the drive home by delivery vans, school buses, and a minivan driver who seems to believe it's okay to drive twenty in a forty zone because she's got her hazards on. When I finally reach Dad's street, the mailman jerks his Jeep into my path without looking or even offering a chagrined apology wave. He squeals to a halt at our box as I turn into the driveway.

I haven't thought to check the mail since arriving Sunday. But it doesn't stop just because its recipient does. The box is jammed so full the door won't close tight. The envelopes cling together when I draw them out. Inside, I peel each piece off the stack and lay it to dry until the entire tabletop is covered. There are fundraising pitches from libraries and nature conservancies and the alumni association at the University of Washington, where Dad got his Master's. His *Newsweek* and *Popular Photography* magazines sandwich a package marked "Do not bend—postcards" and a statement from TIAA-CREF Financial Services.

The TIAA-CREF envelope disintegrates when I rake my finger through it. I flatten the folded sheets on the kitchen counter and stare unbelievingly at the bold number in the center of the first page. Kerry and Audra were way off. The balance on Dad's retirement account reads $695,454.29. Divide that by three and … this can't be right. I can't really be about to come into two hundred something thousand bucks. Plus my share of the house, which even in its run-down state ought to fetch another three hundred grand.

I shimmy out of my jacket and hang it on a chair, remove my tie, and unbutton my shirt down to my waist. The clamminess has traveled up my arms to my torso and the open air feels good on my skin as I flap the cloth against my chest. I take a beer from the door of the fridge and pop the top. My eyes are locked on Dad's balance as I sip. $695,454.29. I can't even fathom what I would do with that much dough. Even a third of it sounds like a fortune, like winning the lottery.

I know it's wrong to celebrate, but I can't suppress the first scream that comes out. They keep coming, building in volume. Some are just noise, others deep and meaningful expressions like, "Fuck, yeah," and "Daddy need a new pair of boxers, baby." I pause to ponder the likelihood of a) ghosts in general, and b) Dad's ghost in particular, and whether it might be nearby, watching me moonwalk in my socks across the kitchen floor. Or whip my shirt off and twirl it around my head. Or floss my crotch with it like a drunken groomsman at his sister's wedding. (If the stories are to be believed.) I'm doing the sprinkler when the doorbell rings, or at least when I hear it, which I can't guarantee is the first time it's chimed on the wall above the stove.

Mrs. Holt looks like she hasn't made up her mind whether she's dismayed or amused. She raised four kids and has no doubt witnessed her share of idiotic exhibitions. Still, the discomfort is mutual as I open the door. If she hadn't troubled herself to bake the pie she's shielding from the elements with an umbrella barely big enough to cover her head, perhaps she'd have retreated unseen to the serenity of her own home.

"Mrs. Holt," I say, hastily buttoning my shirt.

"Sorry we missed the service, C.J.," she says. "Darrin's dermatologist appointment had already been rescheduled twice."

"He's okay, I hope."

"Oh, yes. It's just a rash, as it goes. But it's so hard to get in to see the doctor, he didn't want to let this one go."

"We understand," I say, as if I speak on behalf of my family. Which I suppose I do, as none of them would care one way or the other if the Holts had shown.

"I don't want to hold you up," she says. "I know you must be quite busy. I made a strawberry-rhubarb. It was one of your father's favorites."

My throat tightens and I'm forced to nod until I can swallow and clear a path to say, "Thank you." The pie is still warm when she places it in my hands.

"Say hello to your brother and sister for us. We've been thinking about them a lot this week."

"I will. Thanks."

She backs awkwardly down the stairs, looking relieved to have completed her delivery.

"Mrs. Holt," I call, when she reaches the driveway.

"Yes, C.J.?"

"Was my dad … okay? I mean, did you ever notice anything?"

She breaks eye contact momentarily and seems to be weighing her response. "It wasn't our business to notice."

"But you did?"

She shrugs uncomfortably. "He had a visitor."

"A woman?"

She nods, then shakes her head. "A girl. Maybe once or twice a week. Sometimes latish."

"Who was she?"

"I don't know. We never met her. I only saw her a few times. But her car was here often. A white Honda. Sometimes it would still be here in the morning when Mr. Holt left for work."

"A girl?" I ask, still incredulous. "What did she look like?"

"She looked a bit like," Mrs. Holt again contemplates her reply, ignoring the rain spilling over the low side of her umbrella and down the back of her jacket, "well, like your mother used to."

EIGHTEEN

In the ten years I lived at home after Mom left, Dad had a grand total of one girlfriend. She was a librarian named Elaine with bowl-cut bangs and wire-rimmed glasses and a fat, round ass like Grimace from McDonald's, and I knew from the first time I met her their relationship wouldn't go anywhere. Not that I did anything to help stoke it along. It wouldn't have mattered. She was nothing like Mom, and I suspect the only reason Dad allowed himself to be set up was to quiet the two or three colleagues who kept encouraging him to "get back out there."

She had two boys, thirteen and five. I had just turned sixteen and was about to start my junior year of high school. It was shortly after Audra left, and Dad and I spent most of our time looking for excuses to avoid each other. I had reached that age where I'd rather coat myself in boysenberry syrup and lie down on an anthill than hang out with my family. (I seem to have never grown past it.) Imagine my delight when Elaine proposed a day trip to Mount Vernon. Dad tried to pitch it as his idea, but as he'd never once shown any interest in gardens and windmills, I called bullshit and he let it drop.

He started hinting again a couple of weeks later, only this time he sweetened the pot, suggesting he might be able to get a deal on an mp3 player at the campus bookstore. I had just started working at Remlinger's, washing dishes two nights a week, and for the first time had enough disposable income to buy it for myself. So he played hardball and made signing the waiver for me to take driver's ed contingent on joining them.

I did my best to sabotage it. I burned Queen's "Fat Bottomed Girls" onto a CD and cued it to play in the car just as we picked them up. Instead of taking offense, she cackled and told how she and her girlfriends used it as the soundtrack for a skit they did in college. So I brooded the entire drive there, which gave Devin, her older boy, the green light to sulk as well. "Whatever" was not an acceptable response in their household. After his third such reply in a fifteen minute spell (he was a quick study), she marched him out of earshot and reamed him out good and thorough, thus ensuring his sullen behavior would continue. Had she ignored his attitude as my dad ignored mine, Devin would have bored of being a rebel and reverted to his mild-mannered self.

It was about that time I switched tactics and focused on trying to make Ricky, the five-year-old, laugh. It wasn't hard. Ten minutes of pull-my-finger, with varying raspberry sounds for each digit, won the kid over. And what could she say? It was her idea to drag me along. So we made fart noises and substituted mildly naughty words into songs he knew from summer camp and the kid was worshiping me by lunchtime. I finally pushed it too far on the drive home, dramatically altering the words to "Daddy Finger," a catchy but annoying ditty equating each finger to a member of the family. "Daddy Finger, Daddy Finger, where are you? Here I am, here I am, how do you do?" became "Middle Finger, Middle Finger, where are you? Here I am, here I am, hey, fuck you." Her skin, from the collar of her cable-knit sweater to her hairline, went crimson. I couldn't make out the first few sentences she screamed at me from the front seat; the words jumbled on top of each other until she caught her breath. My father shot me a defeated look in the rearview mirror, and I knew I'd never be welcome on another blended-family excursion. No one uttered a syllable for five miles. The silence was finally broken when I extended my index finger toward Ricky, who grinned and pulled it. When I trumpeted, Devin laughed so hard he broke wind for real, which set everyone off but his mother. Elaine seethed all the way home.

They dated for several more months, Dad typically seeing her one night every week when the boys were with her ex-husband. Over Columbus Day weekend they went out of town together, staying two nights in Anacortes. Home alone, I did what most kids would do: stayed up half the night and ransacked his private quarters. My search came to an abrupt halt when I found a half-empty box of condoms in his night-stand. I promptly rerouted to the kitchen and tapped into his wine. That was the first time I ever got drunk. I woke up Sunday morning on the bathmat and immediately emptied what was left of my innards into the toilet. Despite my vow to never drink again, by nightfall I was back in his hooch. No amount of homemade Shiraz could purge the mental image of my dad mounting Elaine.

Their relationship skidded to its preordained end the following month. She came to realize that despite their common interests and general compatibility she was competing with a memory. I overheard her comment one evening on a photo of my parents that still hung on the living room wall eight years after the divorce. It was taken the week they met, in front of Nevsky Cathedral in Bulgaria. "Warren," she said, "perhaps we should get our picture taken so you could update your décor." By Thanksgiving they were through. Kerry came home from school for the weekend and her name never came up, at least not until Dad went to bed. My brother predicted that night Dad would never date again.

Apparently, he was wrong.

Could the girl Mrs. Holt described be the girl from the funeral? Who was she, and what the hell would she be doing with my dad? I've never pictured my father as the sugar daddy type. Then again, I never imagined his retirement account would be pushing seven figures.

A cold sensation washes over me, settling in my stomach.

His note. What if?

Of course, I'm jumping beyond conclusions here. I have no idea who that girl was. She might have just been a student. I can't even remember exactly what she looks like. When I try to picture her, it's my mother I see, young and pretty and rarely smiling. I take the stairs two at a time and dump the box of loose photos on Dad's bed. Flicking them one by one into a reject pile, I scan through several hundred prints in a matter of minutes. She doesn't appear in any of them.

Down the hall in his office, I shake the mouse on his computer and the monitor comes to life. The cursor pulses in a box in the middle of the screen. It wants a password. Fuck. What if it's her name? Talk about a vicious circle.

I type in my dad's birthdate. It doesn't like that. I try Kerry and Audra and Christopher. I try Northpoint. It seems futile. I could have the right name and my rudimentary hacking will still fail if he's added any numerals or punctuation. My fingers hover over the keyboard, seeking a place to start. They touch S first. Then v. And e. And without consciously thinking it out, I've spelled my mother's name. Svetlana.

I'm in.

I open Facebook as my father, his tiny mug staring at me from his profile picture. He's only got thirty-seven friends, including myself, Kerry, Audra, and a couple of people I recognize from the memorial service. She is not among them. I click each person on his list and tab through their photos to see if she might be a friend of a friend, but find no trace of her.

His email is organized exactly like his file cabinet, with dozens of named folders, many of which contain only one or two messages. I work my way down from Angela Radcliffe, one of Dad's distant cousins, to Youngman's, which turns out to be a business that deals postcards through an eBay store. None of the names sound Russian. None sound foreign at all. I scroll through his sent mail, reading the first few lines of each message before moving on. Either he wiped his tracks clean or they didn't email each other. There will be no text trail, either. He was one of the few remaining Americans without a cell phone. He wasn't much of a gadget guy generally. Not because he didn't care for the technology. Because he was cheap. I was surprised when he showed up at Audra's wedding with a digital camera. It was a nice one, too, a pocket-sized Canon with a 10x zoom lens.

I scoot my chair across the floor to his roll-top desk. The cubbies up top are stuffed with papers and letters I read just long enough to ascertain they're not from her. I find the empty camera case in a small drawer stocked with extra batteries and memory cards. But the camera itself is not here. My search takes a tangential turn when I open the wide, flat drawer just under the desktop. The first item that catches my eye is a woman's gold choker necklace. Dad's old wedding ring, which he wore for nearly two years after Mom left, rests in the pencil tray among the small change and lockless keys. There's a rubber-banded stack of postcards, a dozen ballpoint pens, a pad of Post-it notes, a book of stamps, a bag of M&Ms, a deck of playing cards, a *Penthouse* magazine dated July of last year, and a worn leather wallet.

The bill compartment contains forty-two dollars in cash, two twenties and two singles. Nestled in with the money I find a folded index card, upon which my father has printed a dozen phone numbers, some crossed out and updated, Kerry's twice. My number is here, as is Audra's and his doctor's. The last name at the bottom of the list is Petra. No last name. The ink is fresher and darker than most of the faded entries above. Is it her? It's a 425 area code, somewhere either immediately north of here or on the east side of the lake. I flatten the wallet and rifle through the credit cards and shoppers club IDs. From a pocket beneath them, I extract a spare house key, a quarter, and a single photo in a protective plastic sleeve.

Her eyes are less intimidating than my mother's and her skin a shade or two darker, but from a distance she could easily pass for a young version of Mom. The girl in the photo is in her late twenties by my guess. She wears a reluctant smile and an expression that suggests she merely tolerated having her photo taken. And diamond teardrop earrings that match the one I found in the Charger.

I want to call Kerry and say I told you so. I was right. It wasn't Mom. Not the original, anyway.

NINETEEN

Jimmy studies the photo, tilting it up and back as if it might reveal different secrets depending upon the angle at which it's held, like a holographic 3D postcard.

"Maybe he was just tutoring her." He passes the picture to Patrick, seated at his right elbow, as he was the last time I was here. Despite Jimmy's denial, I suspect they are the Norm and Cliff of Izzy's, regulars so regular their stools sit vacant on the nights they stay home. "It might not be what you think."

"Maybe he was paying her," Patrick suggests.

I would hit him if the same thought hadn't already lodged itself in my own mind, right next to the equally plausible possibility she was worming her way into his retirement coffers. Stretched to its illogical conclusion, the lost earring placed her at the scene of his death, which may not have been a suicide after all. There were a few holes in the theory, namely his note and the physics of a 120-pound girl dragging her much larger victim out to the car against his will and holding him still until he stopped breathing. Not to mention why he called to say good-bye. Untethered, my imagination tends to float away like a helium balloon. Which is why, after pacing the living room inventing one wild scenario after the next, I texted Jimmy to reel me back to earth.

"He wasn't paying her," I say, to myself as much as him.

"How can you know?" Patrick asks.

"He was too cheap."

I'm still in my funeral clothes, minus the necktie, my shirt rumpled just enough to convey I've had a rough day. I picked up on a sympathetic vibe from the girl working the tap when I ordered my beer. I'm not above playing any card that might dispose people to be nicer to me than they otherwise would. Maybe I'll dress in black from now on, maintain a two-day growth of facial hair, and practice smiling wearily as if strangers' random acts of kindness are all that keep me from throwing myself off the Aurora Bridge.

"How'd your lunch go?" Jimmy asks. "Sorry I couldn't make it. If I hadn't missed work yesterday I could have stretched things out a bit longer today."

"Total disaster. I don't want to talk about it. My mom's a mess. Leave it at that."

"What'd she do?" Patrick plows his thick fingers through a bowl of beer nuts and pops them one at a time into his lips like a chimpanzee eating fleas.

"She drank her weight in vodka and started planning her own funeral, then nearly passed out and had to be driven home. It was tons of fun."

"She do stuff like that often?" Patrick asks.

I shrug. I don't really mind talking about my family with Jimmy. He knows them from way back. It's usually cathartic and he's detached enough to let me blame everyone else for the dysfunction. But Patrick's ears are pinned back for entertainment's sake. My life isn't a reality show. It's not *Passive-Aggressive House.* We're not whoring out our lives for eyeballs and marketshare. "No more than anyone else's mom. Let's talk about something else. What were you guys talking about before I got here?"

"You." Patrick's neck jiggles when he laughs and his doughy complexion goes pink. Though he outweighs me by twenty-five pounds, I could take him in a fight. He'd be absolutely zero use in a bar scuffle, which is a good reason for him to limit his evening carousing to Izzy's.

Jimmy looks like he wants to crawl up into the heating

duct and disappear. I don't blame him, though. Who's ever tactless enough to admit gossiping about you? We all do it, we all deny it. That's just the way it works. For most of us, anyway.

If I cared about baseball, or followed it even a little, I could skate us through the awkward silence by making small talk about the Mariners game. But I couldn't name a single player on the team. I have no idea whether they're in first place or last. I haven't actively watched a game since I dropped out of Little League. I stare at the big screen for thirty seconds trying to figure out if Seattle is the gray team or the white one before giving up and scanning the late dinner crowd. Unlike Monday, when I didn't get here until after ten, the dining room is nearly full and most of the tables in the bar are occupied. With no conversation to busy my mouth I knock back my first pint in under fifteen minutes. I haven't even worked through the foam head on its replacement when Julianne and her two friends from the other night stroll through the front entrance.

"Fantastic," I mutter.

"Just ignore them," Jimmy says. "They usually sit down ..." He stops when they blow past the hostess stand and up into the bar area. Julianne hesitates when she notices me, but instead of detouring to the opening at the far end of the bar, she drops her purse on the counter two stools down from mine.

I nod at her as coolly as I can, earning a smirk in response.

"Didn't recognize you without the holes in your pants." She's so pleased by her own wit she can't suppress her grin. "What's the special occasion? Did someone die?"

I let her hold her condescending expression to the five-second threshold where my dad used to warn me my face would freeze. "My father," I reply, just loud enough for her and her friends to hear.

Her face blanches. She looks past me to Jimmy, who nods

solemnly.

"I'm sorry, C.J.," she says. "That was … I didn't know."

Whether she's sorry for my loss or just sorry for crossing the Cruella de Vil line on the bitch scale is debatable. I suspect it's mostly the latter. Even her friends look embarrassed for her.

"That's why I've been home. His funeral was this morning. I'll be going back soon, so you won't have to worry about running into me anymore."

"I wasn't worried about it. This is a big enough town for everyone. Move back if you want. Won't bother me."

Though she looks me straight in the eye when she talks, her pupils are an unfocused inky black, cold and out of synch with her words. She may as well be wearing sunglasses. The rational portion of my brain wishes she would just walk away. But there's still a nostalgic fraction in there that wants her to slide her stool next to mine so close I can feel the sprigs of her Aqua Net-crisped hair against my neck.

"Move back. Yeah, right. Everybody hates me here. That's why I left."

"I don't hate you, Neubs. I love you, man."

"Everybody but Jimmy."

"Life's too short to hate," Julianne says, with all the sincerity of a Facebook meme that's been shared 143,627 times by people who ran out of kitten videos with which to fill their timelines.

I raise my glass in toast. Inside I'm mocking her, but I do it credibly enough Jimmy and Patrick lift their drinks as well. The three girls raise their empty hands as if they held daiquiris or appletinis or whatever it is they come here to blot out their day with.

The bartender sets three drinks on the counter with nothing more than a smile having passed between them. The girls take their usuals to a table on the fringe of the bar seating area, about forty feet away. Every so often I peek over, invariably catching at least one of them averting their gaze.

When I order my next refill, the girl sets a pitcher on the bar. "It's on her," she says, nodding toward Julianne's table. I want to pour some for Patrick first to see if it's been poisoned, but his glass is already full, so I top my own off and offer the girls a wave. Julianne winks back. I can count on one hand the number of girls who have winked at me in bars. Julianne makes four. The first one was back in college. I wound up going home with her. Mindy was the second, but we had already been dating for two weeks, so it doesn't really count. The third one was her boss on one of her office nights out. She was married, and drunk, so I didn't chance it. Those three all felt different. They were flirtatious. Julianne's is unnatural, almost robotic. As if she's closing one eye to find me in the scope of a rifle.

I consider packing it in for the night when the pitcher runs dry. Until a second one shows up. I mouth a "thank you" across the bar. Julianne smiles and twirls a finger in the hair above her right ear. Again it feels forced, as if she's talking herself through the mechanics of manipulating both her cheeks and her hands. But free beer is free beer. We might be about even now for the change she pocketed at the grocery store.

"You all right?" Jimmy asks, when I set my empty glass down on the counter. Though he and Patrick have helped drain both freebies, I've put away at least a pitcher's worth myself.

"Straight shot home up the hill."

"They'll call you a cab," he says.

"I'm good." I nod several times to emphasize my lucidity as we shake hands, which probably only undercuts my message. Patrick, too, insists on planting his moist palm in mine. My first impulse as I walk away is to wipe my hand on my pants. Sober, I'd wait until I was out of sight to avoid insulting him. But I'm barely three strides away before I'm drying my hand on my thigh. I look back and wave, then turn toward the girls' table and salute them as well. This time Julianne's smile is expectant, the first stage in a laugh for which I'm to serve as the punch line. I concentrate on my footwork, down the step to the level of the main seating area, around the hostess stand, and out the door. I won't stumble tonight.

Outside, I pause to light a cigarette. Too late I realize I should have hit the head one last time before leaving. I'd look like a dork walking back in now. It's only a five-minute drive home. I can manage. I continue on across the parking lot, pausing momentarily to distinguish my father's Outback from a station wagon several spaces over. I wonder anew if I have the correct car when the door doesn't open. I thumb the key fob again and it audibly clicks once more. It's only after I lift my thumb I realize I'm depressing the lock button.

"C.J.," calls a voice behind me. "Wait."

Jimmy races toward me, waving his arms above his head like he's warning me away from a rental van packed with plastic explosives.

"Don't get in," he yells. "Don't drive."

"What's up?"

"Don't drive home." He grabs my arm so tight I can feel his fingernails through my jacket. "It's a setup."

"What?"

"Julianne's brother-in-law's a cop." Jimmy points across the street to the shopping center parking lot. "She set you up. As soon as you pull out, he'll pull you over."

I can make out a sedan with a rack of lights mounted on the roof. There appears to be someone sitting in the front seat. Waiting for me. I walk toward him. Jimmy follows. From the sidewalk I distinguish a patrol officer's cap perched upon a freakishly tall head shaped like the upper portion of my thumb. He's watching me.

"Why?" I ask. "How could someone possibly hate me this much?"

TWENTY

Julianne's first words to me were, "You're in my seat." It was the first day of first grade and our classroom was arranged in islands, four desks, set up in squares, two facing two. Mine was in a group by the aquarium in the back. I wanted to sit closest to the fish tank, so I cunningly switched my nametag with hers. She stood there in her electric pink dress, hands on her hips, as if I should move just because she said so. I pointed to the construction-paper nametag in front of me. She trumped me by lifting the desk lid to reveal a Little Mermaid notebook and a transparent plastic case stocked with a rainbow assortment of pencils and markers. Perhaps if I hadn't left my backpack on the kitchen table I'd have discovered her stash when I first sat down and saved myself some embarrassment. Not to mention the humiliation of begging her for a writing utensil when Mrs. Immink began publicly shaming the slacker contingent.

"Preparation, preparation, preparation," she bellowed. "The three P's of success. Jimmy has his pencil ready. Where is yours, Christopher?"

I looked up into the paisley caftan clinging to her ample hips and chest and shrugged meekly.

"It fell," Julianne declared, bending down toward the floor and coming up with a red pencil in her hand. "Here it is."

She preferred to be the one to make me tremble. Mrs. Immink was free to rule the rest of the class, as long as Julianne reigned over our island, populated by myself, Jimmy, and a tiny Asian girl named Sandra Kim, whose static-charged hair danced above her head as if led by a party balloon. When spelling games or math competitions pitted us against the other tables, woe be the weak link who let down our team. Julianne was captain, and she played to win.

Jimmy and I were the only boys invited to her birthday party. He came down with chicken pox that week, leaving me on my own, outnumbered ten to one. They kept winding a fluffy, purple boa around my neck and trying to get me to dance to Paula Abdul. I spent most of the afternoon petting her dachshund, who peed on the rug every time he got excited. The knees of my slacks were soaked through with dog urine by the time my mother picked me up.

Our elementary school being populous enough to house three classes for each grade level, I escaped Julianne's shadow until fourth grade. There were no islands anymore. The desks were in rows, every man for himself. She was into girly things like Barbies and glittery nail polish. I was obsessed with Transformers and my BMX bike, the first set of wheels I got new and not handed down from Kerry. I skidded out in some gravel on the shoulder of the road when she was walking home from school one afternoon toward the end of spring. Showing off, like boys do. Only I wiped out and bloodied my arm from wrist to elbow. Julianne laughed and kept on walking.

It was another couple of years before we shared a classroom again, this time in French at the junior high. She was tops in the class, one of the few who didn't go tongue twisted when Monsieur Blanchet called on her to read from the text. On the rare occasions he partnered us off to work on vocabulary, I was transported back to first grade, trying my darnedest to get the words right to impress her. She had breasts now and braces and wore blush and mascara, and I wanted to hold her hand and walk her home and pet her instead of her leaky dog. She indicated no interest in any of the above, so I kept my yearnings to myself. When Eric McFarland asked her to the eighth-grade prom I was so jealous I jammed a thumb tack in the tire of his mountain bike.

Her father's company transferred him to California, and they moved away for the first two years of high school. She returned our junior year a peg or two down on the social ladder, everyone else having already established their place among the various cliques. Even after the Elizabeth Dunning debacle, she was within my reach. Status wise, anyway.

In part, she owed her decline in rank to the new identity she'd acquired in San Luis Obispo. She came back with her hair frosted platinum, chopped to her shoulders and swept across her forehead, veiling the metallic, green-apple makeup shading her eyelids. She blended punk and preppy better than any of our peers, accessorizing her blouses with funky, metal collar tips and layering cardigans over bustiers. But behind the aloof gaze, she still burned to wreck the grading curve, as much for the satisfaction of succeeding as the joy of causing the B students to slip to C's and the C students to panic. She didn't consider anyone in the entire school, faculty included, worthy of kowtowing to. She simply wasn't interested in playing politics and pretending to be pally with cheerleaders to boost her own profile. Which made her something of an anti-establishment goddess in my eyes.

She would greet me in the halls if I said hello first, but wouldn't otherwise go out of her way to acknowledge me. I reworked my routes to class to increase my odds of bumping into her, but before I could work up the stones to ask her out she was spotted hanging on the arm of Shane Timmerman, a senior who radiated a parallel don't-give-a-shit vibe.

We wound up in the same homeroom second semester. I dropped my book bag on the seat next to hers the first day, and when she didn't object I sat down. "How's your dog?" was the first thing I could think to say. She looked at me as if I'd just asked about her great-grandmother or her period or something equally random and out of bounds. "Fine." "He still pee all over the place?" After another couple of seconds of incredulous staring, her face broke into a smile as that distant birthday came rushing back. For twenty minutes she told me stories of Skippy the wiener dog and his exploits over the past decade, from surviving a tumor on his back leg to accompanying her on her flight to California.

We chatted every morning the rest of the spring. Though Mr. MacDougall never bothered with attendance and didn't show up half the time himself, I was never late to homeroom. I was one of the first people she told when she broke up with Shane over Memorial Day weekend. I think she used me to practice on. It wasn't that she wanted to cry on my shoulder, though I'd have been glad to let her. It was more of a test to see how casually she could slip it into conversation. It was finals week before I finally found the courage to ask if she'd like to maybe catch a movie "or something" over the summer. She squinted at me skeptically, then drew a fine-tip marker from her backpack and scrawled her number on the back of my hand. "Now, don't wash that," she said. "I'll be in California until July."

I cruised by her house every day on my bike until one morning I saw the garage door up. I pedaled furiously the two miles home, not wanting to be spotted and branded a stalker. I waited another twenty-four hours to call, just to play it cool. We made plans to see *High Fidelity* the Friday after the Fourth of July. As I waited in the front foyer for her to come down, her dog piddled on my shoe, drizzling a dark, wavy line across the brown leather uppers. He could have lifted his leg and pissed on my pants and I wouldn't have cared. I was finally taking her out.

I remember nothing about the movie. I spent the entire two hours scheming ways to extend the evening once we left the cinema. As it turned out, she suggested Starbucks. She told me stories about her trip as I sipped my Italian roast and pretended I was sophisticated enough to like it. When I dropped her off, she kissed me on the cheek, near enough the corner of my mouth I could reach the spot with my tongue and taste her lip gloss all the way home.

Five days later we progressed to mini golf and pizza. We kissed for a couple of minutes in the parking lot after dinner, exploring the insides of each other's mouths with our tongues. She stared straight into my eyes when we said good night like there was something more she wanted to say. Or ask. Instead she planted her hand on my cheek, thumb nearly in my ear, and guided my mouth to hers for one final smack. I could still feel her fingers in my hair as I lay in bed later, counting down until our next night together.

We didn't bother with golf or movies. I suggested Richmond Beach, one of Kerry's favorite high school haunts. I figured we could walk the shore and, if things unfolded right, maybe find a driftwood log to camp on for a bit. Turned out it was a bit more crowded than either of us anticipated. We strolled a mile and a half up the beach as the sun faded over Puget Sound, never reaching a secluded enough place for me to feel comfortable pawing at her. Either the windows of the houses above were too clear or there were other like-minded souls occupying nearby perches. We wound up temporarily on a picnic table in a shelter, where we kissed for a few minutes until a raggedy man rolled a shopping cart in and began rifling through the trash bins.

The car was her suggestion. By the time we got back to the parking lot, it was dark enough to provide us cover. I unlocked Dad's wagon and opened the rear door. The mere act of lying in the backseat with her surpassed my expectations. When she let me work my hand under her blouse I was content to stay right there the rest of the evening. It was more progress than I'd ever made with a girl. It seemed greedy to expect more. And terrifying. I think I stopped breathing for a moment when she slid her hand down to my fly. It was all I could do to hold back the tide long enough for her to bust my little soldier out of the barracks. I came all over her hand so quickly I figured I must have lost track of time; in truth there probably wasn't much to lose track of. Counted in earth minutes, it couldn't have lasted more than two and a half.

Then it was my turn. My heart was pounding so hard when I unbuttoned her jeans I couldn't hear anything other than the pulsing of my own blood. I kissed her deeper and deeper as I unzipped her pants because I kind of knew how to kiss. Well enough we'd advanced past it, anyway. Pants were foreign territory. And panties, well, it was as though I'd never felt cotton before. She was soaked by the time I worked my fingers beneath the waistband. I went in straight down, kissing, exploring, kissing, probing, kissing, worrying. What if she realized I didn't know what the hell I was doing? My middle finger disappeared inside her as if sucked into a vacuum. She stopped kissing back and moaned. I slipped my index finger in next. When I opened my eyes hers were closed and she was shivering. In and out I worked my fingers. Warmer, wetter, braver they got. When she reached down and touched the head of my cock, I nearly passed out. This was it. The big moment even bigger than the moment I was just enjoying. She was about to make me a man. I hoisted myself up far enough to align our privates and aimed for pay dirt. I was inside her, but clueless what to do next. I tried to kiss her and wound up banging my teeth against hers. I thought about what I'd seen people do in movies and started thrusting in and out. Her breathing grew heavier, almost frantic. "No, don't stop," she said. Then again louder. I didn't. I pumped harder, faster. "Please," she screamed. At least it sounded like a scream burning into my ear from such close proximity. Then her hips bucked so hard I thought she broke my pelvis. She fell silent on the seat beneath me, blouse open, breasts roaming free of her lace bra, tears slipping out the corners of her eyes.

She didn't kiss me when I dropped her off. I couldn't understand her reply when I said I'd call her. I took it for an mm-hmm, as in, yes, you will, and I can't wait until you do. Apparently it wasn't. She didn't return my messages that next afternoon. I left two, just to ensure she knew I was thinking about her. When she finally answered the following day, she claimed she had to help her mother with something over the weekend. In hindsight, I realized she only agreed to a fourth date to get me off the phone. She broke it with a string of excuses. Eventually my calls were diverted to a recording informing me my number had been blocked.

The indignity deepened as the summer wound down. I wanted to drop out of school just to avoid seeing her. My mind raced with the wild rumors that would greet me on campus. But none did. That almost hurt worse, as if she didn't want anyone to know we'd meant something to each other, if only for a blink.

Has she explained to the silhouettes flanking hers in the window as Jimmy guides his car out of the lot? I can make out their figures through the tinted glass to the right of the front entrance. Laughing, I imagine. Disappointed, perhaps, that Jimmy rescued me from her trap.

The first word I growl as we start up the hill starts with a C. Lacking the vocabulary to top it, I repeat it several times on the short drive home. "Tell me how you really feel, Neubs," Jimmy laughs with every expletive. "Let it out, brother."

I let Jimmy help me upstairs. Not that I'm not capable of staggering to bed. That's practically routine. I don't even have to navigate Mindy tonight. Shit, I was supposed to call her this afternoon. It's only one o'clock in Baltimore. She might still be up. But I feel so comfortable with the sheets pinned under my sides I don't want to get out of bed. Even when my bladder presses. I finally cave, knowing I won't drift off with that nagging at my subconscious. When I emerge from the bathroom, the light rising up the stairs catches my eye. Jimmy didn't turn the kitchen light off on his way out. Downstairs I shuffle in my boxers and t-shirt. I test the deadbolt, kill the light, and make my way back to bed.

Again I cocoon myself under the covers. It's so dark I have to concentrate to make out the doorway. Too dark to see shadows or ghosts or vindictive exes or cop cars or my mother's young doppelganger or the dresser in which I stashed Dad's retirement statement. They're all still there when I close my eyes, rotating through my mind like slides in a View-Master. They pursue me to the threshold of sleep, and follow me through.

I have no idea what time it is when I wake up. I could have been asleep an hour or five. All I know is my mouth is dryer than my t-shirt, and there's a faint beam of light stretching across my floor from the open door to the foot of my bed.

TWENTY-ONE

The house was never this quiet when I lived here. It had its own soundtrack: the buzz of the refrigerator, the hum of air blowing through the baseboard vents, the lament of the very walls and joists as they settled around me. All I hear now above the scratching of my hair against the pillow is my own breath escaping in bursts through my parched lips. Then a car stereo, getting louder as it approaches from the west until I can almost, but not quite, place the song thumping through its speakers. It recedes to the east, leaving me in the screaming silence to ponder the light stealing into my room. Maybe a deer triggered the floodlight in the driveway. But why hasn't it gone out? Maybe it's still out there. I'm not sure exactly how the trigger works. If the sixty seconds are extended by subsequent movement, a large animal could cause the light to stay on for several minutes or more. There are so many deer in the woods behind our lot, my mother used to spray fox urine around her flower beds to keep them from being devoured.

It's pitch dark out when I nudge the curtain open. The only light is a ball at the top of the lamppost beyond Holts'. As the drape falls back into place, I hear the creak of the stairs, then a lighter squeak as weight comes off the spongy plank. I have nothing with which to defend myself. Not even a sawed-off broomstick.

Burrowed under the covers, I tent the blanket just far enough above my head to see and hear. The footsteps aren't heavy enough to be Kerry's. They grow more audible, coming now through the wall separating my room from Dad's uncarpeted office. The hallway outside my door brightens, awash in the light streaming from his floor lamp. Can I get to my phone, charging atop the dresser by the door, without being heard?

Careful not to rustle the sheets, I slowly fold the covers away, pausing every couple of seconds to listen. I hear Dad's chair roll across the floor until it crashes into the wall. And a voice cursing. A woman's? It's not loud enough to be sure. I stand, pause, step, pause, step again, pause. Trembling, I untether my phone from its cord. If I called 911 would I get the police in Baltimore or here? Would the Baltimore police put me through to Lake Forest Park? Would they send Julianne's brother-in-law?

I can't wait for them. I stoop to retrieve my slacks from the floor, stepping first into the right leg, then the left, heart pounding as I fumble to secure the button at my waist. Buckle clutched tight in my palm, I slide my belt free one loop at a time until it dangles at my side. Out in the hall, I advance in baby steps, back flat against the wall to avoid throwing a shadow. "Come on now, where are you?" the voice asks. It's definitely a woman's. This shouldn't boost my confidence as much as it does. There are plenty of chicks that could kick my ass. I'm not envisioning one in Dad's office. I take a deep breath when I reach the door frame. And another. And, dammit, I can't stand here all night. I poke my head out just far enough to peer into the room.

And there she is, hunched over the wide, flat drawer of my father's roll-top desk. Waves of raven hair protrude from beneath a black bandana. She wears a skintight black sweater, zipped as high as the valley between her breasts, black jeans, and black boots. Clearly a precaution meant for the sneaking in and away portions of her mission, as her outfit provides no cover here with the lights on.

"You must be Petra," I say, stepping fully into the doorway.

She stiffens. Her head swivels in slow motion until her almond eyes meet mine. More startled than frightened, they drift south from my face to the belt hanging from my hand, then move beyond me to the stairs, constantly calculating her next course of action. At her full height she stands about five-foot-six with just a hint of paunch straining her sweater in the belly and shoulders. Her hips, too, are rounder than my mother's. The similarities are strongest in the face: the arching eyebrows, prominent cheekbones, and firm chin. And the thin, ironic smile intimating she's sized me up as a minimal threat.

"Hello, C.J." She speaks calmly, in an accent as lush as her eyelashes. She can't have grown up here. Folding her arms across her chest, she leans back against the desk. "What is the belt for?"

"Self-defense." I crack it to illustrate, realizing as it snaps the door frame how laughable a weapon it is, how laughable I am. "Or maybe to bind you until the police arrive."

"I'm not a burglar. I'm only looking for," she pauses to parse her words, "something of mine that was lost."

And it hits me instantly what it is.

"I have it."

She appears both disappointed and perplexed. I have regained control of the interview.

"What do you have?"

"I found it in the car. Where my dad …"

"My earring?"

"The earring *my father* bought you."

She bristles at my emphasis, as if I've insinuated ownership should now revert to his estate. I was merely fishing for confirmation he'd given it to her. A gift I can only assume was intended to make his fantasy a little more tangible.

"May I have it, please?"

"I need something from you first."

"What?"

"I want to know what was going on between you and my dad, why none of us knew you existed, why he, you know … why he's gone."

"So this is all my fault? How convenient for you to find somebody to blame."

"I wasn't—"

"You should point the finger at yourself first. Your father was a very lonely man."

"Until you came along."

"No, even then." She pushes herself up from the desk and starts toward me. "I'd like some coffee if we're going to be awhile. I'm not a night person." When I don't budge from the doorway she adds, "Don't worry, I'm not going to make a run for it. I want my earring back."

I detour to my room and retrieve her diamond from the top drawer of my dresser. When I arrive in the kitchen, Petra is in the pantry, more at home in my house than I am. It's a quarter to twelve by the clock above the stove. My buzz from Izzy's having worn off, I take the last beer from the door of the fridge and pop the top.

"Coffee keeps me up."

"Warren, too," she says. "He wouldn't drink it after dinner."

I watch her for a while, searching for a tactful way to word the $64,000 question, pretending she's not pretending my gawking is making her uncomfortable. Eventually, I abandon any hope of cleverness and launch in. "I don't get it. How and why did you hook up with my father? I mean, you're young, you're very good looking, and he was an old math teacher who spent most of his disposable income on postcards. I understand why he'd be attracted to you. I don't get it from your side."

"You're making certain assumptions about the nature of our relationship."

"Assumptions based on the fact you spent a lot of time over here, including the occasional overnight, that you went to the theater with him, and that he bought you expensive jewelry."

"You know so much, yet you know so little." She reaches into the cabinet and selects a mug that says "Mathematicians do it ad infinitum." "You have somehow all of these details, but lack the overall picture."

"Then please enlighten me. How did you meet my father? Were you in one of his classes?"

Steam rises from the carafe tilted over her cup. She pours slowly, the coffee trickling in a stream so thin it dances as her hand wavers. "He responded to my ad."

"What, like a personal ad? 'Hot twenty-something seeks nerdy older gentleman for discreet fun'?"

"Not like that at all. I offered companionship. He replied."

"Companionship? You mean an escort." Fucking hell, Patrick was right.

"It wasn't like that."

"How is it different? Did he pay you?"

Petra doesn't look up as she stirs two teaspoons of sugar into her coffee. After dropping her spoon in the sink, she slides a chair out from the table and sits down with her back to me.

"I'll take that as a yes, then. How much did he pay you?"

"One fifty," she says softly.

"A night?"

She nods.

"My dad, the cheapskate, paid you a hundred and fifty dollars a night, for who knows how many nights, for what? What does a hundred fifty dollars get a man?"

"Company. Friendship."

"That's what you call it?"

"You know, C.J., I could tell from some things your father said that you must be kind of a prick, but I didn't expect quite so much." She pushes her chair back and rises from the table. "Keep the fucking earring. I don't want to answer your questions."

"No, wait." I shuffle into her path. "Please. I'm sorry. I won't be such an asshole. I promise. Please stay."

"Why?"

I dig my hand into my pocket and pull out the diamond. She stares at my open palm without reaching for it. Her contempt is palpable.

"I need to understand my father. I didn't make the effort when it mattered, but I need to piece it together now. I owe it to him. And to myself. Take the earring, please."

Glowering, she pinches the diamond between her thumb and forefinger. After a moment's examination, she stuffs it into the breast pocket of her sweater.

"I'm not an escort. I never wanted to post my picture on a site like that. I was out of work at the time and my friend said it was a way to make some quick money. The messages I got were horrible. Your father was different. He was the only one that didn't scare me. He wasn't looking for … sex. He only wanted someone to talk to."

"But you still charged him full?"

"Don't judge me, C.J. If you and your brother and sister had cared even a little, maybe he wouldn't have needed me."

"He still would have contacted you. You look so much like my mother he'd have thought it was fate. He loved him some Russian women."

"I'm Czech."

I shrug to indicate the distinction is lost on me and she shoots me a withering, "stupid American" look.

"That didn't creep you out at all, knowing why he was so attracted to you?"

"By the time I saw her picture I knew him well enough to understand."

"Did it bother you knowing he was in love with you?"

"How do you know that?"

"Call it a hunch." I may have lost touch, but I knew him well enough to know he would love her. Combine my mother's looks with someone who cared enough to listen, how could he not?

"It did." She applies a thumb to her glistening eye and bows her head. "I didn't realize quite how taken he was until it was too late."

"Too late for what?"

Petra buries her face in her hands and breathes heavily into her palms. If I hadn't pissed her off so much already I'd comfort her, but I'm fairly certain that would earn me a knee in the nuts. I let her stumble back until her butt meets the counter, offering support that can't be misinterpreted as a half-dressed drunk copping a feel. "He asked me to marry him."

It's my turn to stagger. My wildest speculation had stopped well shy of proposals. Surely, Dad was more realistic than that.

"When?"

"Two weeks ago."

"What did you say?"

"Nothing. I thought he got the message. Then he asked again. Last Thursday. I had to explain to him that I couldn't . . ."

She's sobbing too hard to speak any further. This time I do embrace her. She doesn't kick me. Her wriggling is unintentional and not meant to break free of my hold.

"It's not your fault, Petra." It sounds like a television cliché coming out, but it's not really. She'd have to be batshit loco to shackle herself to a man so fragile he couldn't withstand such an outlandish proposal being politely rebuffed. Never mind the forty-year gap in age. Was it my fault for not realizing he was so far out on that branch, for not reaching out? Kerry's? Audra's? Somehow we all grew up devoid of compassion for our parents. For each other. Whose fault was that? Why were none of us programmed to care?

The longer I hold her, the more awkward I feel. Five minutes ago she made it plainly evident I wasn't on her hugging list. She can't really relish my arms cradling her shoulders or my hair dangling against her cheek. I lead her back to the table and lower her into her chair. Not knowing what to say, I take her cup and refill it, allowing her some space to bring her breathing under control.

"Thank you," she says softly, when I place the mug and sugar bowl in front of her.

I pull a chair out, spin it around, and sit with my chest against the backrest. "Thank you. For keeping my dad company. And for not being what I thought you might."

"So there's something worse?"

"I figured you were after his retirement account."

She gives me a look like she can't imagine his savings would be worth her trouble, though she must have had some suspicions if he dropped a hundred and a half every time she stopped over.

"You'd never guess to look around here, but he had a lot socked away. A lot. A lot more than I ever imagined. I was sure that was what you were poking around after. That was you here Sunday night, right, when I showed up?"

She nods.

"Where'd you hide? I looked everywhere."

"I went out his bedroom window. I could have sworn you heard me when I hit the ground."

She's gone up in my estimation. Shame she didn't meet my father forty years ago. She'd have been better for him than my mom.

By her third cup of coffee, Petra no longer seems to hate me. Respect may be stretching it, but I'm picking up a commiseration vibe, rooted in our mutual grief. Between the sleep deprivation, alcohol, and personal trauma, I'm convinced I might actually have a shot at coaxing her to stay the night. Platonically. Clothed. Though it's the contrasts between her and my mother I notice now—her softer accent with soothing s's and fewer hard k's, the pensive pucker as she contemplates before speaking, the roundness of her ear lobes—it's impossible to disassociate them long enough to imagine anything beyond spooning, and even that just to fend off the loneliness. I sift through several approaches on my way to the bathroom, settling on an appeal to her compassion as I offload everything I've drank since she interrupted my slumber. I will ask her, in essence, to take pity on me.

And it might have worked, if she was still there when I returned to the kitchen. I find instead the door slightly ajar and the driveway awash in the beam of the motion light. As I poke my head outside I hear a car starting and see her headlights filtered through the bushes separating our yard from the street.

It's just past two when I lock the door and douse the kitchen light. In less than an hour Mindy will be getting up for work. Desperate for human interaction, friendly or otherwise, I resolve to sit up and call her. I tote Dad's nearly empty wine jug to the sofa, turn on the television, and promptly fall asleep.

TWENTY-TWO

I awake face down on the couch, my hair fused to my pasty lips, hungover and alone. Outside, the sky is the color of wet cement. The rain is leaking in and pooling on the sill in the corner of the big plate glass window. I guess it's seven-thirty and convince myself to go back to sleep until I check my phone and find I'm off by more than two hours. If I have any hope of retrieving Dad's car before it's towed, I need to move now.

I get sick twice in the shower, cursing myself and everyone I know as my stomach muscles draw me into a spitting question mark. What little actually comes up is beet red and stings my throat. I thought the old rhyme said wine after beer put me in the clear. Maybe it was *before*. Maybe this is why anyone with any common sense doesn't mix.

The entire concept of food repulses me. It's a chore just downing a glass of water to chase the four ibuprofen tablets I'm hoping will rehumanize me. The fresh air doesn't help nearly as much as I'd hoped it might. Its restorative effect is counteracted by the constant rat-a-tat of rain peppering my umbrella.

Out on the main road, the spray of passing cars bumps my throbbing head from the top spot on my list of complaints. The shoulder is barely wide enough in places for a bicycle, putting me on spongy lawns when I need to jump out of splash range. If I'm lucky. Where fences or sheer dropoff restrict my path I'm helpless to avoid it. The left side of my body is spattered with mud before I'm halfway down the hill.

I can barely hear my phone ringing in my pocket above the traffic. I bet myself a nickel it's Mindy, and lose.

"You find Dad's will yet?" Kerry asks before I can even mumble out a hello.

"Didn't really have time to look last night."

"What the hell you been doing?"

"Things came up." Including a couple I'm dying to drop on him as soon as my head clears enough to enjoy his reaction.

"I've got an appointment with his lawyer Monday. We've got to submit his will to kick things off."

"You said you didn't know who his lawyer was, or if he even had a will."

"Well, he does. I got a call from him about twenty minutes ago. Apparently I'm the executor."

"Doesn't he have a copy?"

"Of course he does. I'd like to see it before Monday, though. I want to know what's in there. Can you go dig it out?"

"I'm not home."

"Where are you?"

At least that's what I make out over the roar of the Metro bus passing so close the draft nearly tugs the umbrella out of my hand. The phone gets separated from my ear momentarily as I turn my back to the traffic. "Long story," I say, flinching as another coat of road spray soaks into my jeans and sweatshirt.

"Never mind. I'm coming over. I'll find it myself."

I re-pocket my phone, letting my hand linger in the warm, dry, cotton lining. I'm two-thirds of the way down the hill, nearly to the school we used to walk to in good weather and bad from the time I was six until I was twelve. The canopy here is thick enough the rain drips through only in spots, like a leaky roof. In the breaks between the cars it's almost pleasant, or would be if I didn't feel like someone had set my head on fire and stamped it out with snowshoes.

The windows of the school are obscured by condensation and construction-paper masterpieces. I served time in three of the rooms facing the street. I can still remember staring out the window at the parking lot in third grade, convinced each morning that Mom would arrive to take her turn as classroom assistant as she had the second week of school, shortly after she left. That one appearance caused me months of heartache. Had she not shown, I'd have never expected an encore. Is there a little boy down there gazing up at the road this morning, waiting, wishing, wondering where the idiot battling the umbrella is going?

What would I have thought of grownup me back then? Would I think I was cool? Or would third-grade me, who dreamed of becoming a stunt skier—don't ask me why, I only ever went skiing once—be as unimpressed by my resume as a part-time barista as everyone else? Would third-grade me toss grownup me on the loser pile?

I don't have to stay a barista. With my share of Dad's money I could start over. Maybe I could buy my own coffee shop. There's nothing lame about slinging espresso if you own the joint. Or I could go back to school and major in something practical. Oh, the cosmic irony, using Dad's money to finally do what he asked me to the first time around. Or I could just bank it all, rent myself a loft somewhere, and write. Stay up all night banging away on a new manuscript. Sleep all day. If I scrimp there'll be enough to last me ten years. If I can't produce something with commercial potential in all that time I'll give up and become a garbage man.

The rain tapers off as I reach the bottom of the hill, where I finally have a sidewalk under my feet to put me out of range of most of the puddles in the street. The parking lot of the shopping plaza is virtually empty. Most of the shops are only now opening for the day. The breakfast crowd at Danny's Forest Park Diner has thinned, leaving just a dozen vehicles clustered around the entrance as I pass. My view of the Izzy's parking lot across the street is blocked by the wooden fence separating it from the neighboring bank. Through the drizzle I make out a blinking orange light reflected off the side windows. I pull my umbrella down and break into a run, pausing on the concrete median just long enough to let the oncoming traffic pass. The final hundred feet are a blur of sidewalk squares disappearing under my pumping legs. My fears are confirmed when I at last clear the fence. A flatbed tow truck is lined up in front of Dad's Outback, business end descending toward the blacktop.

"Wait," I call. "Stop. That's my car."

From under the hood of a dirty yellow rain slicker, the goateed operator studies me through oversized brown eyes. His too-small head runs straight into his overlong neck with barely a discernible chin to distinguish the two, and his hips flare out like he's wearing saddlebags beneath his coat. He looks like a llama. "You belong to this?" he asks, not bothering to halt the bed's progress.

"Yes. All set. You can go."

"Don't work that way." He spits a brownish stream at the base of his rear tire. "They call me out, I come out, I gotta get paid."

"Why? I'm here. You don't have to do anything."

"Time is money, bud. I could'a been doing another job. I got kids to feed and a wife with an eBay habit worse than heroin."

"What is this, some kind of shakedown?" I glare at him through the rivulets of rainwater washing over my brow, trying to look fierce and worldly, like the kind of guy who won't put up with shit from tow-truck drivers. Or mechanics or plumbers or any of the multitude of tradesmen who seem to lump me in with the rubes and middle-aged women they invariably bill at a higher rate for service calls. "Fuck yourself, dude, I ain't paying you shit. I'm going in to talk to the manager."

"Good luck," he laughs. "We got a contract. He knows how this works. Unless he wants to pay me his own self."

"How much?" I sigh.

"Ninety-three dollars. But I tell you what, I'll cut you a deal this morning. I'll let you squeak outta here for ninety."

Pinning the umbrella under my arm, I dig my wallet out of my back pocket. I tab through the stack of bills and pull out two fifties. "Here's a hundred. Keep the change. Buy yourself a fucking sense of compassion."

He shrugs and smirks, like, hey, I'm not a bad guy, why you so upset, and I want to punch him in his smug llama face and break his teeth. But he's half again as big as I am and would wipe the parking lot with me and kick my remains down the storm sewer. I walk toward the sidewalk and light up a cigarette as I wait for him to restore the bed of his truck to its horizontal position. The rain has picked up again, but I'm too wet by now to bother raising my umbrella. I part the hair clinging to my face and watch the cars slosh past, glancing back every half minute to monitor his progress. A white Celica fishtails around the corner, hydroplaning briefly before finding its footing. The panicked face behind the wheel belongs to Julianne Wilkes. She slows and turns into the shopping plaza, accelerates through a four-way stop, and disappears around the other side of the diner. I flick my damp butt into the road and stride back to my car.

"Done?"

"Just about."

"Hustle." I open the car door. "I need to go."

He stands there patting his pockets like he's looking for his pipe. I have zero doubt he's busting my balls and could have towed every car in the parking lot by now if properly motivated. I throw the wagon into drive, pull forward until I hit the cement footer, crank the wheel hard to the left, and shift into reverse. In the mirror I can make out his amused grin as he watches me back toward the rear bumper of his truck. His expression changes when I tap fenders. I rock the car forward again until my tires once more make contact with the barrier. This time when I swing back I'm perpendicular to his truck. Middle finger to the glass at my left, I hit the gas and squeal around the flatbed. Adrenaline racing, I stomp the pedal, narrowly avoiding an oncoming minivan as I turn left onto the street. Another hard right and I'm in the plaza lot.

Julianne's car is parked by the shopping cart corral, in the same spot it occupied Sunday night. My heart is pounding so hard the resultant rush of blood seems to have neutralized my hangover. My senses are keen—and keenly aware I have no plan, no idea what to say when I catch up to her. I jog through the rain to the front entrance and grab a small cart. Without discernibly turning my head I sneak a peek into the security office. The shock of white hair sweeping out from under the guard's cap eases my fear of being recognized.

Julianne isn't among the cashiers at the tills up front. She's most likely clocking in somewhere in the back of the store. I push my basket by the checkout lines and aim for the frozen foods. After pitching in a couple microwave dinners, a pizza, a box of egg rolls, and some waffles, I steer toward the beer cooler and add a case of Rainier. Julianne is still counting out her drawer when I pull into her aisle.

"Sorry, I'm not open yet," she says, without looking up.

"I'll wait."

The glare she throws me is her generic customers-suck scowl. It softens momentarily when our eyes meet, until she masters her emotions and smothers the rising guilt. Without waiting for her blessing I place my items on her conveyor belt.

"You must have been disappointed when Jimmy saved me from your buddy last night."

"I have no idea what you're talking about." She jams the change tray into her drawer and slams it shut.

"What did I ever do to you, Julianne? Why do you hate me so much?"

"You really don't know?" she laughs, as she drags my waffles across the scanner.

"I really don't."

She drops the box into a bag and stares hard into my eyes. "No means no, C.J."

"What does that—"

"Richmond Beach. Your car. I didn't want to go that far."

"What?" I'm fumbling through old memories, trying to conjure up the one she's referencing. All I can see are two naïve kids exploring uncharted territory in the back of a station wagon.

"I was scared. I was pleading with you, 'No. Don't. Stop.' You kept right on going until you got what you wanted."

The eyes challenging me are hardly recognizable as the ones I gazed into that night, so hopeful, so innocent, so young. I cue the tape and wind to the moment she's describing. Not once in the hundreds of times I've played it back have I seen it from any vantage but the original.

"That's not how I heard it," I say, voice cracking. "I was just excited to be with you … I wouldn't have done anything to … you were all ever I thought about."

She doesn't say anything else as she finishes ringing my groceries. I hand her three twenties. This time she gives me my change.

"I'm sorry, Julianne." I stuff the bills into my wallet without counting them. "I never realized."

She folds her arms across her chest and turns her eyes toward the pharmacist's counter behind us. "Forget it."

I can't. It has just retroactively become the defining moment of my adolescence.

TWENTY-THREE

Kerry's car is clogging the driveway when I return home. Instead of pulling all the way up to the wide part by the garage, he parked next to the kitchen door to avoid running fifty feet through the rain. Dad once cracked the driver's window of my Charger when I left it in a similar position, rolling it down just far enough to teach me a lesson. On any other day I'd be tempted to pay it forward, but I'm too depressed by the morning's revelation to pull anything cheeky. I haul the groceries out of the back seat and up the steps. Lacking a free hand to turn the knob, I kick at the aluminum base of the screen door until my brother appears.

"Who the fuck is Petra Bednarik?" he demands.

I grunt past him and drop my load on the table. Kerry makes a dive for the beer as I shed my sweatshirt. By the time I kick off my shoes he's got the first can raised to his slurping mouth. It's still twenty minutes shy of noon.

"Take a guess." I extract a can for myself and crack it open.

"Mom girl."

"You got it."

He cocks his head as if to ask how I would know. Instead of waiting for an answer, he swipes a sheet of paper off the counter and thrusts it into my chest. "Why the fuck is she walking away with Dad's retirement?"

"What?" I set my drink down and flatten the page on the table. In bold letters across the top it reads, "Change in Beneficiaries." Droplets from my hair speckle the paper as I lean over it, trying to absorb its message. Petra's name is listed on the first line. The line below reads Northpoint College Tomorrow Scholarship. Kerry read it wrong. Petra's out. As of last Friday. In his final hours Dad dropped her in favor of the scholarship fund. When did he drop us? "Where did you get this?"

"It was hanging on the door handle with the rest of that shit." Kerry motions toward a blue and white U.S. Postal Service bag on the counter. "I can't fucking believe she walks off with half a million bucks and we're left with nothing. Bullshit. I'm bringing this Monday."

"It's seven hundred thousand, not half a million." I collapse into the chair Petra sat in last night. "Six hundred ninety five, actually. And you read it wrong. Petra's the before. Dad left it all to the college."

Kerry snatches the notice from my hand and stares at it as he paces the floor. "This can't be valid. He clearly wasn't in his right mind when he did this."

"Doesn't really matter, does it?" I run my hand through my wet hair and bunch it behind my neck. "Undoing this would just give it all to her. We're still out."

"Who the fuck is she?"

"Dad's …" I shrug, unsure of the appropriate designation. I settle on "special friend." Kerry's expression shifts from dubious to pained as I detail my late-night encounter.

"He was obviously mental," he says when I finish. "Unsound mind, they call it. We have clauses covering it in some of our policies. Nothing he signed should be legally valid."

"How do you prove that?"

"Pretty fucking obvious, isn't it? He thought some hot twenty-something was going to marry him? He's off his fucking head. Then he kills himself. Good lawyer could cut right through all this and get things restored. That's why I want to see his goddam will."

Kerry slams the rest of his beer, chucks the can into the

sink, and snatches another from the carton. I take another for myself and follow him upstairs. Before joining him in Dad's office I strip off my wet clothes and change. I find him kneeling over the bottom drawer of the filing cabinet, a manila folder spread open across the top of the rest.

"Subtract ten bucks from the garage sale. He left the penis lamp to Mom."

Nothing should surprise me anymore, but this does. Had Mom stuck around long enough to negotiate, Dad would have let her take the lamp and its partner, which wouldn't get broken for another four years. But she slipped out when he was at work and we were at school and took only what she could fit in her car. Maybe she didn't want to explain to Keith how my father purchased the lamps when she asked the shopkeeper about their history, how neither of them understood a word of his response, how Dad spent more to ship them home than they cost.

"I hope she didn't have her heart set on it," I say. "I kind of … shattered it the other day."

I tell Kerry the broomball story, minus the part about the treasure, which suddenly makes a hell of a lot more sense. He wasn't hiding it from anybody. He was stashing it for her, in essence leaving her nearly ten grand without explicitly spelling it out. Only I crapped all over his scheme. And I'm not necessarily sorry.

Kerry's laugh sounds like a zebra on helium. I can't tell if it's intended for Dad for his seemingly sappy bequest, for Mom for not receiving it, or for both of them for importing such ass-ugly artwork in the first place. He kills his beer and fires the empty out into the hall. Lips moving, he scans through the rest of the double-spaced text, flipping pages every fifteen seconds until he comes to the end of the will.

"Doesn't say a goddam thing about his retirement. Probably wouldn't matter anyway. The beneficiaries on the policies we sell override most wills. Looks like all we get is the house and everything in it."

He flings the document at me and stalks out of the room. I hear his steps going down the stairs, then ascending a short time later. He slaps a fresh beer in my hand and opens one for himself.

"What about his bank accounts or other investments?" I ask.

"Depends on who he listed as the beneficiaries. I think he held most of it in the 401K, though, so there's probably not much else worth worrying about. What a dick. He fucked us." Kerry's beer sloshes out the top of the can and down his arm as he hoists it toward the ceiling. "Thanks, Dad."

"Well, we still got the house, at least."

"Not that we'll get shit for it. He let it go."

"Couldn't we fix it up a little? I could do a lot of it myself."

"You?" His bemused expression confirms what I've long suspected. In his eyes, I'm still the kid who failed to restore the Charger rotting out in the garage. The one who couldn't even change the belts. The one who quit.

"I could get this place looking pretty decent. Clean it up, fresh coat of paint, maybe some new appliances."

"Honestly, I'd rather just move it. I could kind of use the money. I've got a wedding to pay for, and I can't be bothered with this shit. We wouldn't get back what we put into it, anyway."

Equal parts relieved and resentful of his lack of faith in my ability, I hand him back the will. He folds it in three and stuffs it in the breast pocket of his jacket.

"So who won broomball?"

"No one. Jimmy was up one when I nailed the lamp. That kind of ended it."

"Fifty bucks I can take you."

I don't have to say "you're on," or otherwise verbally acknowledge his challenge. It was offered in confidence it would be accepted. Once more the living room furniture is rearranged, recliner, ottoman, and end tables all packed tighter than tuna in a can. Kerry drags the couch into place without waiting for me, sliding it with no regard for the hardwood floor beneath. The taped-up sock from Tuesday's match still rests under the goal, where Jimmy booted it when we cleaned up the lamp.

There are no gentlemen's allowances in a contest with my brother. I won't offer him the courtesy of first possession, nor will I accept it from him, as he'll use it as leverage on any and all questionable calls throughout the game. It must be decided by coin toss, which he wins. In our teens he talked smack from opening tap until the final goal—longer if he won. Today he's all business, glowering at the ball as he bats it back and forth before him. I hang just close enough to rattle his broomstick with mine, back-pedaling down the field, watching his eyes and hands alternately. When he winds up to shoot I easily block his ball with the head of my broom, poking it halfway to the open goal across the floor. As I start after it, he chops at my shins. If there were rules, that would clearly be against them, but there aren't and there's no point in complaining.

"Dick move," I mutter, as I hack at his stick.

"What's the matter, sport?" Kerry laughs. "Can't handle it?"

When he swings for my leg again I sidestep the blow and slip past him to reach the ball. With a flick of the wrist, I slap it neatly between the chair legs for a score and the lead. I try the same move two minutes later and wind up checked into the couch so hard I flip over the back of it and land on the pillow upon which I woke this morning. In my absence, Kerry taps the ball into the goal to tie the game. It's not an unprecedented move, though in the old days he'd have been grinning like he just shit in my hat. Instead he's scowling. He's pissed off about the retirement and needs to inflict pain upon someone. I happen to be handy.

I co-opt Jimmy's moves as a matter of survival, spinning until I make myself dizzy. My shooting isn't as accurate coming out of the pirouette as Jimmy's, but it's good enough to maintain a lead while keeping my limbs intact. When I slow down I get hit. Kerry wants to win, but it's almost incidental to his primary goal of working off his rage. I realize now how dickish it was to go physical against Jimmy. Broomball was never meant to be a blood sport.

We take frequent breaks to drink, allowing me to numb my new bruises and Kerry to numb what passes as his conscience. Despite the punishment I've absorbed, I forge a 9-7 advantage. I want the final goal to be spectacular and pass up several opportunities for routine shots, any of which could end the contest. It's not enough to win. I want to punctuate it with a highlight-reel maneuver, make a statement that will pierce even Goliath's thick skull. Kerry's tired legs present an opening, literally. I slap the ball between his feet off the back of the couch, passing it ahead to myself. With one final spin I whack it home. It hits the wall under the chair with a satisfying smack about the same time Kerry's shoulder finds my throat. I collapse like I've been downed by a sniper.

There are a few seconds I can't account for between the moment my head hits the floor and the time I realize Kerry's standing over me with his hand extended. Too dazed to slap it away and tell him to fuck off, I take it and let him pull me to my knees.

"Good game," he grunts. No apology for the multiple assaults or possible concussion. He places my warm beer in my hand and takes a slug of his own, then draws his wallet from his back pocket. "All I got is a ten. I'll have to owe you."

"Never mind." I take a long, slow swig of my drink, feeling it trickle through my caved-in esophagus to my stomach, pleased they're still connected.

"I'm good for it." He looks insulted, as if this forgiven

debt will sully his honor.

"Fuck the fifty bucks, man. There's something else I'd rather ask for."

"What?"

"Don't call me 'sport' anymore."

He stares at me like a cow trying to comprehend a little green man emerging from the spaceship that has just landed in its pasture. "What's wrong with sport?"

"You mean aside from the fact it's insulting and insincere and you only do it to piss me off?"

"No, I don't. I've always called you sport."

"Yeah, and I've always hated it."

He grins and shakes his head, in disbelief I could find his condescension objectionable. "Don't be such a fucking girl. What the hell you want me to call you?"

"What's wrong with C.J.?"

"Everybody calls you C.J. I'm the only one that calls you sport. We're brothers. I thought that meant … fuck it, whatever."

"No, what? You thought what?"

"You're my little brother. I've called you that as long as I can remember. I didn't realize it was such a sensitive issue. I mean, shit, I figured we're brothers and we fuck with each other a little, because that's what brothers do. It's not like I call anyone else sport. You're sport. To me. But if you don't want me to call you that, forget it, man, I'll call you C.J. Or Chris. Or maybe Chrissy if you keep menstruating on me like this."

He's actually hurt. I was wrong calling him insincere. This is as sincere as I've seen Kerry in decades. Possibly ever. While it may have originally been rooted in disrespect, somewhere along the line his pea brain filtered out the irony and came to see it as endearing. Chrissy won't be endearing, however. It will be mean spirited and unrelenting, and there's no way I'll survive another broomball match to win the right to request he cease and desist.

"Forget I said anything," I say. "I'll take the fifty bucks."

TWENTY-FOUR

There are eight empties in the kitchen sink and a ninth on the table. I mentally wind back through my afternoon and decide my brother had the five and I had the four. He crushed his last can against the refrigerator door as he left in renewed histrionics over our lost fortune, vowing loudly to right Dad's wrong. I've already accepted we'll never see a dime of his retirement, providing justification to crack open a fresh beer and even the score. As if I need an excuse.

I pull the couch just far enough out of the jumble to clear a path and lie down. The remote control's signal won't penetrate the mountain of furniture blocking the cable box. From any angle I aim it, it fails to bring the TV to life. I entertain myself with my phone instead and discover Mindy called during our epic battle. Though she didn't leave a message, I've been tagged. I'm it. Still. I tap her icon and speculate on her mood as it rings.

"Hey," she says, so curtly I can't get a read on the frosty-meter. My gut says eight.

"Sorry I missed your call. Kerry and I were working some things out."

Mindy huffs out an exasperated sigh that could be mistaken for a laugh by someone who doesn't know her as well as I do. Eight might be a conservative reading. She's probably been stewing like a slow cooker all afternoon. It's not the missed call. It's that I didn't call her yesterday after promising to. It's that she had to call me again. We've played this game before.

"I meant to call you last night, but nothing really went like I figured. All day. My mom got hammered at lunch after the funeral. Then I ran into one of my ex-girlfriends when I was out with Jimmy. That was a real hoot. And then—"

"Yeah, I bet it was."

"No, it wasn't, is what I'm saying. She tried to set me up for a DWI. Haven't seen her since high school, but she still hates my guts, so that's been fun. Cost me a hundred bucks to keep the car from getting towed this morning. What else … my dad's girlfriend—if that's the right term, she's younger than me—broke into the house last night when I was asleep. So I got to meet her, and surprisingly she didn't seem to care for me much either, so I can only wonder what Dad told her. And then come to find out today that he cut us all out of his retirement, so the scholarship fund at the college gets seven hundred grand and we're out stone cold. So, sorry I didn't call, but my life's been kind of falling apart out here."

This time she laughs for real. The at-you kind, not the with-you variety.

"Thanks," I say. "Appreciate your sympathy. Means a lot."

"Sorry. It's just, you have a way of fucking things up like no one I've ever known before. Only this time you're actually reaping what you sowed."

"How? How is this all my fault? What did I sow exactly?"

"You don't even get it. You didn't talk to your dad for, what, a year? Haven't visited him in the entire time I've known you. And you're surprised you were disinherited? I'm guessing your brother and sister are just like you. And what a shock, your dad didn't feel like any of you were entitled to his money. Sorry, C.J., but you guys got exactly what you deserved. Nothing."

"We get the house."

"Oh, well, there's something then. Maybe you can all live in it together and commiserate."

"Don't be such a …" I manage to corral the c-word before it leaps off the tip of my tongue and adds homelessness to my list of laments. I settle instead for "smartass."

"Look, I'm sorry you've had such an awful time this week. But it's hard for me to be very supportive when you can't be bothered to call, or even text. I'm in the dark out here, C.J. I can only call so many times before I give up."

"Well, I'll try to call more. I can't really guess when. This trip hasn't exactly gone according to plan. I just want to be done dealing with—"

The crunch of metal hitting concrete, like a ship slamming into a pier, erupts through the exterior wall, shaking the couch beneath me. Then comes an explosion, like a shotgun firing twice in quick succession, followed by the wailing of a car horn.

"Tell me you heard that," I say, as I watch the framed Escher print swing on its hook.

"I heard it," Mindy says. "What the hell was it?"

Phone clutched to my ear, I scramble over the back of the sofa. I pull the curtain back from the window to reveal the rear end of a Nissan sedan.

"My mom just crashed her car into the porch. I gotta go."

The driver's door is pinned against the wrought-iron railing and looks like it's been beaten with Thor's hammer. Mom's bloodshot eyes plead with me through the fogged window as her elbow flaps at the airbag billowing in her face. The cab reeks of vodka-laced vomit when I open the other door. Holding my breath, I take Mom's wrist and pull her from the front seat. The cacophony of horn and engine are slightly quieter inside when I slide in to take her place. I lean my shoulder into the airbag until it has deflated enough I can reach the gear shift and throw the car into reverse. The undercarriage grunts against the cement stoop when I depress the gas. After a few inches, the car gets stuck. I press harder on the pedal and feel the rear wheels spinning in the gravel. When I gun it, the car lurches back with a loud crumpling sound. The mangled bumper rises up above the profile of the hood. Why didn't I wait for assistance? Would Kerry have done this? I kill the ignition and let her keys fall into my hand. The heavy ring is loaded with two long car keys, a miniature flashlight, a blue rabbit's foot, and three souvenir charms embossed with Cyrillic letters.

Fingertips to her downturned forehead, Mom ascends the stoop and enters the house, leaving me alone to assess the damage. Well, not totally alone. Mrs. Holt is spying through the trees that separate our driveways. I offer her a shrug and a head shake, then turn and follow Mom into the kitchen. She's digging through her purse, strewing receipts and breath mints and loose change across the table, words tumbling from her lips in a pidgin blend of Russian and English.

"I can't find my damn pills," she says, without looking up. "Can you go check the car, C.J.?"

"What pills?"

"My medications."

Her antidepressants. Or depressants. There's clearly no evidence they relieve depression. Perhaps they cause it.

"Jesus, Mom, you don't need pills. You need to dry out. How the hell did you even make it this far? What else did you hit along the way?"

"It was the damn phone." She mimes holding her cell phone in her right hand. I can just see her checking it as she plowed into the house. "Bring that, too. I must have dropped it."

I find her phone in the cup holder between the front seats. There are two pill bottles on the floor in the back, both duloxetine, both half full. I pocket one and hand her the other when I reenter the kitchen.

"Thank you." She shakes two pills into her palm and slaps it to her open lips, swallowing them without so much as a sip of water to chase them down.

"What are you doing here?"

She looks into my eyes as if she's debating how much to tell me. Then her eyelids droop and her jaw firms. "I had to get out of the house."

"Why didn't you go to Audra's? She's right down the street."

"That's the first place he looks for me."

"Keith?" Apparently this isn't an isolated incident. What happens to make her run, and how often does he come after her?

Mom nods. "I tried Yulia's, but she wasn't home. I was practically here. I thought maybe I could visit with you."

"What if I wasn't here?"

"I have a key." She waves toward her purse. "Somewhere in there."

"Who doesn't have a fucking key to this house?"

"What?"

"Nothing." I have no idea where I left my beer. It could be in the living room. Could be outside for all I remember. I pull another from the box that may never make it as far as the refrigerator.

"I could use one," Mom says.

I stare at her for a moment, gauging her blood-alcohol reading from the lines in her eyes. Somewhere around .12. It wasn't her phone that caused her to veer into the stoop. Not by itself, anyway. I reach into the carton and grab her a can.

"No." She waves it away. "Cranberry and vodka. Please."

She answers my puzzled expression by pointing to the pantry. "Top shelf. Behind the pancake mix."

It's there, exactly where she said it would be. The vodka is three-quarters full, with an unopened twin waiting in line behind it. I examine the date on the cranberry juice. It doesn't expire until March of next year. It would be easier for me to comprehend all of this if it were a dusty relic from the early '90s. The sheepish look my mother offers when I set her drink in front of her erodes what little confidence I had that I was even beginning to understand my father's death.

"You're judging again." Mom rises from her chair and retrieves an ice tray from the freezer. The cubes have withered to half their original size. A twist of the tray forces four of them onto the table. She plucks them with her fingernails and drops them into her glass.

"How can I judge? I don't even know what the fuck is going on."

"You never used to curse so much. You were my angel." A tear leaks down her right cheek, causing my own eyes to fill. "So earnest and eager to please, so sweet."

Maybe I'd have stayed that way if she hadn't left. This doesn't feel like the time to point that out.

"Your father offered me a safe place to collect my thoughts," she says, as I sip my beer and stare through her. "Sometimes, when he was here, we talked about you. Wondered what you were doing. He missed you. We all did."

The tears breach my lower lids and spill down both sides of my nose. I try to wash the salty taste off my lips with my beer, but it's difficult to drink when you're crying so hard you can barely see the can in your hand.

"I miss him, too, Mom. I wasn't sure I would, but I do."

"He wasn't the kind of man you appreciate when you have the chance." Mom picks up the vodka and tops her drink off, turning it from red to a faint pink. "It's a shame I never loved him."

"Never? Not even when you met?"

"No." She rattles the ice in her glass and smiles wistfully. "I was only ever in love once. In Sevastopol. He joined the fleet and came home with all the sensitivity stolen from him. He would call me late in the evening when he was out drinking with his friends. Typical sailor. So I showed him. I left."

"How did you wind up with Dad?"

"It's a long story."

"I got time."

"I'm tired." She slides her chair back and pushes herself to her feet, clutching her glass, still two-thirds full. She starts toward the stairs like she's done this before, then pauses to look back at me. "Help me up?"

Taking her elbow in my right hand and her hand in my left, I accompany her upstairs. She glances in my room, notes the rumpled state of the bed, and continues down the hall. After setting her drink down on Dad's dresser, she makes her way across the hall to the bathroom, leaving me in the dusk to ponder how my family came to exist. She returns two minutes later, hair fastened behind her head and her blouse unbuttoned, revealing a lacy camisole. She stops at the dresser and drains the last of her vodka. When she sets her empty glass down, her blouse falls away from her shoulder, exposing a purple and yellow patch that radiates from her underarm toward her breast.

"Oh, Jesus, Mom."

She stares at me, guiltily, and adjusts her top.

"Does Keith hit you?"

"No." Her eyes won't meet mine. "Not hit. No."

"But he did that?"

"I'm very tired, C.J." She sits down on the edge of the bed and unbuttons her slacks. "Please let me sleep."

TWENTY-FIVE

I want a gun. I want to put it to Keith's temple and blow his fucking head off. I want to drive to his house, put a crowbar through his front door, and batter his brains into a bisque. I want to reroute the wires from his home theatre to his testicles and amp up the juice until his ball sack explodes. But mostly I want to cry. For my mom. For myself. For what might have been. I retreat to the kitchen and resume my place at the counter. Turns out drinking and crying aren't mutually exclusive. I master it in under ten minutes.

Somewhere between beers seven and eight I text Kerry. "Mom has bruises on her chest from that fucktard." I stare at the screen anticipating his response, eager to ride shotgun with my brother and pound some retribution out of Keith's hide. Or at least watch Kerry beat him silly. After waiting ten minutes for him to respond, I head upstairs to Dad's office to pursue the other matter niggling at my brain. Somewhere within these four walls, I'm convinced I will find a clue as to how my parents came together.

But Dad's filing system doesn't seem to account for her. There's no folder for her under her maiden name, Demchenko, nor anything under Neubauer. There's not even one under Svetlana. I tab through all four drawers of the cabinet and draw a blank. She doesn't exist.

To the right of the cabinet sit three cardboard file boxes. I tip open the lid of the top one and find every pay stub my dad ever received, dating back to the days when he caddied at the golf course as a teenager. The second box looks much like the first, leading off with folders labeled "Taxes 1976" and "Taxes 1977," and running through several decades of returns long overdue for the shredder. There is literally nothing my father didn't keep. Which is why I felt certain all along I would hit a jackpot like the fat folder simply tabbed "Letters" midway through the third box. I recognize my mother's handwriting immediately, her densely packed characters slanting ever so slightly leftward. The postmarks on the airmail envelopes are so faded as to be illegible. Fortunately, she was conscientious enough to date her letters. The first one was written on August 8, 1978.

Dear Warren,

I get your letter. It was very pleasant and decide at once write you my letter.

Thank you very much for your nice kind letter. I like your letter and your photo. You are a rather handsome man. I'd like to continue our correspondence.

I hope this letter will be the beginning of beautiful relations between you and me. I live in the Crimea in Sevastopol. Our city is situated in the south of Ukraine near the Black Sea. I was born on the 24 of October in 1957. My height is 174 cm, weight is 53 kg. I've graduated from Polytechnical College two years ago. My profession is a secretary.

I'm very kind, sincere, tender, womanly, caring, faithful, dedicated, warm, romantic, affectionate, charitable, sensitive, tactful, with sense of humor, family oriented.

I love children very much.

I am fond of traveling, swimming, seaside, walks, nature, music, reading, flowers. My leisure interests are art, theatre, museums, exhibitions. I like animals very much. I am dreaming about a happy strong family. I believe in real love and I hope that you too. I am very family person. I believe that the family always comes first and every things else is not as important.

I want a harmonious family life above all, as I believe it is the only way to true happiness. I appreciate only faithful and reliable man, because I am a very dedicated girl, and of course I suppose a man must be noble, honest and sincere. Are you such?

I hope you are such.

I would like very much to know more about you, your family, your views on life, your hopes for the future.

With tender wishes,

Svetlana

If the house erupted in flames all around me, I'm not sure I'd even notice. I'm too busy trying to comprehend the mail-order origins of my existence. Mom must have worn the pages in her Russian-English dictionary thin compiling all of those honorable attributes. I notice "honest" didn't make the list. Art? Theatre? Exhibitions? Happy strong family? I call bullshit across the board.

From the second envelope I extract another letter on similarly thin and brittle paper.

Dear Warren,

Thank you very much for your kind letters, which both I got today morning. It was a wonderful surprise for me to receive your letters. I'm so glad! I share your views and hope to learn you more closely.

I think you would like to know some more information about me. I live with my parents. My mother is a teacher of linguistic in the college. She is a very sociable and good-natured woman. My father is a teacher of policy subjects at the academy. We have loving and strong family. I have two brothers and one sister, which all live here in Sevastopol. My grandparents live in Kiev. My grandfather was a pilot aviator in the past. Now he is retired and lives in the center of Kiev.

I want to have a family very much. I had a very happy childhood with my family and would like to recreate that atmosphere with a family of my own. I believe I can find a happiness in a dedicated family group where that group is the prime reason for all that you do. I need a kind, sincere, faithful man, who helps me to be happy. I want to make my future husband happy and our home cozy. I want to admire my husband and be proud of him. I want a person who I can have real love with and a person who I can share life with, both in bad times and good times.

I'm stop here and hope very much to hear from you as soon as possible. I think of you and send my best wishes.

Yours,

Svetlana

Eight more letters carry on the same theme, dreaming of family bliss with a man who will make her proud and honor her. None of which synchs up with anything I ever heard from my mother's own lips. But it's all in her handwriting, scrawled in blue ink on bleached white paper, hinting at a harmonious future with a man she'd never, at that point, met. I don't know who I feel sorrier for, the 1978 version of my dad or the 1978 version of my mom.

Dad's the one who would have had to shrug off the stigma of importing a wife. The whispers at the college, around the neighborhood, among his family, his cousins, his brother and sister, his parents. What did they say when he told them? How did he break the news he was giving up on the traditional methods of finding a mate?

Dad fit the mold, the calculus-obsessed egghead who would rather read Carl Sagan and Isaac Asimov than ask a girl out. The gawky, uncoordinated nerdlinger who counted math-club socials as dates to pad his collegiate scorecard. I may not have all the details spot on, but he dropped enough hints about his university days to paint a sad picture for me. Of course, at the time, he meant to provide a contrast to my decidedly less disciplined academic approach at Wazzu. Was there a mold for Mom? She might have escaped it. She wasn't the stereotypical foreign bride, the tiny Vietnamese or Laotian woman automatically assumed to have been summoned from a catalog. Mom's photo would have stood out among the rows of faces. She must have heard from dozens of suitors.

And she picked Warren Neubauer?

It wasn't sight-unseen, of course. That trip to Bulgaria immortalized by the Nevsky Cathedral photo and the infamous penis lamps—they didn't meet there by chance. How could I never have picked up on this before? Did Kerry and Audra know?

Their relationship suddenly seems a whole lot more plausible to me, and its unraveling even more inevitable. If all the men she knew in Sevastopol were drunks or sailors—or drunken sailors—Dad must have looked mighty dependable by comparison. Had his dot-your-i's-and-cross-your-t's personality leached through during their week in Sofia, it may even have provided her some sense of reassurance. Here was a solid provider, a man who would never blow his paycheck down at the bar or disappear for three days without telling her he went to Vegas, or wherever the Crimean equivalent was. Maybe boring was originally a selling point. Then again, maybe I've undersold him. Maybe he was more lively back then. He was only my age when they met. What was he like at thirty-two?

And what's my excuse? It's easy to mock him for ordering a wife through a catalog, but he wanted to start a family and had exhausted his options. My clock has ticked down just as far. Mindy and I aren't about to start knitting booties. We never will. She's made comments from time to time, when friends or co-workers go out on maternity leave. They usually wind up as barbs about how she can't bring up two kids at once—meaning me as the other one, of course. She's on the pill, just as terrified of me getting her pregnant as I am.

What if I never have kids? I've always figured I would, at least in the "I'll do things completely differently" kind of way. In my head I'm always best friends with my son, who grows up with the benefit of my inside scoop on school and girls and life in general. He never rebels because he doesn't need to. At the same time, he's his own man, cooler and more mature than his classmates. Like me as a teen, only the complete opposite. It's not a son I've dreamed up. It's a do-over.

There are no do-overs. I'm thirty-two and I'm barely responsible for myself. I spend all my disposable income on cigarettes and beer. By my age, Dad was a tenured professor with a mortgage and a car and a wife. And who the hell cares how he met her? I should be so lucky to land a Russian girl. I suspect you need to have more money than her first, though, or they might make you move there instead of the other way around.

I hear music from somewhere downstairs. It's one of those ubiquitous songs that seems to seep from every speaker I pass. I've heard it at the coffee shop and when I've been out with Mindy. Someone was even strumming it last week in the Metro station. Before I can place it, it stops. As I sit with my back against the wall, staring at the insides of my eyelids and tapping notes against the side of my empty can, the song starts over, in the exact same place as before. There are violins, maybe, with a strong bass line, some piano, and a male vocalist who sounds like he's being maimed by a polar bear. Arcade Fire or Coldplay or some uber band that's way too popular for reasons I can't fathom. And then it stops again.

It begins a third time before the rotting synapses in my brain finally recognize it as the ringtone on Mom's cell phone. The song erupts anew in my hand as I pull it from her purse on the kitchen table, Keith's ugly mug lighting up the screen when I thumb it to life. I let the tune run its course, then check the call log and confirm my suspicion he authored all four calls. As well as three texts.

"Where are you?" demands the first.

"When will you be home?"

"Answer your gd phone."

What a charmer.

I crack open a new beer and wait, Mom's phone in hand. This time when it rings I answer it.

"Hello."

"Who's that?" He pauses a couple of heavy breaths and takes a stab. "David?"

Two short syllables on a cell phone aren't much to gauge by, but I don't sound at all like David. Keith figured as Mom expected he would, that she'd run to Audra's. How often did she flee? Did he smack her before she left or when she came back?

"C.J."

"Where's Lana?"

Lana. My father celebrated Mom's culture when we were young, even finding a restaurant downtown that made authentic Crimean food for Old New Year. He seemed to care about her heritage more than she did sometimes. Keith, on the other hand, made a point of Americanizing *Svetlana.*

"She's resting."

"Can you go get her?" His tone is condescending, as if he's speaking to a small child or a dog who fetched the wrong slippers.

"She's asleep."

"I need to talk to her."

"I didn't really get the impression she wanted to talk to you, Keith." Despite the dizzying surge of adrenaline, I nail the line. It comes out cool and calm. Cocky even. As cocky as I've ever spoken to him since the night I busted him peeping on Audra's friends.

"Do you get the impression I give two shits what you think? Tell your mom to get her ass home right now. Remind her we had dinner plans. And she's late."

My hand is shaking as I raise my can to my lips. I probe the edges of the metal with my tongue, then tip it and let the room-temperature beer spill into my mouth.

"She's not really in any condition to drive at the moment."

"Then I'll come get her."

He hangs up before I can reply, which is just as well, as nothing witty or even halfway sensible is coming to me. My brain's not producing much beyond "oh, fuck" on an infinite loop. Psycho Keith is on his way. I have thirty minutes, tops, to come up with a plan, and somehow I don't think he's going to fall for turning the lights out and bolting the door.

Still clutching Mom's phone, I pull my own from my pocket and scroll to Kerry's number. He lives nearly as far away as Keith. If he leaves immediately without asking questions, he might get here in time. But that would require him answering, which he doesn't do. After five rings I hang up on his voice mail.

Maybe Lauren … shit, I don't have her number. But Mom does. Right there on her home screen. Four faces, Keith, Audra, Kerry, and Lauren. I didn't make her Mount Rushmore

The second ring is interrupted by Lauren's cheery voice. "Hey, Mom."

"Lauren, it's me." Realizing I may not be her first guess, either, I add, "C.J."

"What's wrong? Is your mom okay?"

"I need Kerry. He didn't answer his phone. I need him over here now. Keith's on his way. I'm not letting her go home with him. He hit her. I know he did."

"Your mom?"

"Yeah. She denied it, but I saw the bruises. He did that. I need Kerry. Where is he?"

"Calm down, C.J. I'm on my way. I'll be right down."

"Where are you?"

"At work. I'm on my way out. It's dead in here. I'll leave Brandi in charge. I'll be there in fifteen, okay? Deep breaths, buddy. I'll call Kerry. I'll find him. We'll be okay."

It's times like this when it really hits me what a fuckup I am. I need my brother to protect me so I can protect my mom. I pace the kitchen floor, cradling my broomstick like a rifle. Should I call the cops? How would I even explain all this? Unless they pulled up at the precise moment he was kicking in the door, it would somehow boomerang on me and I'd be the one hauled off. I jog upstairs, hoping to find my mother awake. Maybe we can slip out before he gets here. But she's fast asleep, sheet pulled up to her neck. Would she wake if I lifted it just enough to confirm I really saw what I think I did? I reach for the edge and freeze when I hear the popping of gravel under car tires. Oh, shit. How long has it been? I consult Mom's phone. He called at 6:28. It's been fourteen minutes. He can't possibly get here that fast. Mario Andretti couldn't. "Please be Lauren, please be Lauren," I think, as I rush down the hall.

She's to the kitchen door by the time I reach the bottom of the stairs. "Kerry's coming," is the first thing she says. But it's in that good news, bad news tone and my eyes give away my panic.

"Where was he?"

"At Grayson's. Don't worry, they're both coming. And Grayson is," she spreads her arms wide, "a big boy."

"How far away are they?"

"Just breathe, C.J. Calm down. We'll be fine."

I nod vigorously in response, which does little to quell the pounding in my chest.

"Where's your mom?" She starts upstairs before I even respond.

"Dad's room."

I pace the kitchen again, eyes drifting to the deadbolt every few seconds, my muddy brain working out anew each time that up and down is locked. It's been twenty-seven minutes since he called. The way he drives he could literally be here any second. Or be dead in a ravine somewhere.

The high-pitched whine of an over-revved engine draws me out to the living room. Headlights flicker through the trees, approaching fast. The Pontiac's tires squeal as Keith fishtails into the gravel driveway, halting in a cloud of dust just shy of Lauren's rear bumper.

"Lauren," I call.

"Is that him?"

"Yes."

She thumps down the stairs and pokes her head around the corner. "Do you want me to handle this?"

"No."

"I could try to talk to him. He might—" She gasps. Following her eyes to the kitchen, I see Keith's head and shoulders through the window in the door.

It's me he's glaring at as he rings the bell. I stare right back at him, advancing as far as the center of the kitchen. He raises his hands in a shrug, playing like he's honestly surprised I haven't let him in. The knob wiggles but holds. I shoot him a middle finger. He grins in reply and raises a shiny, brass key to the window. Is there anyone in the Greater Seattle area who does not have a key to this damn house? I step toward the door, then stop. What can I do? I can't hold the deadbolt in place.

It snaps open, falling impotently horizontal. With a second click the knob turns free and the door explodes inward. Keith pauses at the threshold, cocks his head to the side, and narrows his gaze in that way that has always made me want to splash hydrochloric acid in his eyes.

"Where is she?"

"I told you she doesn't want to talk to you."

"And I told you I don't give a shit what you say." He points at the broomstick in my hand. "Is that for me? Give me an excuse, C.J. I'll fucking wreck you."

"Go home, Keith," Lauren calls from behind me. "I'll bring Svetlana by in the morning and we can talk things over when everybody's … sober."

"I thought that was your car." He steps forward far

enough to see into the hallway, nearly within reach of my broom. "What are you doing with this jackoff? Tell him to get out of my way, so he doesn't get hurt."

"No, Keith," she says. "You should leave."

"Not without my wife."

"Kerry will be here soon." She speaks calmly but earnestly, as if she still believes she can talk him out the door. "You should go."

"You called for reinforcements, C.J.?" he mocks. "You're such a fucking pussy. You always have been."

Focused on his mustache, I wind up and swing like I'm aiming to bust open a piñata. Keith parries with a forearm, neatly snapping my broomstick in half. As the head clatters harmlessly to the floor, I dance back a step, eyes roaming from his face to his fists.

"Tried to warn you," he grunts. His first swing grazes my shoulder just enough to knock me off balance. I took better shots from Kerry this afternoon.

I shuffle my feet and consider whether to jab at him with the broken broom handle or punch at his jaw. Can I buy enough time for the cavalry to arrive? His mouth proves too inviting a target to pass up. I thrust my right fist at his chin. So intent am I on offense, I neglect to duck out of the way of the knuckles approaching my own face. He reaches his target first. I feel his booze-infused breath on my skin as my head snaps back.

"Stop it," Lauren screams. Her cool façade has melted into hysteria. "Leave him alone, Keith."

I wobble a step and take another unsuccessful swing at, I'm not sure, exactly. Him. Any part of him. I'd like to at least leave a bruise someplace. Maybe on his elbow, which crashes into the bridge of my nose. The crunch of cartilage and bone echoes through my head as I collapse to the floor. My hands are slick with blood when I lift them from my face. It tastes salty and sweet and reminds me a little of drinking from the hose in the backyard growing up. I'm just enough aware of what's going on outside of my head to register that Keith is no longer in the kitchen. Lauren is screeching in the hallway beyond, begging him to stop, to go home. I want to close my eyes and pass out. To wake up with all of this gone. Mom, Lauren, Keith—all of them somewhere else. I tried to help. I gave it my best. I'm simply not hero material.

But I can't give up. I can't let Lauren down. I draw in a deep breath, cough, sputter, hack up a bloody loogie the size of a walnut, and scramble to my feet. Grabbing the jagged broom handle, I set off for the stairs. Lauren stands her ground, arms stretched from rail to rail, pleading with Keith. "Sorry, sweetie," he laughs, and pushes her aside. After a brief stumble, she rights herself and grasps ahold of his thigh, clinging to his leg as he proceeds up the stairs.

One hand to my nose, the other clutching the remains of my pathetic weapon, I charge up after them. I stab at his calf when I'm high enough to reach it, but the wood won't penetrate his jeans. He kicks my hand away, driving my knuckles into the wall. I reach out with my other, sinking my nails into the flesh above his ankle.

"Goddammit," he bellows. "Say good night, C.J."

He shakes Lauren off and kicks at me with his newly freed leg, connecting just above the back of my ear. The stars I see are not like the ones in cartoons, but more like a meteor shower inside my head. Bursts of white light explode against a tomato-soup orange sky. My stomach muscles contract and send a wave of tangy, warm beer upward, erupting first in my mouth, then on the stair beneath my cheek. I'm barely cognizant of Lauren's screams or the shadowy figure stepping past me. Kerry, I reason, as I spit into the carpet. He made it. But the tassled loafers shuffling just above my head aren't his. Nor are the khaki slacks so sharply creased they could slice bread.

It's David who lands the kidney blow that halts Keith. It's

David who knocks him off stride. It's David who yanks Keith backward by the shirt collar and brings both of them crashing down upon me. I rotate as best I can so it's my back absorbing the flailing knees and feet as they wrestle atop my body. Keith's cussing provides a real-time account of the bout, his initial f-bombs and "goddammits" progressing to cocksure "pissants" and "cocksuckers," frequently paired with a determined grunt from my brother-in-law. I seize the black and white sneaker wriggling on the step below my face and torque it until Keith howls. Score one for C.J. Finally. He kicks free of my grip and nails me twice in the shoulder and three times in the hand covering my face before his foot suddenly disappears. Along with the rest of him.

When I peek out through the crook of my elbow, the hallway below is crowded with bodies. Keith's is immobilized by the massive hands of a shaven-headed Filipino with colorful tattoos winding from his neck down his exposed arms. His chest is nearly as wide across as the refrigerator, and Keith's thrashing feet inflict no noticeable damage as they glance off the giant's shins. My brother, fist drawn back and ready to fly, is grinning so wide I can see his molars. His first blow lands in Keith's abs, eliciting a groan and a shower of saliva. Kerry tunes him up with a couple more gut shots, then finishes the barrage with a roundhouse to the left eye.

Grayson's blinged-out paws are all that hold Keith upright. Kerry grabs him by the slumped chin and forces his head up far enough to level their eyes. "If you ever lay another finger on her, I'll break your fucking neck." He gives Keith's face a quick slap as he lets it go, then glances in my direction. "Sport."

"Wudd?"

"Your turn." He beckons me with his right hand. "Get your licks in. Looks like you owe him a couple."

Keith's head snaps up. The skin around his eye has turned gray. He can still open it enough to glare at me, though it's only a matter of time before it swells shut. David, who by now has risen to his knees, extends a hand and helps me into a seated position. I've dreamed of hitting Keith back since I was fifteen. Still, it seems wrong to take my shot when he's being held still by a monster big enough to play offensive line for the Seahawks. Then again, no more wrong than a grown man decking his wife's scrawny teenage son. Leaning on the rail, I work my way down to the hall.

I've never actually landed a good punch on anyone in my life. I'm not even sure what the proper mechanics are, though I remember once hearing someone on TV say you have to snap through and fully extend your arm. Keith sneers at me as I study his face, seeking the perfect place to leave my mark. I picture crushing him in the jaw hard enough to knock a tooth out and decide to go for the left side of his mouth. I dance in place a couple of steps to channel my inner boxer, but instead of Rocky I feel like Bullwinkle. My nose throbs with every movement. I can't focus.

"Just do it already, Sally," Keith says.

But I can't. I want to hit him so hard. For what he did to me as a kid. For what he's done to my mother. For breaking my nose. For pushing Lauren. But it's not going to hurt. Maybe me. Not him. I'll probably break my knuckles and he won't even feel it.

"Forget it," I say. "Just get him out of here."

Kerry's eyebrows creep north. He shoots me a look like I've just passed on a chance to sleep with Miss America. He's never been me. There's no way to explain it and no point in trying.

Keith rolls his shoulders up out of Grayson's relaxed grip. The sweat-soaked hair ringing his dome shines in the hall light as he shakes his head at me. I'm already beginning to regret my choice when he starts with the clucking noises. I'm a chicken. He's the only one to make the connection. I drop my gaze to my fists, still balled uselessly at my waist. Would it work? Could it work? No.

I take a shuffle hop forward and kick him instead. My foot connects with his crotch with enough force to drive in a door. He staggers back and crumples to the linoleum.

"Fuck you, Keith." I relish the way it sounds coming out. I'm dismissing him. I got the last word.

I raise my scabbed hand to my brother, who high fives me so hard I can feel it in the clot in my nose. Determined to play down the pain, I lift my palm to Grayson. It's about now I notice the two cops out on the stoop peering through the screen door.

TWENTY-SIX

A female officer knocks on the frame of the door as her partner pulls it open. They enter without waiting to be invited, hands casually resting on the butts of their holstered weapons. Grayson steps back from Keith, writhing on the floor, and places his hands behind his head.

"Stay cool, man," he says, just loud enough I can hear him. "We're the good guys."

I can't. Both cops are fixed on me as they approach. Me, the one they just saw kick a battered man in the jewels. Me, the guy bleeding from both nostrils and behind one ear. Me, the aggressor.

"What's going on, gentlemen?" the male officer asks. The gold bar on his breast pocket reads "P. Falcone," and I wonder if he might be related to the Tom Falcone who was a grade ahead of me in high school. He's pushing forty, judging by the salt sprinkled among his otherwise pepper hair. How many hundreds of houses has he entered over the years? How many times has he left without hauling anyone away? "Why are we fighting three on one? That hardly seems fair."

"Five on one," Keith mumbles, rolling himself into a seated position against the hall wall.

"I'll go solo any time you want," Kerry says, earning a pointed finger from the other cop. She looks like an ironman triathlete, with strong sinewy arms and legs and neck muscles tighter than cello strings. She crouches down to examine Keith, whom they clearly regard as the victim based on the snippet they witnessed.

"He broke in," I say. "I told him my mom didn't want to talk to him."

"I didn't break in. I've got a key."

"Whose house is this?" Falcone asks.

"Mine," I say.

"My father's," Kerry says.

"Why, he don't look old enough to be your father." Falcone cracks. He places a hand upon Grayson's shoulder and spins him 180 degrees. Without saying a word, Grayson spreads his legs wide and sets his palms to the wall. He turns his face toward me and rolls his eyes as the cop pats him down. I line myself up likewise, acting like I've been here before, as if my street cred's at risk. When his hands run over my shirt, I shiver. I may vex everyone who cares about me and a lot of people who don't, but I tend more toward the obnoxious and disappointing than illegal. I've only ever had two speeding tickets, the last one more than a decade ago. The simple act of being frisked makes me indignant. I'm not the guilty one here.

"What's this?" Falcone demands, hand pressed against the front pocket of my jeans.

"Just my phone."

"Awful thick phone."

"My phone and my mom's. What are you looking for? If I had a gun you think he'd have made it in the house?"

He rides my face into the wall with a forearm to the neck and digs into my pocket. "Why have you got two phones?"

"I just said. One's my mom's. Jesus, I have rights, don't I?"

"Shut up, C.J.," pleads Lauren, seated at the top of the stairs.

"I'd listen to your girlfriend, C.J." Falcone hands me the two phones and gives me a gratuitous shove as he moves on to Kerry. The walkie-talkie clipped to his shoulder crackles with static, followed by a voice I can't make out. "Please proceed," he says into the radio. "We could use you."

When I glance up at Lauren she's motioning downward with her hand. Calm down. Were Mindy to signal me like that it would only rile me up. Lauren I'd listen to. I do listen to. I put my hand to my nose and suck in deep breaths as I trace its new, bloated outline with my fingertips. Lauren offers a sad smile and slides down three steps until she's even with David, who's chewing on his bottom lip and staring at nothing in particular, looking offended the cops haven't judged him worthy of a pat down.

"They were only trying to stop Keith from reaching their mom," Lauren offers, breaking the uncomfortable silence. "Because she came here specifically to—"

"Hang on," Falcone interrupts her. "Stop right there. We'll talk to you each separately. You," he indicates Keith. "You're up first. Let's go out here."

His partner, whose badge says "J. Rutting," helps Keith to his feet and turns him toward the wall. His eye resembles a spoiled plum, with a tiny slit just wide enough to leak the fluid crusting on his lashes. "Lana," he growls, staring up beyond me with his good eye. "Don't say a goddam word to them."

At the top of the stairs my mother raises her hand to her face and shudders. "I'm sorry," she says, sliding her fingers just far enough down we can see her pupils. It takes me several beats to realize it's me she's apologizing to, not Keith.

As Falcone leads Keith into the living room, the screen door creaks open. Two more officers enter, followed by my sister, laughing at something one of them said. They grin familiarly at each other, as if sharing an inside joke, and he pats her playfully on the shoulder. I glance at Kerry and shrug. Positioning his hands tight in front of his chest so David can't see them, he makes a tiny circle with the forefinger of his left hand and subtly slides the thumb of his right in and back a couple of times. He hikes his eyebrows conspiratorially and nods.

Eyes never straying from us, Rutting consults with the new arrivals, addressing Audra as if she's somehow in charge by virtue of being the only one she knows wasn't involved. She returns to the base of the stairs and beckons my mother. "Ma'am, I'm going to start with you, so you can get this over with and go back upstairs if you like."

Lauren helps Mom down the stairs, continuing on to the kitchen table. After leading her to her chair, Lauren fetches her a glass of water and sits down next to her. When Rutting suggests she leave, my mother clutches hold of Lauren's arm and protests in her blended English until the officer relents. My gut says it's an act, aimed at bringing a quick end to the interview, but it's possible she's too stressed out by the night's events to speak coherently. Then again, maybe she's still drunk.

"Calm down, Mrs. …?"

"Nevitt," Lauren says.

"Take a sip of your water," Rutter says kindly. "We just want to find out what happened so we can be fair to everyone here."

"Neubauer," calls the cop who was flirting with Audra. Kerry and I both turn. "You." He steps toward me. "Let's talk outside."

My head's spinning so madly it's a challenge simply following him through the kitchen and out to the stoop. I take a deep breath and wait for the fresh air to clear my head. It doesn't. Maybe I'm too enchanted by all the pulsing red lights. It looks like the final scene from *Christmas Vacation*, three cop cars flashing along the shoulder and a fourth plugging the end of the driveway.

"Relax." The name badge on his breast says, "D. Sawyer." He looks older than me, but not by much. There's no gray in the tightly shorn ginger hair or the neatly trimmed mustache. "I'm not going to shoot you."

I figured that much, given the half dozen neighbors lining the fence across the street. Through the trees I can see Mr. and Mrs. Holt standing in their driveway. It'll have been Mrs. Holt who called the police, almost certainly. I guess I can't blame her. She'll be happy as hell when the For Sale sign goes up.

Sawyer pulls a pack of smokes from his shirt pocket and pinches one between his lips. The pack is halfway home before he thinks to offer me one. I accept.

"I've been here before." He raises his lighter and sucks in the flame. "Long time ago. Back when we were kids. I had a cobalt blue Mustang. Maybe you remember it?"

I shake my head.

"I knew your sister."

I let him light my cigarette without pissing all over his memory by pointing out how many other guys "knew" Audra in high school. He pockets his lighter and draws a thin flashlight from his belt. Nudging my chin up with his knuckle, he shines the beam into my nostrils.

"That from tonight?"

I nod into his fist.

"You're going to want to ice that when you get a chance."

"Is it broken?"

"Oh, yeah. Doesn't look like it's out of alignment, though. Should heal okay. I've seen worse." He takes a long drag and vents the smoke out through the corner of his mouth. "So, tell me what happened here tonight."

I start at the start, pointing to the deflated airbag inside Mom's car and re-enacting her collision with the curb. How she was upset and scared of Keith. How I saw the bruises on her chest when she went to bed. I show him the texts and the call log on Mom's phone. Every detail I can think of from the moment Keith arrived until I kicked him in the balls. He interrupts only once, to hand me a handkerchief and point out that my nose is bleeding again. When I dab my face, the cloth sticks to the congealing mess on my cheek. His silence unnerves me and I ramble, going back over what seem to be the key points in my favor, like a lawyer summing up his case to a jury. They don't seem to have any greater impact the second time around. He simply nods and scratches notes on his report, raising his eyes every time I pause as if to ask if I'm done, sparking yet another round of babble. The hope I felt when he reminisced about his carnal explorations of my sister has flickered out.

"Am I in trouble?" I finally ask, stomping my cigarette butt into the driveway.

He looks at me through one eye and shrugs. "I need to compare notes with my sergeant. It's not really up to me."

Inside, Keith, Kerry, and Grayson are seated at the table, heads bowed. The officer who arrived with Sawyer looms over them, like a detention monitor itching for a reason to send them to the principal's office. From Kerry's sullen expression, I infer they have already picked at the cop's last good nerve. Grayson stares blankly at the wall as though he's used to turning himself off. Keith glowers at me, like he'd like to bash my nose even further into my skull.

"Sit," Sawyer commands. The only open chair is within an elbow swing of Keith's. I slide it well back from the table, nearly to the counter. If Keith lunges for me, I'll crown him with the coffee pot.

Sawyer joins the huddling Falcone and Rutting in the entry to the living room. Beyond them, Audra, Lauren, David, and Mom are seated on the couch and recliner, which have been moved back to their approximate original positions. They are free, cleared of their roles in the brouhaha. Our fate hangs in the balance of the hushed discussion taking place on the other side of the room. I catch only pieces, accentuated by the occasional glance or pointed finger. The longer it drags on, the more certain I become I'm about to take my first ride in the back of a police car. Which would be horrific enough if I didn't have to pee. My bladder is bursting so full the discomfort in my abdomen has surpassed the throbbing in my nose. Will they let me go before they haul us off, or will they figure it's a ploy to escape? If they do let me go, will they insist on coming in with me? I'm not sure I can go with someone watching like that. I'll wind up pissing my pants in the back of the car. How will that go over in the holding cell? How do hardened criminals treat kids who show up with piss pants? And, yeah, in prison terms I'm just a kid. I'm new to all this. I wish I'd gone back home to Baltimore already. I miss Mindy. I miss my window bench. I miss getting drunk in the dark and watching Titsy dance around her apartment. At least there I'd have a Gatorade bottle to pee in.

As the huddle breaks, Sgt. Falcone issues orders, speaking into the bent ears of Sawyer and Rutting. I watch them through the curtain of hair adhered to my face by my own sweat and blood.

"Nevitt," Falcone barks. "On your feet."

The detention monitor yanks Keith up by the collar of his shirt. At a nod from his sergeant he produces handcuffs from his belt and clasps the first ring around Keith's left wrist. Even as his right arm is wrenched behind his back, the swollen eye never drifts from my face. As though he blames me for his circumstances. But it's more than that, I realize. He's waiting for my turn.

"I'm writing you up for burglary and assault, Nevitt," Falcone says.

"What about him?" Keith nods at me.

"He won't be joining you."

I brush the hair from my face and examine the sergeant. Does he mean not in the same car, or not at all?

"That's horseshit," Keith explodes. "He took the first swing. He started it all. I want to press charges against him."

"That's not how it works," Falcone grins. "All he's guilty of is poor judgment. His mistake was not calling us. Had you dialed nine-one-one first," he says to me, "you'd still be able to breathe through your nose."

I'm breathing hard through my mouth now, filling my lungs with freedom. I'm not going to be cuffed or booked or humiliated any further by the police. It was worth the collapsed nasal cavities. I'm free and Keith is going to jail.

"And them?" Keith does his best to indicate Kerry and Grayson with his elbow. "You saw them holding me. You watched that motherfucker hit me in the face. That's a freebie?"

"Man's got a right to defend his mother," Falcone says. "If it was my mom I'd have killed you."

"I'd never hurt her." Keith twists toward the living room. "I love you, Lana. You know that. This is all a misunderstanding. Call Ron Barber and get me out of this. His number's in my address book." He sneers at the sergeant. "He's good, too. I'll own Lake Forest Park when he's through with you fuckers."

"Shut him up and get him out of here," Falcone snaps.

I want to pull my phone out and record Keith being hauled away. It feels like we should be popping bubbly or at least clinking beer cans. But the sound of Mom sobbing in the other room kills the buzz. This is only a temporary reprieve. When she wakes up tomorrow she'll still be married to him.

TWENTY-SEVEN

Somewhere in the scrum, David's collar was nearly torn clean off his Oxford shirt. It hangs over his left shoulder like an epaulet, attached at his neck by a mere inch of cloth. His bottom lip is swollen as fat as my thumb, and split neatly down the middle. Eyes closed, he relaxes into Audra's massage, his back resting between her spread thighs as she kneads his shoulders. Perched on the back of the sofa above him, she leans forward and whispers something into his ear. I haven't seen him smile like this since we peeked in on his lap dance the night of his stag party.

The yellow light flashing outside the living room window interrupts their moment. The tow truck is here, and David, parked immediately behind Keith's roadster, needs to move his car. He's the last one in the driveway, Grayson having departed twenty minutes ago, immediately after the cops as if he foresaw their return. I wait for David at the kitchen door, my jealousy seeping beyond the healthy boundaries of a sibling relationship. Audra used to shower me with attention when I was little, dragging me around the house like a favorite doll. She would draw on my back for an hour at a stretch, making me guess the letters she traced with the tip of her finger. Her affection for me dried up about the time I grew too big for her to push in the stroller. So long ago it's easy to forget we were ever close.

It's raining just hard enough I regret not having grabbed my umbrella on the way out. Before I can go back for it, David pushes the screen door open behind me, forcing me down the steps. Kerry sweeps past both of us and starts toward the flatbed rumbling in the street. Its bright halogen headlights cut through the drizzle, outlining the gourd-shaped frame of its operator.

"Who called *him*?" I ask.

David shrugs. "It was the first one in the phone book."

"Fuck me," I say, loud enough to make it clear I'm not just talking to myself.

The driver's grease-splotched rain slicker bunches around his wide hips as he pauses and strokes his silvery goatee. "You again. Heh. Almost didn't recognize you with your nose redecorated. We towing something this time, or you going to pay me to leave again?"

"*I'm* not paying you anything. You can send the bill to," I consider the best way to sum up Keith for someone outside the ring of our family circus and reluctantly settle on "my stepfather."

He closes one eye and shoots a stream of tobacco spit into the grass. "Doesn't work that way, my friend. Not for you, anyway. I'm going to need cash."

"How much?" Kerry asks.

"That all depends where we're going."

"Issaquah," I say, mostly out of curiosity to see how deep he plans to gouge us.

"Two fifty." The accompanying shrug acknowledges even he smells his own stink. "Or I can drop it at the impound lot down the hill for a hundred."

"A bit excessive for a five-minute drive," I say. "Let's call it even for the hundred bucks I gave you this morning."

"Can't. I already spent it. They were having a sale on compassion."

"Look," I sigh. "I just need this fucking car out of my driveway. I don't care if you lose it down the ravine."

"Hundred bucks." He smirks like he knows I'm going to refuse, which I do.

The way he raises his palms as he backs away, one might conclude I'm the asshole. David seems to think so as he watches the driver climb back into his truck. Kerry stoops down and plucks a handful of gravel from the driveway. He selects a stone the size of a bottle cap and fires it at the departing lights. Arm cocked for another throw, he waits for the sound of rock on metal or glass, but we can't hear anything over the truck's grinding engine. His second stone misses as well. This time we hear it clatter against the blacktop and bounce twice before skipping into the brush.

"Let's just put it in neutral and shove it into the road," Kerry suggests.

"Why don't you just drive it back?" David asks. "Doesn't your mom have a key?"

He might be right. There were two car keys on her ring. Did the second one belong to Keith's Solstice? Not that I can ever picture him letting her drive it.

"Change in plans," Kerry announces when we reenter, preempting the question on Audra's lips. Hooking Mom's key chain on his finger, he isolates a long black key with a Pontiac logo and works it off the ring. "This belong to Keith's?"

It takes my mother a moment to realize what he's asking. She answers with a weary nod.

"We're going to drive it back ourselves. That guy was a Grade-A dick. Okay if we borrow your car, babes? We should be back by eleven."

Without waiting for a response, he kisses Lauren on the cheek and digs her keys out of her purse. Out on the stoop he hands them to me. "Careful. Don't even scratch it. She'll notice, and she's a lot stronger than she looks."

"Wait a minute," I say. "Why do you get the Solstice? Shouldn't we flip for it?"

Kerry smirks. "You've never driven it before."

"All the more reason. Flip. I call tails."

"I don't have any change."

"Rock, paper, scissors, then."

He taps his right fist against his left palm twice and fires scissors. I match. We both shoot scissors a second time, before I come out paper to his rock. Kerry shakes his head and places the Pontiac key in my hand. "Don't kill yourself."

I wait for David to back out and climb into Keith's convertible. It's been four years since I've driven a stick. I practice depressing the clutch and letting it rise slowly under my left foot, feeling Kerry's eyes in the rearview mirror of Lauren's Acura. Left heel to the floor, right hovering over the gas pedal, I turn the key and coach myself out loud, knowing even before the gear shifter shudders in my hand that I've rushed the exchange. The engine sputters and dies. Before turning the ignition a second time, I shift into neutral. Allowing the car to start first before changing gears alleviates the self-imposed pressure. This time I find reverse without stalling. I back into the street and push the clutch once again, gaining confidence as I shift into first. With a screech of the tires, I'm off.

At the stop sign, I scan the dials on the dash and rev the engine as I wait for my brother to catch up. The rain has left a patchy sheen on the road. Kerry skids in so close behind I can barely see his headlights through the tiny rear window. When I punch the gas, my tires spin on the wet asphalt until they catch, launching me into a left turn up the hill. The gears grind shifting into both second and third, where I leave it as I ascend through the hairpin and finally reach level ground.

It is as fun as I'd imagined, and I'm not even halfway to the interstate. I slow for a four-way stop just enough to be sure no one's approaching from either side and gun it, feeling my stomach rise when I crest the hill. The buzz from the beer has worn off, replaced now by a livelier high that could only be more exhilarating if I could actually breathe through my nose instead of gasping for breath every time I realize my lungs have emptied. I wind through a stand of tall evergreens, emerging into open sky to find my path blocked by a pickup moving slower than I figured anyone who would still be out would drive. Unable to see around them, I nose just far enough across the double yellow to check for oncoming traffic. The opposite lane is clear as far as the bend a quarter mile ahead. If I go now I can make it before anyone comes around the turn. Hand on the shifter, I start left, catching the outline of the lights mounted on the roof of the sedan stationed on the shoulder ahead just in time to decelerate and fall back into line. As I reach to turn the stereo down, I catch the laughing face of my brother in the rearview mirror.

At the light in front of the Safeway the street widens to two lanes in each direction. I veer right to pass the lumbering truck and nip through on the yellow, pulling Kerry in my wake. The onramp to the interstate is clear and I relish the opportunity to finally open the throttle. I merge at seventy and work my way almost immediately into the passing lane, torn between the desire to drive faster than I've ever driven and the fear of getting busted. Twice I push the needle up past eighty, and twice I let it slide back, eyes constantly searching the median for troopers. Ahead, a low-slung black coupe maintains a constant buffer of fifty yards, give or take. I follow his lead when he brakes, dropping abruptly into the mid-sixties, then slower still when I spot the cop car camped on the overpass, allowing Kerry to draw at last within sight behind me. Sandwiched between the black coupe and my brother, I continue south, emboldened by being one of three to push the speedometer back near eighty.

I take the ramp onto Interstate 90 too fast and drift dangerously close to the concrete barrier, streaked with black markings left by idiots before me who were unable to navigate the curve. A jolt of adrenaline makes me hyperaware of how close I have just come to joining their ranks. Were I to somehow survive such an encounter, it would take the rest of my natural life to pay off the damage. Kerry passes me on my left as I wait out the aftershocks in my chest. I'd be content to let him go if not for the raised pinky he waggles as he pulls away. He's questioned my manhood. If I can't beat him in this car I won't hear the end of it until one of us cashes out.

He's a football field ahead of me before I get back up to speed, eighty, eighty-five, nosing up to ninety, eyes darting from the rearview mirror to the road ahead, constantly on the hunt for cops. I gain incrementally through the S-shaped bend, Lauren's car growing a little bigger with every breath until it vanishes into the Mount Baker Tunnel. A blink later and I too am underground, the roadway illuminated by futuristic strings of lights mounted on the walls overhead. The shoulders here aren't wide enough to hide a police car. The vehicles to my right evaporate, each disappearing in a blurry puff as I pass. By the time we emerge from the tunnel into the cloud-riddled sky, I can once again read Lauren's license plate, REDHOT. Truth in advertising, at least when she's behind the wheel.

The lake is dotted with lights when we reach the floating bridge. To my left, I sense a tour boat. It could be anything from a jet-ski to a cruise ship for the attention I pay it. My eyes are fixed on my brother and the cars in the adjacent lane, into which I'll need to jump to pass him. I'd give anything to feel my neck pop, but I can't afford to turn my head long enough to loosen it. I've never concentrated this hard on anything. I leave a bluish vehicle in a haze and jerk the wheel to the right, placing me in the middle lane as we reach solid ground on Mercer Island. From this angle I can see all lanes ahead. There is no one in front of Kerry. He's going as fast as he can possibly go, and I'm gaining. I travelled this same road three times a year in college, heading across the lake, the mountains, and the desert to Wazzu. It never felt like this. It never felt so alive. I pull even when we finally clear the island, hoisting the bird when our front windows at last align.

My triumph is fleeting. An SUV merges into my lane, forcing me to brake hard to avoid hitting it. Back in the left lane I catch Kerry's taillights as he pulls away. Hot and claustrophobic, wishing I'd had the foresight to drop the top before embarking on this insane race, I force the windows downward. The wind pummels me from both sides, rippling my sleeves like a sky diver. Once more I push metal to floor, intent on catching my brother before the first Issaquah exit, now mere minutes ahead.

I won't get anywhere in his lane. I need to go around him and merge in ahead downstream. I check my mirror and glance over my shoulder to be double sure. Back in the middle lane there are more hazards to negotiate. A string of cars ahead is connected like link sausages. Everyone wants the middle lane. None of them recognize they're barely going fast enough to survive in the right, which I claim as my own. I surge ahead, lost, I'm sure, to my brother, growing overconfident two lanes to my left. He's fifty yards away. He's forty yards away. I cut it to thirty. I'm already eyeing a perfect gap in the middle lane when I spy the trooper ahead. He can only nail one of us. I contemplate the coin flip that would allow me to pass while the cruiser flags my brother and realize it will never play out that way. He's been blessed since birth as I've been cursed. I brake hard and veer off at the exit ramp.

I have no idea where I am, but there are no cops here. I coast into the light and wait out a red, debating whether to turn left or right. My decision is made by the Prius in front of me. He goes left, I go right, and I'm left to wend my way through the back roads and side streets, alternating east and south until things begin to look familiar. I recognize a church and a mini-mart. I think I know the credit union with the bright white sign. I've seen these houses and bus stops. And here is Mom's street. Keith's street. I turn right and follow the bend, steering up at last into their driveway. The house, like the orchard beyond, is dark. I come to a stop in the driveway unsure of what to do until I glance up and notice the garage door opener clipped to the visor. When I press my thumb to it, the panes in the door light up and the panels lift off the ground.

My legs feel shaky when I step out into the garage, as if I've traveled here by star cruiser. I stagger toward the driveway, listening for the sound of Lauren's car. All I hear is the distant bark of a neighbor's dog. I head back inside and try the door. It turns. I'm in. I perk my ears again, not convinced of Keith's absence. Will he be home soon or languish overnight? Who did he call? I make my way to the refrigerator and liberate a beer from the top shelf. The first sip steams down to my barren stomach. After inhaling a couple more, I pull my phone from my pocket and check for incoming texts. There are none. Where the hell is Kerry?

It's almost creepy wandering through Mom's house. I've never been here alone before. The house is silent, the only detectable noise coming from the clock in the living room. I check my phone again, as if someone should have messaged me in the last minute. Nothing. Finally, I hear a car on the street out front.

Kerry pulls into the driveway and infuriatingly sits there until I tire of waiting for him to emerge. He's gazing at his lap when I step back into the garage. I approach slowly, sipping my beer, wanting him to explain his delay, to confirm my suspicions.

"I had you," he says, when he finally opens the door.

"What are you talking about? I've been here twenty minutes."

"I was ahead, and you quit. I win."

On the passenger's seat beyond him lies a thin sheet of yellow paper, folded in half and cratered in the middle as though an object about the size of my brother's fist had met it. Repeatedly. I shouldn't laugh, but I can't help it, even when Kerry shoves the door into my midsection.

"Shut the fuck up and give me a cigarette," he says.

"You don't even smoke."

His look is a nearly exact replica, aged twenty years, of the one he unfurled the day I figured out he and his buddies weren't hiking in the woods behind our house every day after school. I extract the crushed pack from my jeans and drop it in his extended palm. He continues beckoning with his fingers until I produce my lighter as well.

"How did you not see him?" I ask. "He was right there in the flow of traffic."

"I was looking at my damn phone. Had a text from Lauren."

"You're doing ninety and checking your texts? How am I the stupid one?"

Kerry glances up from the flame tickling the end of his cigarette. "Who said you were stupid?"

"Give me a break. I know where I stack up on the family totem pole. I'm the jackass you guys all look down on."

"Jackass, maybe. I never thought you were stupid. You do stupid shit, but so don't we all." He stuffs my smokes into my pocket and gets up. "Come on. We've got to stock up. Boss's orders. Clothes, shampoo, whatever the fuck you can find. And let's hustle. Even that cocksucker's got friends. If he got ahold of one that wasn't too busy beating his own wife it's just possible he's been bailed out by now."

Back inside, we make our way up to Mom and Keith's room. Kerry dumps the laundry basket out on the bed and begins filling it with fistfuls of garments from her dresser. Underwear, bras, socks, and pants. I pull an armload of blouses and sweaters from the walk-in closet and drape them, still on their hangers, over the top. He finds a small, soft-sided suitcase in the closet and tells me to fill it with stuff from the bathroom. Anything, he says, she might need to get ready in the morning. At least a week's worth. I collect hair products, makeup, a pink toothbrush I can only assume is hers, a box of maxipads, and several bottles of prescription medicine. I trip over a shoe on my way back into the bedroom and think to throw a couple of pairs in as well. Down in the kitchen I toss in a bag of Milano cookies and a can of Pringles. I have no idea if Mom even likes them, but I'm starving and they look good. The bottle of vodka she'll appreciate, no doubt.

I find Kerry in the garage, leaning over the side of Keith's car, a beer in one hand, the other planted atop the trunk, supporting his weight. The open gas-tank cover shields what appears from my angle to be an intimate act committed by him upon the vehicle.

"What the fuck are you doing?"

"Taking a piss," he grins. "What's it look like?"

I make my way past and wait for him in the driveway. He drops the garage door and emerges from the side exit, head tilted back, beer can to his open mouth. He underhands me Lauren's keys and opens the passenger-side door.

"Figured we ought to at least get the tank back up to where it was," he chuckles. "Man, imagine what a full bladder could do to an engine. Suppose his mechanic will be able to diagnose that one?"

"Not a chance." I adjust the seat and mirror and back out of the driveway. "Wish I'd have thought of that. I wasted mine inside."

"Stick with me, sport. You just might learn something."

There's an opening here if I dare to take it. The evening—if not the entire week—has chipped away at the bricks in the wall that usually separates us. We've got a long drive ahead of us to get back to Dad's. I glance over and catch him staring at the yellow paper in his hands.

"How bad they sting you?"

"Two hundred forty-seven bucks. Said I was doing thirty over."

"Look on the bright side. At least you won't get dropped by your insurance."

Kerry cracks a wry smile. "I don't get to write my own policies, you know. That's not quite how it works. I wish."

"Is it too late to take out a life policy on Dad?"

"That might raise a few red flags at the central office."

"You have one on Mom?"

He nods. "She's got everything through me. My first and most loyal customer. Life, supplemental health, auto. Got Keith's, too. Thanks for not wrecking his car, by the way. I'm going to cancel his ass, though. Tomorrow morning before that piss hits his engine."

"Did you know she was a mail-order bride?"

It's a moment before he responds, long enough for me to start feeling smart for having scooped him.

"I don't think that's her preferred terminology."

"You knew?"

"I figured it out about the time she left, sport. It just dawned on you tonight?"

"No one ever tells me shit."

"You never asked. I assumed you knew."

"Where's she going to stay?"

"Dad's, I guess. That seems to be what the boss wants." He shakes his head and huffs out a cross between a sigh and a laugh. "It's really sort of up to Mom."

"Where am I going to stay?"

"Thought you were going home."

I thought I was, too. That was the plan. I'd come and say good-bye to Dad, help settle a few things up, and head back to Baltimore. To Mindy. To the coffee shop. To my jackass life. But in the few, fleeting hours between when I first learned about our windfall and when we lost it, it was never Baltimore I pictured. It was here. Even after the jackpot evaporated, my first thought was trying to milk out a rent-free summer playing handyman. Here. I merge onto I-90, the familiar Seattle skyline reaching just high enough into the night to be visible in the distance. I only ever explored the city during the summers I came home from college, when Jimmy and I and a couple other high school buddies would go see bands at night. I wish I knew it better. It's still mine by birthright, the hometown I claim when asked, always leaving out the minor detail of having grown up in the burbs up north.

"Eventually. There's still a lot of Dad's stuff to deal with. I know you're busy."

"You don't really need to stay and clean all his shit up. Lauren'll help me get through it."

"What about the wedding?"

"We'll manage. Her mom would help if the little control freak would let her." His phone buzzes in his hand. He taps the screen a couple of times with his forefinger and chuckles. "She must have heard me. Hates it when I call her that."

He texts with his thumbs, nails clicking against the screen as he responds to her message, mumbling the words aloud as he types. I detect no mention of the race or the ticket. After three or four exchanges, buzzing, clicking, waiting, Kerry's head lolls forward, chin nearly touching the collar of his shirt. I turn the radio up to cover his snoring.

We're well north of downtown by the time he jerks awake, a panicked expression on his face. "Take this one," he says, pointing at the approaching exit.

"Huh?"

"My car's still at Grayson's."

"Why didn't you go back with him?"

"And miss all the fun? Motherfuckit, I had you beat."

He leads me through several stop lights and into a neighborhood in Greenwood I've never been in before. His car is parked on the shoulder of a side street in front of a weary, oversized colonial that appears to have been divided into multiple apartments.

"Don't tell Lauren," he says, stuffing the ticket into the front pocket of his pants.

"I won't."

"She gets a little funny about money. Kind of ironic. Ain't cheap keeping her around." He digs his thumb into his eye as if he just woke up from a long night's slumber. "You still coming back for the wedding?"

"Yeah, why wouldn't I?"

"I know it's kind of late in the game, and I should have asked you before. So I get it if you want to tell me to fuck off." He's looking straight ahead through the front windshield, his eyes darting in my direction just long enough to register I'm still there. He struggles with sincere moments even worse than I do. "But I was thinking it would be nice if you were in the wedding with us. I mean, Gray's my best man and all that, but Lauren won't mind if we squeeze in another usher. If you're into it."

It takes me a moment to respond. Not because there's much to think about. I'm just waiting for the sudden tightening in my chest and throat to recede so my voice won't crack. "Sure. Count me in."

There's just the faintest hint of mistiness in Kerry's eyes when he finally faces me, hand extended. My palm touching his breaks the spell. He's the big brother again, and handshakes are meant to be won. He pins my fingers together before I can even attempt to fight back. I grant him his victory straight-faced, salvaging what I can of my manhood by waiting until he has departed to flex the pain out of my knuckles.

TWENTY-EIGHT

It's a quarter to twelve when I pull in behind Mom's battered Nissan. The kitchen has been tidied, empty beer cans dumped in the recycle bin, dishes washed and laid to dry on a towel next to the sink. The flicker of the television provides just enough light to locate Lauren, asleep on the couch. I sit down on the arm and consider whether to wake her. Her chest rises and falls in rhythm with the popping of the cartilage in my nose every time I breathe. I can feel it shifting as I probe the bridge with my thumb and forefinger, gazing beyond my blurred hand at my brother's fiancée. The little control freak, as he so affectionately referred to her. I wish it was me she controlled. I envision kneeling next to the couch, whispering to her, taking her hand, leading her upstairs. She grins and excuses herself to use the bathroom, emerging a minute later in a nightie that will soon wind up in a ball on my floor. I take her hand again, draw her to me, fall into bed beneath her. She lifts my shirt slowly, and … I shudder back into consciousness when she shifts positions on the sofa, rolling onto her side, her blouse spilling open wide enough to provide an unobstructed view of her right breast, straining against her pink lace bra. I realize after staring long enough to draw it from memory that I've grown erect, and force myself to look instead at the house-hunting couple on the TV. I get up to walk it off, winding up at the refrigerator, from which I pull a cool-down beer.

Back in the living room, I pluck the remote control from the cushion, inches from Lauren's hip, and reassume my perch on the arm of the sofa. I start up through the channels, pausing just long enough to find a reason to reject each until stumbling upon an oiled-up blonde in a loosely tied, red silk kimono and a smile. She's walking through the high-ceilinged foyer of a brightly lit house, much larger than any I've personally been invited to. I can't hear what she says as she opens the door, but it apparently pleases the mulleted fellow on the front step enough that he follows her back to the bedroom. It's one of those soft-core screwcoms that run late at night on Showtime, which I'd figured Dad would be too cheap to subscribe to. I glance down at Lauren to ensure she's still asleep, then back to the couple, who—surprise, surprise—have been joined by an Asian girl in a white towel, which almost immediately falls to the carpet. The volume is just loud enough to make out the smarmy saxophone music and the giggling as the girls blindfold their helpless victim. I peek down at Lauren again. This time her eyes are open, fixed on the TV.

"She's a busty one, isn't she?" she says sleepily. "Funny, I don't remember seeing her on *Property Brothers* before."

I jab at the down arrow on the remote as if it could pull me back in time. The fornicating trio disappears. "Just flipping through, seeing what's on."

"That's what your brother says every time I walk in on him. Once a week, seems like. Could be ten minutes after we just had sex, he's out on the couch 'flipping through.' If there's a girl with her tits out anywhere on cable, he'll find her."

She punctuates this with a laugh and a toss of her hair, as though she finds his rapscallion behavior endearing. If Mindy walked in on me ogling soft-core strumpets she'd fire the first handy projectile either at my head or through the TV screen. Probably my head. She paid for the TV. I get uncomfortable enough during sex scenes of movies we're watching together, worried she's thinking I'm enjoying them more than I should, which only makes me wish they would hurry up and end already.

"At least they're just on TV now," I say. "You can't even imagine how many girls he brought home in high school. Some of them whipped them out right here on this couch." Or so he bragged. I never saw.

Lauren tsks. "Ewww, now you tell me." She sits up straight and scrutinizes the cushions, suddenly wary of the cooties embedded in the upholstery. "Maybe I should get him back a little. What if I show you mine?"

I swallow hard as she undoes the third button on her blouse. She slides her hand down to the fourth, below the curvature of her breasts, far enough to grant a full access pass. Thumb poised to unfasten it, she shakes her hair clear of her shoulders and winks up at me. My heart is pounding so hard I'm sure she can hear it.

"Geez, C.J.," she laughs. "You really thought I was going to, didn't you?"

"A guy can hope," I shrug.

"You're so pathetic." She buttons her blouse back up, this time leaving only the top one free. "You're like a puppy that followed me home from the park. I shouldn't tease you like that. Sorry."

I'm more smitten than I was the day we went to the mall. There's chemistry here. She's different. She's special. I've never gone out with a girl I could really talk to. I usually guard my inner thoughts like prisoners. I'd let them all free for her, confident they wouldn't circle back and betray me. But this is going to get damn awkward for both of us if I don't quit obsessing. It might be cute if she was ten years older than me instead of the other way around. It's only not creepy because she's such a good sport. Even if I could afford her, she could never leave Kerry for me. It would shatter what's left of my family, a unit she alone seems capable of salvaging. I know this logically, intellectually, even if I'm too stupid or stubborn to accept it carnally.

"I wouldn't have told," I say.

"I should hope not," she laughs. "How many times do you need your nose broken?"

"Is it bad?"

She traces under her eyes with her forefinger and nods. "You're purple all in through here. That'll probably be worse by morning. Did you ice it at all?"

"When?"

She shrugs.

"How's my mom?"

"Upset. Scared. I sat with her upstairs until she fell asleep. Poor thing."

"Thanks."

"She's not faking that. She's terrified of him. We pleaded with her to get a restraining order against him. This is ruining her. She was so much livelier last summer I almost don't recognize her. She can barely function. She's such a beautiful woman. It breaks my heart."

"I know." She's right. My mother is a shell of herself. It's no longer fair to accuse her of manipulating us. By now it's learned behavior. It's all she knows. She's sleepwalking her way through life. Coping, not living.

"She should stay here until she can figure out what to do next. Audra's on board. If you guys get the house like Kerry thinks, would you be okay having your mom live here for a bit? I'd be glad to have her stay with us, but Kerry's funny about it, especially with the wedding coming up. Audra would probably take her in if she and David were getting along better. I don't know where else she could go. We don't have any idea how much money she has, but I don't think it's much. I mean, she'd get alimony if we can talk her into going through with a divorce, but that could take months, or longer."

"It's fine. I mean, if she wants to."

It wasn't the house my mom ran away from. I'm no longer completely convinced it was my dad. I suspect in a sense she was running from herself. She was thirty-four, married with three kids, and wistful for a freedom she'd never tasted. She essentially skipped right over her twenties straight into motherhood. I might have wasted mine, but at least when I woke up hungover I didn't have to pack anyone's lunch and get them dressed for school. No, the house was never the issue. Having grown up in a concrete apartment tower subject to nightly electricity blackouts, even our modest home was a source of pride. We often found her tending her little garden out front when we came home from school, pulling weeds, pruning the spent blossoms, and splitting plants when they grew too big. She'd send pictures of it back home to her mother and sister. She kept house like I imagined most Russian women did, throwing open the windows to air out the rooms every Monday regardless of weather, beating rugs out on the clothesline, scouring the hardwoods with stiff-bristled brooms and swabbing them with strong-smelling disinfectants. Old school. Until she snapped. In the few times I visited Keith's as a kid I never picked up on any of these rituals. For a time they actually paid a woman to come clean. Maybe that was part of Keith's recruiting pitch.

Lauren slips her feet into the pumps parked on the floor next to the sofa. I follow her as far as the kitchen, where I wait while she goes upstairs to check on Mom. Selfishly, I hope she'll find her restless, giving her a reason to stay, but when she returns a minute later she reports my mother is still sound asleep in the same position as she left her earlier. She pecks me on the corner of the mouth and grabs her keys from the table. I watch from the door as she backs out the driveway. There are just seven beers left from the case I brought home this morning. I fumble a little with the math, pretending I can't track how many I had versus Kerry versus whoever else might have downed one while we were racing across the lake, but it's got to be ten, plus or minus a can. I can attribute the dullness in my head to lack of sleep if I want, but that's only part of the equation. I'm just as guilty as my mother of enlisting chemical assistance to cope.

Alone again, my feelings shuffle like cups and balls in the hands of a skilled conjurer. There's still a whiff of euphoria at having stolen my mother back from Keith, however temporary the victory may prove. I haven't felt this close to my brother since, well, never. What would life have been like if we'd schemed together in the past? We weren't even close enough to be rivals. Is that my fault? Does it matter? I'm heartbroken for my mother and I miss my father, yet I'm warmed a little by the thought they got back in touch with each other after all these years, even given the circumstances and the open question of whether their reunion influenced his state of mind. And I hate myself for what I did to Julianne. When I play it back now I hear her words as she intended them. No. Don't. Stop. It's what I want to tell my thoughts. Stop. Please. Let me alone long enough to fall asleep.

I remember the pill bottle in my pocket. Are they responsible for Mom's borderline catatonia? Is it the vodka? Or a combination of both? I shake two blue and white capsules into my hand and lift them to my mouth. I want to know what they do. Will I feel different? Happier? The first one sticks to my tongue when I lap at my palm. I wash it down with a swig of beer and drop the second in after it. Nothing happens. They're not magic beans.

I return to the living room and assume Lauren's position on the couch. My thumb tabs the channel upward, back to naked land. Different girls, possibly the same house, definitely the same music. I sip my beer and watch their robes slip open and slide off their shoulders, watch the redhead unbuckle the cable guy's belt, watch the girls lure him to the bed. Why do I watch porn? Is it meant to make me feel better or worse? And shouldn't I feel *something* by now? I'm soft as a ragdoll. What's wrong with me? Is it the pills? It's too soon to blame them, right? I'm just exhausted. I'm buzzed. I'm asleep.

I'm driving the Charger, only it's not the Charger, exactly. It's bigger, and redder, and a lot faster. I'm racing down a hill, unable to brake, unbothered by the consequences. I'm alone, and then I'm not. To my right sits my father, his beard as white as God's. The road falls away. We are dropping off a cliff, tumbling, flipping, drifting. There is no more road. No more car. We are walking now. I follow him into the garage. The haze is so thick I can barely see the station wagon behind him. It's not just a station wagon. It's a hearse. He smiles and nods. I understand. I open the door and sit in the driver's seat. I turn the key and breathe.

And breathe.

And stop.

TWENTY-NINE

My t-shirt is drenched when I wake, unsure whether I'm still alive or if the light from the television is the one I'm meant to follow to the next life. But here's the remote, and the couch, and my half-finished beer on the floor beneath me. The clock on the stove reads 4:36. I feel more tired than I did before I fell asleep. I lock the deadbolt and down an entire glass of water to rehydrate my cottony mouth. Upstairs, I strip off my sweatshirt and jeans and fall into bed. The sheets are so frigid I hug myself to generate warmth, bringing my knees up toward my chest, curling into a ball for protection from the cold. From the world.

I die three more times, twice careening down precipitous highways that drop off sharper than roller coasters, my tiny yellow ragtop breaking contact with the pavement and hurtling into nothingness, once torn life from limb by a raging mama grizzly in parkland that bears a striking resemblance to my father's backyard. I linger a little longer in each successive tragedy, my subconscious increasingly vexed at being jolted awake to find the room still cloaked in dusk. When I finally crack my eyes to daylight I'm in the midst of a dream I don't want to leave about a woman with long, platinum-frosted braids stretching down below her breasts, wearing nothing but a silver medallion on a rope chain around her neck. She is summoning me, and I am eagerly following—and so very disappointed when I'm unable to locate her after having opened my eyes just long enough to register the sunlight. I'm relieved by the hard-on tenting my shorts. Last night's impotence was temporary, the affliction receding along with the pills, alcohol, and general haze of exhaustion. I lie in bed speculating what time it might be, one hand gingerly probing my nose, the other sneaking through the fly of my boxers to gauge the viability of my erection. I close my eyes and try to conjure up the woman in the necklace, but all I can think of is the voice floating up through the floor. My mother, singing in Russian. If that won't fizzle a boner, nothing will.

I taste bacon when I open the bedroom door. I can't smell it, however. I can't smell anything. My nose might as well be cemented shut. Downstairs, Mom stirs the contents of the frying pan, her back to me as I enter the kitchen. She doesn't hear me over her singing and the popping of the grease as she ploughs her spatula through a mass of hash browns. This is what I longed to wake to those first few weeks of third grade, when all I wanted in the world was my mom to come home. She doesn't turn as I wrap my arms around her midsection, just under her ribs.

"Good morning," she says. She's already made up and dressed in slacks and a cashmere sweater I recognize from the laundry-basket haul. Clearly, she's been up awhile.

"Morning," is all I say in response. It feels like I should add something more, but it's too early in the day to understand what I'm feeling, let alone articulate it in a coherent manner. Instead, I kiss her quickly on the temple and take a seat at the table.

She scoops the potatoes into a chipped ceramic bowl and lines the bacon strips out to drain on a folded paper towel. From the cabinet above, she draws two mugs and fills them to the rim with dark roast so strong it penetrates the clot in my nasal passage.

"Hungry?" she asks.

I nod. I haven't eaten since breakfast yesterday. I shovel the potatoes into my mouth like an escaped hostage, forking in the second and third bites before swallowing the first. The bacon is firm but not crisp, just the way I've always preferred it. The way no one has cooked it for me since Mom left.

"How'd you sleep?" I ask, after washing down the first gulletful with my still-scalding java.

"Better the second time." The wrinkles deepen around her eyes as a wry smile takes hold. She pulls out the chair next to mine and sits. "I'm sorry he came. I didn't think he'd look for me here."

"I shouldn't have answered your phone. He just kept calling. I should have turned it off."

She seems uncomfortable looking me in the face, and I wonder what color it is this morning. I imagine a shade between purple and green.

"Does he always come looking for you when you're not home?"

"Not always, no. It's not usually so … dramatic. I usually just go to Audra's for a coffee until things calm down. Yesterday, I'd just had enough. All the things he's said about Warren." She presses her thumb to her eye to suppress her rising emotion. "And you."

"You have to leave him, Mom."

She stares into her mug and hunches her shoulders into the faintest of shrugs.

"You can stay here. Kerry and Audra are fine with it. We'll change the locks and fix things up a little. We can even dig out your garden again."

"It would be a little weird to move back here after what happened to your father."

"I know, Mom, but Dad would want you to." Maybe not as much as he wanted her to when he was still alive, but he wouldn't want her to be stuck where she was. "It's not your fault what he did. Nobody drove him to it. We all could have done a better job of being there for him. I could have called him more, or emailed him. But it doesn't do any good to point fingers now. Dad made his choice. He wasn't really thinking right at the end."

I wonder if she knows about Petra, if Dad ever mentioned her during their clandestine cocktail klatches. How did my father seem to her, and how much would she have picked up on while bearing such a heavy burden of her own?

"I know," she says. "It's more than that. I've never lived alone. I don't think I could."

"You won't be alone, Mom. I'll be here."

Her eyes and cheeks glisten when she looks up at me. "You'll be going home soon. You've got a girl and a job to get back to."

I swirl my coffee with progressively pronounced movements of my wrist until the maelstrom threatens to breach the lip of the mug. The waves don't calm until I set it back down on the table. "I'm not going back."

"I could never ask you to stay, C.J. What about Mindy? You've been together a long time, no? Four years? You can't leave her to take care of me."

"All we do is fight and make up. She's got to be as tired of it as I am. Probably more. We're only still together because we're too lazy to break up. I'm not leaving her for you. I'm just leaving."

That might not be exactly how I spell it out when I tell Mindy. Assuming I ever get around to it. She might figure it out on her own if I simply don't return. In a funny way I feel worst about leaving the front room half painted. I wish I'd have finished before I left. I didn't mean for her to get stuck with that. She's terrible with the edging. I can hear her cursing me every time she clips the molding with the side of the roller. She'll use one of my shirts to wipe it up with. Assuming she hasn't thrown all my belongings out the window by then. That'll give Titsy something to watch for a change, the angry neighbor girl raining tattered clothes and paperback books down on the sidewalk. Will anyone stop to pick up the pages of my manuscript as they flutter down the street? Maybe I should call my deadbeat agent first and confirm he's still got a copy. He should have it in his email, at least. I'm probably safe.

Mom lifts a strip of bacon from the paper towel and nibbles at the end. "Sorry there were no eggs. They'd gone bad."

"I'll take you shopping in a bit, if you like. We should stock up. We can also stop in at the town hall and ask about a restraining order. Lauren's right. I think you should, Mom."

Lips pursed, she nods. She knows it's the right thing to do but won't pursue it on her own. She rises halfway from her seat and reaches for her handbag on the counter. From the inside pocket she retrieves her pill bottle. Her crutch.

"You ever get funny dreams off those things?"

Palm cupped over the cap, she gazes at me quizzically.

"I found a second bottle in your car yesterday. I tried a couple before bed. I had the weirdest damn dreams. I kept dying. Over and over."

"I don't dream anymore."

"I don't think those things are good for you, Mom. Especially with the vodka. The label specifically says not to mix them. It's messing you up."

"You're one to talk." Her voice is soft, but not soft enough to conceal the defensiveness.

Point taken. I could probably cut back a little. Some days I just feel like getting drunk. Like every time I fight with Mindy. Or Kerry. Or Audra. Or someone pisses me off at work. Or something good happens. I don't only drink when I'm mad. I'm just more determined then. "You're right. I do the same thing you do, Mom. I numb myself. It hasn't worked out any better for me."

She makes no attempt to hold her tears back now. They stream down her cheeks as her head and chest quiver. When I sandwich her hand in mine, the knobs of her knuckles dig into my palm. She grips my bottom hand with surprising strength.

"I'll cut back if you will," I say. "We'll help each other, okay? We're too young to be lushes. Especially you."

The sparkle in her eyes is diffused by a thin sheen of tears as she smiles at me. "I'm sorry, C.J."

"For what?"

"I wish I never left. I was young and stupid and selfish and . . ."

I can't make out the rest because now I'm crying, harder than she was. What if she hadn't left? Maybe I'd be right here having breakfast with her because I stopped by to catch up every week. Maybe Dad would still be alive. Maybe I wouldn't have frittered away half my life running away from my own family. Maybe I wouldn't be a fuckup. When I wipe enough tears away to see again, Mom is offering a tissue. I blot my face, dabbing at the tip of my nose gently until my nostrils no longer feel like they're about to drip. We resume our breakfast, saying little, exchanging half-formed, regretful smiles. She's never said so, not even when I was small and my brother and sister were at school, but I was her favorite. And she was mine. Sorry, Dad. For the first time since she walked out, I feel like I have her back. What's left of her, anyway.

THIRTY

There's a tow truck in the driveway when I emerge from the shower. This one is here at Kerry's request, in his role as Mom's insurance agent. I watch it from the kitchen table as Mom inventories the pantry, jotting her grocery list in a small spiral notebook. I catch her glancing over at me and shift in my seat to obscure the envelope crammed in my front pocket. It's a quarter-inch thick, stuffed with hundreds and twenties, $1,500 in all, a sum it pains me to part with, though it's pennies on the dollar compared to everything I've borrowed or flat-out taken from Mindy the past four years. My flight here alone was over seven hundred bucks, booked on short notice. At least she won't get stuck with the tab for a return trip.

There are three banks in the plaza down the hill. I have accounts at none of them. I don't ask if Mom does, because I don't want to have to explain where all the cash came from. Or what happened to her lamp. She asks no questions as we enter the smallest of the three establishments, my palm sweating in the pocket of my funeral slacks. I couldn't be more nervous if it contained a hold-up note. I settle Mom in a comfy chair and step to the first open window. The teller is young and pretty, if slightly heavy, with black, plastic-framed glasses and chestnut hair pulled tight in a ponytail. I approach timidly, convinced I'll be sent packing, requiring me to either reveal my mission to my mother or abort it.

When I tell the girl I'd like to wire some money, she looks at me like I've just asked for fries and a milkshake. I fan the bills on the counter, mentioning it's all for my girlfriend back in Baltimore. She asks for my account number in a tone that implies she knows I haven't got one. Her smug expression softens when I explain about Mindy's difficult pregnancy and how I wish I could be there to take her to her appointment myself, but at least I'll be back next month to help with things around the house. Way too much information, but that's how you sell a lie. She gives me a sad, sympathetic smile and explains their policy restricts bank-to-bank transfers to account holders, but if I have a minute to wait she'll check with her manager to see if she'll authorize an exception. She makes her way across the lobby, past the chair in which Mom appears to have fallen asleep, to her boss's cubicle. Three minutes later, she returns, her sad smile more pronounced. She's sorry, but due to some provision of the Patriot Act they can't allow it. Perhaps if I'd like to open an account, they could help me, otherwise the best she can suggest is the Transfer Express in the drugstore across the plaza.

I stuff the envelope back into my pocket, thank her for her time, and nearly collide with my mother as I start toward the door.

"Excuse me," Mom says to the girl. "Can he use mine? He's my son."

It's a tough call who's more excited to learn of my mother's account, the teller or me. As Mom and I complete the transfer form, the girl rambles about her sister's baby and how worried they all were during the third trimester, nervous every time the phone rang that something had gone wrong. She asks me whether it will be a boy or a girl, and I explain we want to be surprised but are working on names for both, just in case. I dig Mindy's check out of my wallet and copy the account number neatly on the form just above the line for Mom's signature. The net amount is $1,451, after subtracting the forty-nine dollar fee, which the girl confidentially notes is less than half what Transfer Express would have charged. It should arrive by the end of business today, certainly no later than lunchtime tomorrow. She's nearly in tears, she's so pleased to have been able to assist. The older woman with the mole on her eyelid working the next window over joins in, wishing me the best of luck with the baby. I'm almost sorry Mindy isn't really pregnant as I wave good-bye.

Mom shakes her head disapprovingly as we start up the sidewalk. "I can't believe you'd leave that girl in such a circumstance," she says. "I'm disappointed in you." It's not until I catch her reflection in the window of the music store that I realize she's in on the joke. She has no idea quite how far in she is, however. It was her money she just helped me send across the country. I feel worse about taking it now than I did before I knew how badly and immediately she would need it herself. But I'll use what's left to help her until her alimony kicks in. I'll make sure she goes through with leaving Keith. I take her hand and lead her across the parking lot to the far corner of the center where the town hall building stands. We pass a row of police cars and I wonder which were at our house last night. Which one hauled Keith away? I ask at the front desk where we go for restraining orders. The woman points us to an office down the hall, where a second woman, plump and pink-faced with crooked, silver bangs, offers Mom a thick sheaf of papers, stapled in the upper left corner. She tells us the domestic violence advocate is at lunch, but if we'd like to stop back later we can talk to her and make sure the form is properly filled out. She gazes a moment at my face and asks if I'd like one as well.

Mom stuffs the form into her purse. I know if I don't get her to fill it out today it will stay there, buried under her wallet and keys and the pill bottle she must be jonesing to crack open, assuming she hasn't done so already when I wasn't looking. Instead of taking her to the grocery store, I guide her further up the plaza to a coffee shop with an outdoor seating area. Only one of the seven wrought iron tables is occupied, by a gray-haired gentleman reading a paperback novel, his shirt-sleeves rolled up to his biceps to take advantage of the full sunshine.

Mom indicates the "Barista wanted" sign on the front door as I hold it open for her. "You should apply."

I glance across the parking lot at the Big A. "It's too close to …" but she knows nothing about Julianne, then or now. It seems pointless to delve into it all.

"To what? It's close to home. That would be convenient. I could stop in to see you." She hikes her eyebrows playfully, acknowledging she's aware there will have to be boundaries for our living arrangement to succeed.

It would be convenient. Inside, it's about the same size as Ruth's, with several couches and overstuffed chairs on one wall and a row of booths along the window. The girl at the counter bears an uncanny resemblance to Danielle, one of my co-workers, right down to the thickly clumped mascara and the multiple piercings in her ears. The obligatory goth in every coffee house. She's friendlier than Danielle, however, and seems to think it's cute to see a guy buy a latte for his mother. I order an Italian roast and an orange scone for myself. As she prepares Mom's drink, I ask about the open position.

"Let me get my manager." She takes two steps toward the open door behind her and yells, "Petra."

If we weren't still waiting for our order, I'd grab my mother by the elbow and drag her straight out the front door. Instead, I bury my hands in my pockets and stand my ground. Maybe it's another Petra. There could be more than one in the county. But it's Dad's who pokes her head out of the office.

"What?" she asks, yanking an mp3 bud from her ear.

"He's interested in the job." The goth girl points toward me. "Still open, right?"

Petra's jaw tightens, twin dimples taking root on either

side of her mouth as she grits her teeth and glowers at me through narrow slits. She apparently thinks I'm having a laugh at her expense. It's not until Mom paws at my elbow and asks, "Wasn't she at Warren's funeral?" that Petra seems to notice her.

Ignoring my mother, I raise my right hand as if I'm swearing testimony and say, "I had no idea you worked here. Sorry. Never mind about the job."

Petra's expression softens. "It's filled, anyway. I think. I'm just checking her references."

"You never mentioned you worked here, so …"

"You never asked. What happened to your face?"

"Broke my nose," I shrug. "Well, someone kind of broke it for me. Long story."

"Do you know her?" Mom whispers, loud enough everyone can hear her.

"Petra, this is my mother. She's going to be staying with me for a bit."

They exchange more awkward than usual nice-to-meet-yous, my mother eyeing me as though she suspects I've had some kind of broken relations with Petra. I'll let her think that and leave Dad out of this bizarre triangle. If she doesn't know about his companion, it's not my place to fill her in.

The goth barista slides our order across the counter. As we start toward the door, Petra calls my name.

"We have another store," she says. "In University Village. I think she's looking for someone. You can tell her you know me."

I thank her and follow Mom outside. She sets her latte on the table nearest the door and sits down in the shade of the umbrella. I take the chair opposite and throw my head back to feel the sun on my broken face. Maybe I'll wait until it heals up a little before I get serious about finding a job. No point in wasting legitimate opportunities on a hideous first impression.

The scone is better than the ones we serve at Ruth's. Not as dry and with bigger bits of orange baked in the dough. I tear off a corner and offer it to my mother, who waves it away and pulls the form from her bag. She fills in the first few blanks, then flips ahead to preview the second and third pages.

"So long," she says. "We should take it home."

"No, Mom, do it now. I'm going to go have a smoke. I'll check it over when you're done. We need to turn it in today. This is important."

"You should give them up." She points her pen at the pack of cigarettes I pull from my pants pocket. "Those are worse for you than my pills."

"I doubt that," I laugh. "I don't get crazy dreams off these."

"Your grandfather died of those. Lung cancer. I bet he wishes he'd quit."

"If I don't cut back on the beer first I won't live long enough to get cancer." I wink at her.

She slaps at me, but I'm too far out of range and her fingers only graze my shirtsleeve. "Take it all the way out there. I hate that smell."

I wait until I'm on the sidewalk outside the gate before lighting up. I probably could quit. I've cut way back since Sunday. It's been too hectic to maintain my usual pace. I blow out a ring and watch it spread and fade. My phone vibrates in my pocket. Don't be Mindy, I think as I pull it out. Please, don't be Mindy.

But it is. Does she know about the money yet? When they said end of business did they mean here or on the East Coast?

"Hey."

She doesn't respond. I can't tell if it's meant to be a dramatic pause or if there's something going on there. Finally I hear a sigh, which I take as her initial greeting.

"What's going on?" I ask.

"How should I know?"

"Is this about the money?"

"What money? I told you I've written off everything you ever borrowed, C.J. I know you're not good for it."

Dammit. I shouldn't have said anything. I should have just waited her out. I'm not ready for this conversation right now. I don't know when I will be. But as long as it's here, I might as well stick up for myself. Now that I finally can.

"Check your bank account. I wired you fifteen hundred bucks this morning." Minus the transfer fee. Minor detail.

"What for?"

"The ticket. Everything else. I know it doesn't cover it all, but I always meant to pay you back, even if you figured I didn't."

"Where in hell did you come up with fifteen hundred bucks?"

"My dad."

"How much did you get?"

"Not much. I told you we're not getting his retirement. That's most of what he had."

"Why don't you just pay me when you get home? Don't you know when you're coming back yet?"

This time it's me sighing. I can hear my own breath amplified through the phone held to my ear. Twice. Three times. I'm almost hyperventilating.

"C.J.?"

"I'm going to stay."

"For how long?"

"I'm not coming back. I'm sorry."

"Oh, I get it. You come into a little money, suddenly you don't need me anymore."

"It's not like that at all. I just … it feels like time for me to reconnect with my family. I've been away a long time."

"How stupid do you think I am, C.J.? You haven't said

one nice thing about anyone in your family in the four years we've been together. This isn't about them at all. You met somebody else, didn't you?"

"Yeah, right. I've been here a week, I met someone and moved in."

"Sounds about right. You moved in here the day after we met. So you found some new fool to take pity on you. Poor, down on his luck C.J. needs a place to stay, and she rescues you from the streets like a stray dog. Did you promise to do a little painting, maybe fix a leaky toilet? God help her a year from now when she comes home from work and wonders why you're still in bed. Poor stupid girl will be stuck with you then. Good luck to her, whoever she is."

"There isn't anybody. I told you. Look, I'm sorry. I should have—"

"Oh, I got it. It's that girl from high school, isn't it? The one you ran into the other day? What's her name?"

"Julianne. Hardly. Trust me, it's not her."

"So there is somebody, then. You admit that much. I knew it. I know you too well, C.J. I knew something was up yesterday when you were being all aloof. You've never been half as clever as you think you are."

I gaze at my mother, tapping her pen against the form on the table, and sigh. "Fine, you're onto me, there is someone else." Mom brushes her raven hair from her face and twirls it into a knot above her ear. Her eyes climb from the tabletop to the sidewalk where I stand. "And it is someone I used to know." Her smile when she realizes I'm looking at her is beautiful, early vintage Mom, the one I fell in love with as a kid. I wave and she waves back. "Her name is Svetlana."

ALSO BY JAMES BAILEY

THE GREATEST SHOW ON DIRT

Lane Hamilton takes stock of his life and doesn't like what he finds. His friends are all chasing their dreams, while he's working for a goose-stepping bully on the middle-management track to nowhere. When Lane is fired for sleeping through an important meeting, a high school buddy lands him a job with the Durham Bulls. Despite the grueling hours, it doesn't take him long to realize even a bad day at the yard beats a good one in Corporate America. But is his new gig worth risking his magazine-cover girlfriend? And between jealous co-workers and psychotic relief pitchers, will he survive the season?

NINE BUCKS A POUND

Three seasons into his minor league career, Del Tanner can no longer ignore the obvious: He lacks the power expected of a first baseman. Despite a smooth left-handed stroke and a slick glove, he's regarded by the brass as nothing more than a warm body clogging a roster spot in A-ball. When his aspiring agent suggests he try steroids, Del makes a choice that will shadow him for the rest of his career.

Made in the USA
Monee, IL
16 November 2020

47963828R00142